UNEXPECTED DEFENSE

LAURA SNIDER

SEVERN RIVER
PUBLISHING

Severn River Publishing
www.SevernRiverPublishing.com

This is a work of fiction. Names, characters, businesses, places, events and incidents are either the products of the author's imagination or used in a fictitious manner. Any resemblance to actual persons, living or dead, or actual events is purely coincidental.

ISBN: 978-1-64875-397-8 (Paperback)

ALSO BY LAURA SNIDER

Ashley Montgomery Legal Thrillers

Unsympathetic Victims

Undetermined Death

Unforgivable Acts

Unsolicited Contact

Unexpected Defense

Unconditional Revenge

To find out more about Laura Snider and her books, visit

severnriverbooks.com/authors/laura-snider

PROLOGUE
ASHLEY

April 28

The jury filed into the courtroom, all silent, solemn. Ashley's heart thumped, her blood pressure rising. These moments, the few seconds before the pronouncement of her clients' fate, were the worst part of her job as a public defender. Her work was done. It had been one of her more difficult trials. She'd taken a lot of risks. She didn't have a choice. The facts were the facts. They couldn't be changed. Manipulated, sure, but never changed.

Some lawyers claimed they could determine a jury's verdict before it was announced based on the jurors' behaviors as they entered the courtroom. If the jury convicted, they wouldn't look at the defendant or their attorney. If acquitted, they would try to catch the lawyer's eye, sometimes even smile.

That wasn't Ashley's experience. She'd had plenty of acquittals throughout her lengthy career, and, in her experience, the jury members had always kept their heads down, staring at their feet as they shuffled into the courtroom. Which felt appropriate, at least to Ashley, because she believed—or maybe hoped—that this reaction was due to the weight of their decision. They had been handed a great deal of power, forced to decide the trajectory of someone else's life, and they were taking that responsibility seriously.

No matter the result of the trial, conviction or acquittal, there was no true happiness in the end. Not for either side. Because the verdict didn't change the fact that a life had been lost. A person was forever gone. Those left behind were forever changed, people in mourning. Nothing about the verdict would change any of that. It would only decide whether one more life would be swallowed by the iron walls of a prison.

"Is that everyone?" Judge Ahrenson asked, his eyes sweeping across the jury box and settling on the court attendant. This was his last trial on the bench. He was turning seventy-two, forced retirement age, in less than a week.

"Yes, your honor." The court attendant was a small, round woman, with ruddy cheeks and short, curly hair.

"Very well." Judge Ahrenson turned to speak to the entire courtroom. "You may be seated."

Feet shuffled behind Ashley and the bench seats in the courtroom gallery creaked as the onlookers in the packed courtroom reclaimed their seats. Ashley and her client remained standing until after the entire jury had sat down. The judge and prosecutor did the same. It was a sign of respect, a way to say, *We see you. We understand your responsibility. We appreciate you.*

Once everyone was settled, the judge turned back to the court attendant. "Has the Jury reached a unanimous verdict?"

"Yes, your honor," she said.

He motioned for her to approach, and she came forward and handed him a stack of documents, careful to keep them face down. The jury verdict forms. There would be multiple options, all on separate pages, ranging from, *We the jury find the Defendant, Lucas Mitchell Campbell, guilty of Murder in the First Degree,* to, *We the jury find the Defendant, Lucas Mitchell Campbell, not guilty.*

There were multiple options between the two ends of the verdict spectrum. Second degree murder. Voluntary manslaughter. Involuntary manslaughter. Willful injury causing death. Willful injury causing serious injury. Assault with a dangerous weapon. Assault. Each one of these options, these lesser offenses, had its own page sandwiched between the verdict forms for guilty and not guilty.

Judge Ahrenson put on his reading glasses and looked down at the stack of documents. Then he began flipping through. Nobody in the courtroom moved, all frozen with anticipation. Ashley was finding it hard to even breathe in that moment. Her heart seemed to stutter as she waited for the judge to speak, to say the words that would seal Lucas's fate. She couldn't imagine what he was feeling in the moment. It had to be something far worse.

Once he'd reached the last page, the judge looked up, ready to pronounce the verdict.

1

ASHLEY

Three Months Earlier
Monday, February 3

Initial client meetings always started as a power struggle. At least they did for Ashley. She was the only public defender in Brine County. The term *public defender* held a stigma, one that Ashley felt was unfair, but it existed all the same. Not all public defenders were the cream of the crop, she knew that, but neither were all doctors, yet sick people didn't go into appointments with physicians challenging their every word, questioning their every thought.

It was frustrating, even infuriating at times, but Ashley had grown used to it. That's why she came prepared for every meeting, armed to the teeth with knowledge. Not only because she was a public defender, but also because she was a woman, and she didn't have gray hair or deep-set wrinkles showing age that many believed meant wisdom. It was the trifecta of expectation—age, gender, court-appointed work—and Ashley fell short on every single count. If she was older. If she was a man. If she was in private practice, she would avoid all the scrutiny. *If, if, if*. But she didn't live in the world of *ifs*. She lived in reality, and her reality required her to know more, to work harder, and to be better than any other attorney.

But Lucas Campbell, the client Ashley currently faced through the glass wasn't challenging her. He'd been arrested the day before and appeared before the magistrate in morning court, claiming he had no money to hire his own attorney. That was when the Court appointed Ashley. Now, here he was, sitting quietly in his jail jumpsuit, patiently waiting for...what? She wasn't quite sure.

He didn't fit the mold she'd set based on her experience with so many other clients. Or perhaps he did, she just couldn't tell. She'd been sitting across from him for a good thirty minutes, and he'd yet to utter a single word. He hadn't called her a *public pretender* or asked for a *real lawyer*. He hadn't offered to pay her *under the table* if she'd work harder on his behalf. He also hadn't acquiesced to her authority. He'd simply said nothing.

They were in the attorney/client room at the jail. It was one of five identical rooms, all with partitions, separating attorney from client with a thick piece of glass. There was one other meeting room, a sixth one that was simply a room with a desk and two chairs. No partitions. No phones. Ashley preferred that sixth room, but she wasn't given a choice. It was jail policy. They would be separated until Lucas could demonstrate he was no longer violent—their words not hers. Nonetheless, she'd delved into the appointment like she would any other.

She'd introduced herself as his attorney. He hadn't responded.

She'd told him that she'd known his mother, Minnie, and that Minnie had been part of Ashley's late mother's book club. Still nothing.

She'd told him that she'd read Minnie's obituary in the paper a few years back. She was so sorry to see her go. Cancer, just like Ashley's mother, although not the same type. He didn't even look up.

Then she mentioned that she still lived in her mother's house. An acreage about thirty minutes south of town. That was when he stilled, his eyes slowly tracking upward, his gaze meeting hers for the first time. What she saw there stilled her heart. It was wild, uncontrolled, almost animalistic. Like a domesticated pig, escaped long enough to turn feral, violent.

"You live on the old Montgomery farm?" His words were slow, his voice scratchy with disuse.

"Yes," Ashley said, trying to piece together why that fact had drawn his attention.

"Are you for or against the windmills?"

"I don't know," Ashley said slowly.

"You don't know," he repeated, his words not quite skeptical but also not wholly accepting.

"I don't know enough about them. At least not yet." Ashley had heard that a Texas oil company had started dabbling in wind energy—apparently realizing renewable energy was the way of the future—and they'd chosen Brine County, Iowa, for their first windmill farm project. Ashley had plenty of questions about the project. Like why choose Iowa when Texas had plenty of its own wind? But she had few answers.

"What is your opinion on them?" she asked.

Lucas shook his head, lowering his eyes back down to the floor.

"Were you offered one of the windmill farm contracts?"

"No."

Ashley tried to discern the nature of his "no." Whether it was a, *No, I didn't want those giant metal monstrosities on or near my property*, or a, *No, I wanted the contract, but I didn't get it.* The way he'd spoken hadn't given any real indication which side of the spectrum and more importantly *where* on that spectrum he fell. He hadn't said it with fervor, or with sadness. Not jealousy or fear. He'd uttered the word *no* with a flat affect, so devoid of emotion that it could rival Ben Stein.

"Okay." Ashley paused, trying to think of the best way to word her next question. Phrasing was important in these initial client meetings. Trust between attorney and client was important, but it wasn't automatic. It had to be earned. "Is this windmill project important to you?"

"Isn't it important to you?"

This, she discovered, was his point of challenge. He didn't care that she was a public defender. He didn't care if she was a woman. He cared about windmills, and how she felt about them popping up throughout the Brine County countryside like ginormous metal daisies.

He stared at her, hazel eyes bright with interest, waiting for her response.

She had no idea what to say. She didn't want to give the wrong answer. But any answer could be wrong, not only by the content of the answer, but the strength in her conviction could also be a problem. Deflecting was the only way.

"I'm a lawyer not a farmer, Lucas. I work long hours and I'm rarely home." *There,* she thought, *crisis averted.*

"But you have to see them driving in and out of town. You'd pass the seven that are already up on Gerald's property."

"Gerald's old property," Ashley said, grabbing onto the name to redirect the conversation. "Gerald's dead now, remember?"

Lucas held up his hands, chained together with heavy irons. "I'm not sure how I could forget."

"You understand you'll be staying in here until your trial, right?"

Lucas shrugged.

Ashley decided this was as good a time as any to go through the pending charges. It was never an easy discussion, but anything seemed better than windmills. "You understand that you have been arrested and accused of murdering Gerald Mock."

"Innocent until proven guilty, right?"

Ashley ignored him. Every defendant awaiting trial in jail raised that complaint. If they were presumed innocent, why were they incarcerated? She was inclined to agree with them, but she'd made that argument at enough bond review hearings to know how every judge in the area would rule.

"If convicted, you will be facing life imprisonment without the possibility of parole." Ashley paused, looking up to see how Lucas would react. He seemed unfazed, so she continued. "There are a number of lesser included offenses, including murder in the second degree. How old are you?"

"Forty."

That seemed about right. He'd been three years ahead of her in school. Close enough in age for her to know *of* him, but not close enough to actually *know* him.

"Sometimes attorneys try to shoot for a plea offer of murder second, but that isn't a real option for you. It carries a mandatory fifty-year prison sentence. That would put you at ninety when you are eligible for parole. You'd more than likely be leaving the prison in a body bag, and even if you weren't, you'd be too old to live any real life. If an offer of murder two comes your way, we might as well take our chances at trial."

Lucas shrugged.

"I don't want to discuss the details of your case at this point. I want to get discovery from the State first, get an idea of strategy, and then start going through facts. I know this sounds odd, but if you give me your version of events and I decide—based on the evidence, of course—that a different defense theory would be more effective, I can't use you as a witness anymore. I probably won't use you as a witness anyway, but we aren't going to start this case limiting our options. You are in a bad enough position as it is."

"Okay."

"Now, I know you..." Ashley's voice trailed off.

She'd been all geared up for a fight. To talk over him, telling him that he needed to shut up. To stop trying to tell her his side of the story. That's how it always went with clients, especially those charged with serious offenses. They all wanted to proclaim their innocence, make Ashley understand that they weren't "bad" people. Yet, Lucas didn't seem to care. She wasn't sure if she should be relieved or concerned.

"I need to get going," Ashley said, glancing at her watch. "I have a sentencing hearing in a few minutes."

"When will you be back?"

"I'm not going to make any promises. Maybe tomorrow, maybe later this week."

"Okay."

This, too, was an odd response. Her clients wanted to see her all the time. They wanted her there, focusing on their case. Not off working with other clients. Yet Lucas didn't seem to care. Ashley cocked her head, assessing her client. He was not at all what she had expected, and if his case was going to unfold in a similar fashion, if his odd fixation with windmills when he was facing life imprisonment was any indication, there could be little doubt that she was in for a wild ride.

2

KATIE

It was Monday, but Katie wasn't working. She'd taken the day off, a much-needed hiatus from the constant needs of her clients. It wasn't their fault; they battled mental health and crippling addictions. Which meant they needed more attention than others. Katie was the lead of the Brine County Mental Health Response Team, a project that focused on intervening with mental health clients before they committed crimes rather than punishing them afterward.

She'd once been a Brine police officer, a job she'd truly and deeply enjoyed, but the department's shrinking budget resulted in a layoff years ago. She'd spent a year after that working as an investigator for the Public Defender's Office. That had been, by far, her favorite job. Partially because she got to work with her best friend, Ashley Montgomery, but also because it was investigative work similar to police work. Yet again, the budget didn't support her continued employment, and then she'd been tapped to lead the Mental Health Response team.

The Brine County Mental Health Response Team was a fledgling program which Katie quickly discovered would require lots of work. Katie had worked fifty hours a week focusing on her clients' various needs, and she'd done it for the past seven months. That had turned to sixty plus hours when one of her two assistants, Rachel Smithson, resigned. Now Katie needed a break. Even if it was only for a day.

To celebrate her short staycation, she'd vowed to spend the entire day doing as little as possible. She was not going to get dressed. She would wear her pajamas until midday when she would change into a different pair of pajamas, the ones she intended to sleep in that night. She would stay in bed, binging Netflix episodes while eating a whole sleeve of raw cookie dough. There would be no actual meals. Only snacks. The kind that were the sugary, salty, savory variety that packed a large quantity of trans fats and high fructose corn syrup. Diet be damned. If she was only going to get one day for vacation, she was going all out.

Then her phone started ringing. She opened her eyes and stared at the ceiling as the phone buzzed on her nightstand, wondering if she should look to see who was calling. It was early in the morning, she could tell by the position of the light filtering in through her bedroom window, so it could be a client. They usually called the office, but when dealing with an acute crisis, they often called Katie directly.

Should I answer it?

I should answer it, she decided, but then she reminded herself that it was her day off, and everyone needed time to themselves. It was a mental health thing, and she knew all about that. Overwork translated to burnout, and then she'd be no use to anyone.

But what if it really is an emergency? An overdose or suicidal thoughts? She sat up suddenly, the blood rushing to her head, and reached for the phone, but the buzzing stopped before she could wrap her hand around the device.

Just as well, she thought, lying back down. If it was important, they'd call back.

And they did.

She grabbed the phone, scrambling to answer. "Hello? This is Katie. Is everything alright?"

"Umm, yes. Thanks for asking, but I think the better question is whether everything is alright with *you*." It was Ashley Montgomery, Katie's once enemy, turned frenemy who had somehow wormed her way into Katie's heart, becoming her best friend.

"I'm fine. Did you call a minute ago?"

"No. Why?"

"Never mind," Katie said, pressing the speakerphone button and dropping back down onto her back.

"Seriously. What's wrong with you? You sound like you are still in bed. Are you sick or something?"

"No."

"Then what's the problem?"

"Why are you calling? Is it solely for harassment purposes, or is there a reason you are interrupting my 'do nothing' day."

"A 'do nothing' day. That sounds nice."

"Yeah. But you're interrupting it with whatever this is." Katie lifted her arm and flicked her wrist to indicate around her. Ashley couldn't see her, but her habit of talking with her hands didn't die when she was alone.

"Don't get snippy. It's not my fault you've overdone it. I warned you that you needed to start taking Saturdays completely off, but you wouldn't listen to me. *I've got too much work to do*, you said. *But people need me*, you said. And what did I tell you?"

Katie sighed. "You said I would burn out."

"And what has happened?"

"I've burned out."

"Exactly."

Katie rolled over and looked at the time on her digital alarm clock. It was nine o'clock in the morning. "So, you were calling to gloat?"

"No. I was calling to complain."

"About?"

"Life."

"What are you doing? It sounds like you're jogging or something." Katie could hear the whistle of the wind against the phone, and Ashley's breaths were growing heavy.

"I'm on my way to court. As always. And I just left the jail."

"Yeah?"

"I've got this new client. It's that new murder. The one between neighbors. You've heard about it, right?"

Katie sat up, her interest piqued. "Everyone has heard about that. Lucas Campbell. I didn't know the guy well, but I would see him in passing. He always seemed shy. A bit of an introvert, but kind. I wouldn't have pinned him as the type to shoot his neighbor in the face. But I guess that's why they say you can't judge a book by its cover."

"I think that's a book thing, not a people thing."

"You know what I mean," Katie said with a sigh.

"Yeah, I know."

"So, what about Lucas Campbell's case?"

"I need an investigator. I hardly know anything about this case—it's early days—but I agree with your assessment of Lucas. He doesn't seem the type who would walk a mile to his neighbor's house, knock on the door, and shoot him in the face the second he answers. Maybe that's what happened—and I'm not saying that it was—but even if it was, that's got to be vastly oversimplifying the situation. There is a deeper undercurrent of issues here. An affair. A land dispute. Harassment of some kind. Something. I just don't know yet. And once I start digging, I know this thing is going to get much bigger over the coming weeks and months. These kinds of cases always do."

"Maybe there are some mental health issues," Katie suggested, trying to keep her tone from growing too hopeful.

The mental health response team, or MHRT for short, didn't get involved until after conviction and sentencing, but she wondered if she could bend the rules a little. She was still technically part of the criminal justice system, but her job lacked the excitement that came with investigating crimes. These days she was overworked, but she was also bored. She wanted to get back into the exciting stuff. This seemed like a way back to it.

"I don't think so," Ashley said.

Katie's heart sank.

"I mean, he's probably depressed. Who wouldn't be? He's looking at wearing one of those depressing onesies and staring at cement walls for the rest of his life. But so far, I'm not seeing any indication of severe mental illness. At least not enough to be helpful in his defense."

"Oh."

Virtually all criminal defendants suffered from some sort of mental illness. Addiction. Schizophrenia. Bi-polar disorder. Post-traumatic stress disorder. Personality disorders. There was always something. It was one of the first things Katie learned when she spent that year working with Ashley as an investigator. Most of them weren't bad because they *chose* that life-style. They were that way because of their medical, mental, and environmental history.

But those mental health disorders did not excuse their behavior. Not unless the defendant was so mentally ill that they were deemed incompetent, meaning they couldn't assist in their own defense, or insane, which meant that they didn't understand the nature and quality of the act they were committing. It didn't sound like Lucas was either incompetent or insane, so a mental health defense was likely off the table.

"But I *need* an investigator," Ashley said, cutting through Katie's thoughts. She said the words with enough force to make it clear that Ashley didn't want just any investigator, she wanted Katie to do it.

Katie sighed heavily. "You know I would love to help you, but I can't just leave my steady employment to investigate one case with you. What would I do after that? I've got a mortgage. And a cat. I've got responsibilities."

"A cat. Those things can feed themselves. Just let him outside."

Katie's gaze shifted to the giant orange fluffball lying at the end of her bed. His belly was so round that he looked very much like a basketball, especially when he was curled up like that. He'd been smaller when she adopted him a few months earlier, but he'd steadily gained weight as the days passed.

"I don't think Mr. Jones is going to catch anything."

"Then he can live off his fat pad for a while."

"And what do I live off of?" Katie paused and then added, "And if you say my fat pad, I'm hanging up."

"You don't have a fat pad."

Logically, Katie knew that Ashley was correct. Or at least that was what she told herself. She wasn't a tiny woman. She wasn't large either, but she definitely had curves. She was nothing like Ashley, who was all sharp angles, straight up and down with jutting cheek and hip bones.

"I don't know," Ashley said with a hint of frustration. "The head office in Des Moines has waved their magic wand and granted me funds to hire an investigator for this case, and this case only, but I don't want just anyone. I want you. And I get where you're coming from, I do. I just don't like it."

"I wish I could help." And she did. Katie wished so much that she could be back in that world, working with Ashley. That year they'd worked together, culminating in the fire down at Frank Vinny's property, was the best year of her career.

"Alright," Ashley said with a heavy sigh. "I've got to go. I have a sentencing hearing that starts here in a few minutes. Thanks for chatting with me. Even though you can't help, I feel a little better."

"Anytime," Katie said.

She hung up, dropped the phone to her side, and laid back down, ready to fully embrace her *do nothing* day. Then there was a knock on her door. She ignored it at first, but it came again and again. It grew so incessant that Mr. Jones even lifted his head, meowing plaintively for her to get the door.

"Fine," she said, standing up and stalking out of the room. She headed straight for the door, wrenching it open. "What do you wa— " she said, words escaping her when she saw who stood behind the door.

It was her father. Michael Michello. They had a sordid past and a tumultuous relationship. He'd gone to prison for financial crimes when Katie was only sixteen, leaving her to fend for herself. She was an adult, and a police officer, when he was released and showed up on her doorstep the first time. It took over a year to form even the slightest bond, but then he disappeared. Just *poof,* gone. She'd heard nothing from him for a full year. What he'd been up to was anyone's guess and definitely not something Katie wanted to discover.

"Look what the cat dragged in," Katie said.

"Hello, Katie," Michael said, giving a sheepish wave.

Katie was reluctant to invite him inside. But he was her father, after all. She couldn't just leave him standing out in the cold. She also didn't know what to think, how to receive him. He'd been involved in an illegal smuggling operation the last time she'd spoken to him. If he was still a part of that, she didn't want anything to do with him.

"I've got a proposition for you," Michael said.

And those were the six words Katie hadn't wanted to hear from her father's mouth. Especially on her "do nothing" day. It was barely nine o'clock, and the way her morning was shaping up, she knew her day off was going to turn into an all-out circus.

3

ASHLEY

Ashley's client was waiting for her when she reached the second floor of the courthouse. He was a middle-aged man, wearing a pair of gray slacks and a dark blue button-down shirt with white pearl buttons. He was seated on one of the benches outside the district courtroom, watching the stairway. When he saw her, he stood and started walking toward her.

"Ms. Montgomery, thank you, thank you for coming," he said, grasping her hand and giving it a firm shake.

"Sure, Ben," she said. "But it's part of my job. I *have* to show up."

"All the same," Ben said.

Benjamin Harris was not Ashley's typical client. He didn't use illegal substances or overindulge in alcohol. He also wasn't mentally ill. He was a regular guy who had fallen on some hard times. He'd been working to get himself out of it, burning the candle from both ends, and one day he'd just snapped.

"Are you ready for this?" Ashley asked, nodding to the closed double doors that led to the courtroom.

"Ready as I'll ever be," he said, tugging at the collar of his shirt.

"Don't worry. It'll be a quick hearing. We are asking that you receive a deferred judgment, and the prosecutor is making the same request. I don't see any reason why the judge wouldn't grant it."

A deferred judgment allowed a person to plead guilty to a crime, and the person would be placed on probation for usually a year or two. If they stayed out of trouble and complied with the terms of probation, the offense would be expunged from their record once the probationary period passed. Deferred judgments were reserved for those with clean criminal histories, and people were only allowed to use two in their lifetime.

"Anything you want to discuss before we go inside?"

Ben shook his head.

Ashley grabbed the handle of one of the double doors and pulled it open, motioning for Ben to enter first. He did, and she followed close behind. The courtroom was vast, with high ceilings decorated in intricate crown mouldings and carefully painted designs. The judge's bench took up the entire back wall with its dark wood reaching up to the clear white of the ceiling. The room itself held such power that it automatically induced the same kind of reverent silence found within the walls of cathedrals.

It was Ben's first time inside the courtroom, and he froze as he crossed the threshold. Ashley tried to keep clients out of this room as much as possible, preferring to handle most hearings in writing, but Judge Ahrenson had set this one for an in-court hearing. Which could be bad for Ben. The judge could have handled the sentencing in writing and chose not to, which could be a signal that he was going to reject the plea agreement.

She hadn't warned Ben of her concerns because it was too late to take back his guilty plea. A Motion in Arrest of Judgment—the motion that said *Judge, for whatever reason I'm backing out of my guilty plea*—had to be filed five days before sentencing.

"This way," Ashley whispered, motioning for Ben to follow her up the long aisle toward the attorney tables.

They stepped through a small partition and then left to the defense table. Charles Hanson, the prosecutor, was already seated at the desk next to it. He didn't greet Ashley, and she was just fine with that. Their working relationship was shaky, at best, and it had always been that way. She didn't see a need to force social niceties, and he seemed to feel the same way, which she appreciated.

Ashley motioned for Ben to sit at the left side of the table, and she sat to his right, both facing the bench where Judge Ahrenson would soon sit. The court reporter poked her head out of the door that led back to judge's chambers.

"Is everyone ready?"

Ashley nodded.

"Okay, then. We'll be right in." She disappeared back into chambers, then reappeared a moment later, carrying her black stenograph machine. "All rise."

Ashley stood and motioned for her client to do the same.

"The Honorable Judge Ahrenson presiding," the court reporter said as she set her steno machine down and settled into her seat in front of the judge.

Judge Ahrenson entered the courtroom, his black robe billowing behind him. "Have a seat, have a seat," he said as he made his way up to the bench. He waited a few moments for everyone to get situated, and then he turned to the court reporter and said, "Are you ready?"

She nodded, her fingers poised over the small keyboard.

"We are convened today in State of Iowa vs. Benjamin Harris, Brine County Case Number FECR019453. The Defendant was originally charged with Willful Injury, a Class D Felony. That charge was amended by the County Attorney to assault causing bodily injury, a serious misdemeanor. The Defendant has entered a guilty plea in writing to the amended charge. Today is the date set for sentencing. Are the parties ready to proceed?"

"Yes, your honor," Ashley said.

"Yes," Charles echoed.

"I don't see any pending motions, so we will proceed with sentencing. What is the State's recommendation?"

Charles slowly rose to his feet. He'd always been a big man, wide and tall, but lately he'd been packing on the pounds at an alarming rate. It was likely stress. Judge Ahrenson was retiring at the end of the month, and Charles had officially filed his application for the position. It wasn't more than five minutes after Charles had hit the *send* button before the gossip started. Suddenly every attorney within a fifty-mile radius had something to say about Charles Hanson. Half of them didn't even know the prosecutor. At least not well.

"The State is recommending that the Defendant receive a deferred judgment with informal probation for one year. It is my understanding that he is between jobs, so the State has no objection to the court waiving the fine."

"Very well," Judge Ahrenson said, before his laser sharp focus swung to Ashley. "And the Defense? I assume you join in the State's request."

"Yes, your honor," Ashley said.

"Well, sir," Judge Ahrenson said, focusing on Ben who was hunched over, trying to make himself as small as possible. "Do you have anything you want to say? You have the right to allocution, which means you have the right to tell me anything you want me to know in mitigation of sentence."

"Umm, yes, sir," Ben said.

"Go ahead and stand and make your statement."

Ben stood and wiped his sweaty palms on his slacks. "I'm not here to make excuses. I know what I did was wrong, and that's why I pled guilty." His voice started out shaky but gained strength as he continued. "I just want to give you, the court, some background on why this happened."

Ashley froze. This was not the carefully prepared speech they had spent weeks writing and practicing. She didn't know what, exactly, it was, but she felt sure it would take this hearing off the rails in a hurry. Yet there was nothing she could do about it. This statement was Ben's constitutional right. Even she, as his attorney, was powerless to shut him up.

"I am a farmer. Or, well, I was a farmer until the cost of materials skyrocketed. I was already struggling from the last five years of constant droughts. Every year it was getting harder and harder to hold on. Then someone approached me about a year ago, a realtor representing an undisclosed entity. He offered to buy up my farmland. The guy wasn't local. He had a Southern drawl. But he said his client was moving to the area and wanted to farm up here."

This was all information Ashley had never heard before. She discouraged clients from going into these kinds of stories with her. Partially, because she didn't want them to accidentally say something that could ruin some potential defense, but also because it was a waste of time. The reason for the assault didn't create a legal defense unless it rose to the level of self-defense, which was rarely the case. In Iowa, unless a defendant was in their own home, they had a duty to retreat before responding to violence with violence. If there was any space to retreat and the defendant hadn't done so, self-defense didn't apply.

"I sold my farmland to him. I was a bit surprised when he didn't want the farming equipment, but I assumed, quite wrongly I might add, that his client already had equipment of his own. It wasn't until a few months later that I found out that his client was an executive in a Texas oil company, and they were coming to this area to put up windmills. Now that land I sold to him has fifteen of those things on it, all hovering over my little house that is still at the corner of that property. Have you ever been beneath one of those suckers? You can feel it, right here," Ben pumped his chest with a closed fist. "It gets into your soul, the very base of your existence."

Ashley's gaze darted toward the Judge, trying to gauge his reaction to the story, but she saw none. As usual, his face was blank. A mask worthy of any professional poker player.

"Don't get me wrong, I'm not completely against windmills. Or I'm at least undecided on them. What bothered me so much about this incident was the deception. He lied to me about his intent."

The courtroom had always been silent, but you could actually hear a pin drop in that moment.

"And that's why, when I saw Mr. Larson, the realtor I dealt with when I sold my property, down at Mikey's Tavern trying to buy up some more land from Frankie Pitch's grandpappy, I lost it. I walked right over to him and punched him straight in the face. I know I shouldn't have done it. I know that he lost a couple teeth, but I just couldn't stand there and listen to him spewing those same lies he'd sold to me." He paused, wiping his hands on his pants a second time. "And that's all I really had to say."

Ben dropped back down into his seat, his body falling like dead weight. Like he'd expended every ounce of energy exercising his right of allocution, leaving barely enough to remain upright.

The judge was silent for a long moment, then he shuffled through a few papers before looking up. "What you did was wrong, Mr. Harris. That's why you are here today. No matter your reasoning, it is illegal to strike anyone. Especially with enough force to knock teeth loose. But I'm not going to leave you in suspense for long. I'm going to go along with the recommendation of the parties. I am doing this partially because I respect the opinions of the prosecutor and your defense attorney. I am also doing this because those assholes putting up those windmills are not blameless. They have been a scourge to this community since the moment they arrived."

Ashley started at the word *assholes*. Not because she was offended. She was known to have the mouth of a sailor. But because she'd never heard Judge Ahrenson curse. Not in chambers and certainly not in a courtroom on the record.

"Is there anything else?" The judge asked, his gaze darting from one attorney to the other. They both shook their heads. "In that case, we're off the record, and I'd like to speak with you, Ms. Montgomery, back in chambers on an unrelated matter."

Ashley stood, patting her client on the shoulder. She gave him a brief rundown of the things he needed to do next, and then she headed toward the door the judge had used to exit the courtroom. She was walking slowly, taking her time, all but dragging her feet. She knew what this was about, and she wasn't quite ready for the upcoming conversation. He was bound to pose a question to her. To ask her about her application for his position.

She had been intending to submit it, but she was not so sure about it anymore. She'd had enough scrutiny over the years, and she didn't want to end up like Charles Hanson. Stress eating her way through all the food in Brine while others gossiped half-truths about her career, belittling her in a desperate attempt to make others believe she was unqualified for the position.

Especially when she was just getting started with Lucas's murder case. There was so much to do. Hearings, depositions, her own investigation. She couldn't do it all, at least not on her own. Time was not an item that came in unlimited quantities. More could not be purchased or bartered for. If she was to apply for this judgeship, something would have to give. That something would probably come from the zealousness of Lucas's defense. He would suffer for her choice to apply for a judgeship.

Was it worth it?

She didn't know.

4

KATIE

Those six words—*I've got a proposition for you*—were perhaps the worst possible things for Katie's father to say. They caused a sudden, visceral repulsion to rise within her.

"You have two minutes to tell me what the hell you are doing here," Katie said, blocking the door with her body.

This wasn't the father she'd known and adored when she was a child. He'd been released from prison over a year ago, and there were moments she thought they would get back to those early days. Then he'd started going down the wrong path, committing crimes to get ahead. That had bothered her, but then he'd disappeared from her life for a full year, once again choosing money over a relationship with his daughter.

"I already told you. I have a proposition."

"A proposition," Katie repeated, her words like acid.

"Yes. Can you let me in so we can talk?"

"What kind of proposition?" She was fine leaving him out in the cold.

"A job offer."

"A job. If it involves committing crimes, you can turn around and walk your happy ass back to Stephanie Arkman." The Arkman family was local to Brine. They practically owned the county and were influential throughout the state. Stephanie was their matriarch and someone who didn't shy away from a little criminal activity if it generated enough revenue for her businesses.

"Oh, come on," Michael said, running a nervous hand through his thinning crop of partially grey hair. "You work with Stephanie, too."

"No," Katie corrected. "I work for the city. Stephanie makes donations to our organization, but I don't work *for* her."

"And those donations come from Stephanie's income, which is based on the profitability of her businesses. The work I *did* for her assisted in the profitability."

"The work you did?" Katie said, placing her hands on her hips. "So, you aren't trafficking people anymore?"

"I wasn't ever trafficking people. I was bringing workers north from Texas. That isn't trafficking. It's transporting. Like a bus."

"Like. A. Bus," Katie repeated.

It was a justification. That while the immigrants were illegal, they were hard workers. Law abiding citizens who were far more likely to behave than their citizen counterparts like her father. Ashley would agree with Michael on this point, but to Katie it was still breaking the law. No matter how it had occurred. If he wanted to change the law, he needed to go through the proper channels.

"Anyway," Michael said, pulling Katie out of her thoughts. "We are getting off topic here. I want to discuss a business plan with you, and it is one that I think you will want to hear."

"How do *you* know what *I* want to hear?"

"Can we stop with the jabs for five minutes? Yes, I have made mistakes. I disappeared for a while, but I did that for your own good. You didn't want to know how I was making my money, and I needed to raise some capital to start a new business. So, here we are."

"A year later."

"A year later."

Katie held his gaze, her arms crossed, and her jaw set. She wanted to turn him away. To make him feel the same way he made her feel. Abandoned. Yet she felt herself stepping away from the doorway and motioning for him to enter. He was still her father. Flawed as he was, she still loved him. At least he kept coming back, unlike her mother who had disappeared when she was sixteen and never returned.

"Thank you," he said, walking past her and into her living room. He stood there for a moment, hands in pockets, looking around. "Nice place you got here."

"I can't tell if you are being sarcastic, or you mean that." Katie's house was tiny by Michael Michello standards. His last home—aside from his prison cell—was a mansion twenty times the size of her small, two-bedroom city bungalow.

"I mean it. It's very homey."

Katie stared at him, trying to decipher what, exactly, he meant by that. Homey could easily be a compliment, but it could also be backhanded. She hadn't spent enough time around him yet to determine the difference. She almost challenged him on it, but she changed her mind at the last moment, shaking her head and shifting topics.

"So, what's this important proposition?"

Just then Mr. Jones came sauntering into the room, his green eyes locked onto Katie's father.

"You have a cat," Michael said.

"Obviously."

"I'm allergic," he said with a sneeze.

"Then it's a good thing he isn't *your* cat."

"Sheesh. You're worse than you were as a moody teenager."

"I'm surprised you remember me as a teenager."

"Well, don't be. I remember everything about you. How do you think I made it through all those years in prison? It wasn't thoughts of my ex-wife, that's for sure. It was you. I kept reminding myself that one day I'd be back out and I could spend time with my little girl."

He sounded sincere, but Katie didn't want to believe him. She was angry, and she wasn't quite ready to let go of that anger. She needed a little more time to stew in it.

"And that's what brings me to you today."

"The proposition has something to do with spending time with me?" She was trying to follow his train of thought, but she couldn't quite connect the dots.

"Yes."

Katie walked into the kitchen and poured herself a cup of water, suddenly feeling flushed. She didn't know where this was going, and it was starting to make her nervous.

"I'm going to open a private investigation firm."

"A what?" Katie said, choking on her water.

Michael came over to her, clapping her on the back as she dissolved into a fit of coughing.

"What do you know about investigations?" She croaked once her coughing was under control.

"Nothing."

"I feel like this goes without saying, but I'm going to go ahead and say it anyway. Just because you have been investigated, charged, and convicted of crimes does not mean you know how to conduct investigations. It makes you about as qualified as you are to practice as a lawyer."

Michael chuckled. "You're right. That's where you come in. I can run the business side, and you can do the investigating."

Katie stared at him, studying his expression, trying to discern his angle. Did he truly want to make up for lost time? So much so that he'd invest every penny he'd saved in a business that would bring them in contact day in and day out. Could they handle that kind of closeness?

"I know it seems odd. I get that," Michael said, raising his hands in a gesture of surrender. "But this isn't a knee-jerk, sudden reaction. I've been saving and working on the business side of this for a while. This part of Iowa needs someone skilled to help out on the defense side of investigations. Plus, I know how much you liked working with Ashley Montgomery. I'd planned on coming to you with this idea in a couple months after I'd had a chance to reestablish our relationship, but then I heard about this new arrest. That Lucas Campbell guy. And I heard that your buddy Ashley was appointed to represent him. Then I figured there was no better time than the present."

"You really want to do this?" Katie said, her heart leaping in her chest. It sounded almost too good to be true. "It would be profitable?"

"I've crunched some initial numbers. And, yes, I think it would be profitable. We can charge sixty dollars an hour and rent a small space in downtown Brine. It'll be rough going at first, but I'm confident we can make it work."

The idea was attractive despite Katie's recent frustration with her father. She'd be back in criminal investigations. Sure, she'd have to do some civil stuff, some investigations into cheating spouses and people lying about injuries, but she'd be willing to sling some shit to get back into investigations. Then she remembered how things had gone with George when he'd been a supervisor to her. She didn't like George telling her what to do, and she certainly wouldn't take well to her father doing the same thing.

"I would be free to handle cases how I see fit?"

"Yes. As you so eloquently put it earlier, I don't know anything about investigations. I wouldn't know how to boss you around. But I will be setting a budget, and you'll have to do what you need within the financial parameters I choose."

"Alright," Katie said, nodding. She stuck her hand out to shake. "I'll do it."

Michael grasped her outstretched hand, and shook it, putting his other hand on the outside of hers like he was cradling it. His eyes sparkled, filming over with unshed tears.

It was touching to see him so happy, but that wasn't the primary thought filling her mind. Her head was filled with the same idea on a loop. *I'm back.* And she couldn't wait to tell Ashley.

5

ASHLEY

"The application deadline is in two days," Judge Ahrenson said.

Ashley had just arrived back in chambers and had barely set one foot in Judge Ahrenson's office before he was already starting in on her. "I know, I know."

She was growing frustrated. They'd been over this countless times. He knew the process of applying for judgeships—obviously, since he was currently sitting on the bench—but he'd never applied while working for the public defender's office. She was already overworked and overstressed. Adding one more thing to the pile felt a little like a straw dangling over a sagging camel's back.

"Is that an 'I know' because you are keeping tabs on the deadline so that you can get your ducks in a row, or is it an 'I know' you are watching the deadline, waiting for it to pass so I'll leave you alone?"

"Both."

"Sit down." He motioned to the two leather chairs across from his desk and removed his reading glasses, tossing them in front of him.

Ashley did as instructed. She was irritated with him like anyone would be with a nagging parent, but also like parents, he had authority over her. He was a judge. He would be right up until his retirement, and even after that if he chose to continue as a senior judge.

"I'm not pushing you to apply for the fun of it. You *need* this. And so does the judiciary. Look around you. There are very few female judges in the State of Iowa. None in our district aside from magistrates, and those aren't *really* judges. They're like quasi-judges."

"They're magistrate court judges," Ashley said. He gave her a hard look, and she relented. "Okay, okay, you're right. Magistrates aren't really allowed to do a whole lot."

Magistrate Court was for simple misdemeanors and small claims. They handled the lowest of the low hearings. They sometimes held preliminary hearings, which were probable cause hearings for the more serious indictable offenses, but once probable cause was found, those cases were out of the magistrate's jurisdiction and passed along to district associate court and district court judges.

"I'm an old man, but even I can recognize that it is time for change. I want my position to be the start of that," Judge Ahrenson said. "You have the experience, the intelligence, and the desire to do good. You lack a judicial temperament at times, but that's something you can work on."

"I don't know what you are talking about," Ashley said with a sly grin. "Everybody loves me."

"You never miss an opportunity to take a jab. That's what I mean."

"I can't say that'll change if I ever do take the bench."

"When, not if. And you'll just have to learn to issue your jabs fairly."

"I can do that, but..."

It was not a fact lost on her; women needed to be part of the judiciary. They made up at least fifty percent of the population, so they should fill fifty percent of the judge positions. That, of course, was not the case, and she did agree that it needed to change. She just didn't know if she was the right one for the job.

"What is holding you back?"

"Politics."

Judge Ahrenson nodded and leaned back in his seat. "I thought that might be the issue."

"Look at Charles Hanson. He applied, and all of a sudden he's the topic of conversation in every circle. I heard someone down at Genie's diner discussing his weight. Saying that he undoubtedly has a clogged artery or two, so he shouldn't get the position because he might die soon."

"I heard that, too."

"I don't like Charles Hanson. Not even a little bit. But really? People are predicting his death and debating his health all because he's applied for a position that he is fully qualified to hold." She paused, biting her lip. "And don't tell him I said that last part."

"Your secret is safe with me."

"And then there is the stuff about his wife. Everyone keeps saying she had an affair fifteen years ago. *Fifteen years.* Why on earth does that matter? If she did—and I'm not saying it's true—then who cares? It has absolutely nothing to do with his ability to be a fair and impartial judge. It happened a long time ago. They have kids together. If they chose to make it work, then it's really none of anyone else's business."

"It's politics," he said, threading his fingers together and putting them behind his head. "The process sucks. I won't deny that. Everyone's skeletons come out. But it doesn't last forever. Only until you are selected for the job and then it all stops. Abruptly. I guess people don't want to disparage the person making decisions."

"What about the others? The ones that don't get the job. What happens to their skeletons?"

"People stop caring. Gossip is like strawberries."

"Strawberries?"

"Yes. Strawberries. Attractive at first, but it grows moldy rather quickly."

While Ashley appreciated his effort in trying to ease her mind, he was missing the mark. "I have so many skeletons. All of which were once public knowledge but have since died down or grown moldy, or whatever. Arnold Von Reich and Victor Petrovsky are just a few. Those stories aren't like strawberries. They won't stay moldy."

"You'll get scrutiny over Von Reich and Petrovsky's cases again. That's true. People will relitigate it. But they will also remember how you were victimized by a local law enforcement officer, and the county attorney at the time. They'll also remember your work with Rachel Smithson. You were the only one willing to dig deeper to find the truth about her. As a result, she was exonerated, and her father went to prison."

"I don't know," Ashley said with a heavy sigh. "Rachel just came out of the limelight. I don't want her thrust right back into it. Especially when it would be my fault."

Rachel was once a client of Ashley's, but she'd become more than that over the past few years. She was like a daughter to Ashley now. The closest thing she'd ever have to a child.

"Rachel isn't around anymore, right? She moved to Des Moines for school, didn't she?"

"Yes," Ashley admitted.

After Rachel had been kidnapped by one of Ashley's clients, she'd decided to get out of Brine. Ashley had agreed that it was time. Rachel had been taking online classes, but she moved to Des Moines to enroll full time in classes at Drake University. She was close to graduation, and her ultimate goal was to go to law school. Ashley hadn't encouraged Rachel to follow in her footsteps, but she hadn't discouraged it, either.

"She won't be back for another couple of years, right?"

Ashley nodded.

"So, now is the time. The gossip will go around, sure, but it's local gossip. It won't make it all the way to Des Moines. They aren't in our district, so they won't care about our choice of a district court judge."

He had a point. If there was any time that would protect Rachel emotionally, this was it. "Okay," Ashley said. "You've convinced me."

"Good. Now, get out of here and finish that application."

"Thanks," Ashley said, nodding and rising to her feet.

On her way out of the courthouse, she started making a list of the things she needed to do for the application process. She was almost done with the paper application, but that was only a start. She would need to start reaching out to other attorneys, requesting support. She'd need to schedule meetings with everyone on the judicial nominating committee. She would need to go to those meetings and then she'd have to prepare her speech for the committee meeting. And those were just the first steps.

Then there was Lucas's case. She was going to have to go through the application process while providing him with a zealous defense. It all felt like too much. There was no way she could effectively do everything.

Unless she intended to forgo sleep, which was not an option. She needed help. She needed an investigator.

6

KATIE

Michael and Katie did not waste time celebrating their newly forged father/daughter business venture. There wasn't time. There was a lot to do in the coming days to get the office up and running, especially if they wanted to be ready in time to offer assistance to Ashley. They would have to secure office space and buy equipment and office furniture while sending out feelers to potential clients. But first, Katie needed to inform her current employer of her departure.

So, she and Michael parted ways, both leaving Katie's house with a little extra spring in their step. He was on his way to file documents to officially form Mickey & Michello Investigations, PLLC, and Katie was on her way to the Mental Health Response Team's downtown office. As excited as she was to get back into the world of investigations, she did not relish the thought of informing Tom, the only remaining employee, of her departure.

Their office had contained three original members. Katie, Rachel, and Tom Archie. Rachel had resigned in December and moved from town. She had claimed she wanted to focus on her education, her future, but Katie knew it was more than that. Rachel had been through a lot of trauma while living in Brine, and she needed a break from it and to step away from the town so that, hopefully, she could one day return, this time with her head clear.

It had been hectic after Rachel's departure. Tom and Katie had barely managed to keep on top of their caseloads. Now that Katie was leaving, Tom was going to drown. There was no way around it. Especially since he'd be thrust into the lead position and required to oversee the hiring process, something he had never been eager to do.

Katie parked out front of the MHRT office and shut off the engine, studying the newly remodeled front of the building. Rachel was a member of the very rich, very influential Arkman family. So, when she'd joined the team, her aunt, Stephanie Arkman, had poured a lot of money into the project. Hundreds of thousands on the low end, and millions on the high. As a result, the gleaming façade of the building made it one of the most attractive buildings in courthouse square, second only to the ornate courthouse itself.

She was stalling. She knew it. Trying to build up the courage to march inside and inform Tom of her plans. He was going to try to talk her out of it. To him, it would seem like a sudden departure, as if she had changed her mind about MHRT overnight. It wasn't true. She still believed in the mission of the team, but she'd missed the excitement and challenge of investigative work for quite some time now.

"No time like the present," she told herself. She took a deep breath, sucking it in through her nose and releasing it through her mouth. Then she forced herself to get out of the car and walk into her soon-to-be former office.

"It's just me," she called as she walked through the front door.

There was no receptionist—Katie hadn't had the time to hire and train someone—and there had been some trouble a few months earlier when some clients became far too interested in a MHRT worker, so Katie had security cameras placed in the office. Every time someone came through the front door, a buzzer would go off in the offices and the person there would know to check the cameras and see who was there. Katie was calling out to save Tom that second step.

"I thought you had the day off," Tom said, coming down the long hallway with a wide grin on his face. "Something about a lazy day vacation. Or did you miss me too much?"

"Yes, I did have the day off, but something came up and I needed to be here. To, uh," she swallowed hard, "talk to you."

"Talk to me?" Tom raised his eyebrow. "I'm not in trouble, am I?"

"No, no, nothing like that."

"Oh, good," Tom said with a sigh of relief.

They had been friends before working together, but Katie was still technically his boss. Their friendship complicated the boss/subordinate line. It could have been a problem if an issue had come up requiring her to reprimand him. Fortunately, Tom was the ideal employee, so their relationship had remained intact. At least up until now.

"I do have some...news." She wasn't quite sure how to characterize what she was about to tell him. It felt like good news for her, and Tom would likely understand the benefit to her professionally and emotionally in forging a bond between herself and her father, but he would not welcome the extra responsibility thrust on his shoulders.

"News. Most news is bad."

"Is it?"

"Yeah," Tom crossed his arms. "Turn on any TV news station and I bet you one hundred bucks that whatever story they are discussing is a negative one. Conservative or liberal, local or national, foreign or domestic, it doesn't matter. All *news* is bad news."

"And here I thought the saying was no news is bad news."

"That's no news is good news, and that means that not hearing the news means you can't hear the bad things. It literally makes my point."

"Oh. Well, anyway, we are getting a little off track here," Katie said.

"You're the one who used the word."

"Whatever," Katie said.

He was messing with her. It was a playful banter common between adult siblings who were close, which was practically what Katie and Tom were, but it was starting to irritate her. She had come for a serious conversation, not to shoot the shit and waste her only day off work. They could do that any day. Or at least they used to be able to.

"So, seriously. What's brought you in?" Tom's typically smiling demeanor had grown solemn, like he knew what was coming and he'd already braced himself for it.

"I'm going to resign."

"What? Why?"

"I'm going to start working with my father."

Tom blinked several times in rapid succession, his long, blond eyelashes fluttering like tiny butterflies, apparently speechless.

"He's opening a firm for private investigators. He wants me to be his partner."

Understanding dawned on his face, bringing a lighthearted twinkle to his eyes, but that darkened almost immediately.

"I'm sorry. I just need to do something different. I need a challenge. I'm tired of managing people. Keeping their schedules and making sure they've taken their medications. I thought there would be more excitement, but there isn't. Sometimes I feel like a glorified babysitter in this job, and I don't babysit. Not even when I was young. I'm not good at it."

Tom was silent for a long moment. Then he nodded. "You have always been kinda terrible with the clients." His smile returned, but this time it did not reach his eyes.

"Gee, thanks."

"Sometimes the truth hurts."

"Everybody hurts."

"Everybody cries," Tom said, drawing the syllables out in lilting tune.

"We're getting off track here with song lyrics," Katie said.

"You have a point. Have you told City Council about your impending departure? Forest Parker is going to be pissed."

Forest Parker had been a member of City Council for several years, and MHRT had been his pet project. He had handpicked Katie for the lead position. Of course, he'd first caused her to lose her job at the police department by cutting the budget over and over again, but she tried not to think about that particular manipulation all too often. It made her blood boil.

"He'll be fine," Katie said. She sounded a lot more confident than she felt.

"If you say so. Will you stay until I hire someone?"

"I'll stay as long as I can."

"That's a cryptic answer. Do you intend to go into politics next? You seem to have developed a knack for answering questions with non-answers."

"No politics, and I don't know the answer, so I'm trying to be as honest as I can without selling you something as truth when I don't know."

"How noble of you. So, when are you going to tell City Council?"

"Now if I can. I wanted to tell you first, though."

"That, I appreciate. Thank you."

"You're welcome."

"Do you plan to go over there now?" Tom asked as Katie started to inch her way closer to the door. They'd worked closely for a long time now and he knew her far too well.

"Yeah."

He glanced at his watch. "They're probably at lunch. You should wait an hour or two."

"Okay. I guess I'll pop over to Ashley's office to kill some time."

A flicker of something passed Tom's expression, but it was gone before Katie could discern what, exactly, it was. He and Ashley's romantic relationship had ended a long time ago, but neither had moved on, so she sometimes wondered if they continued to hold a flame for one another.

"Tell Ashley I said hi," Tom said.

"Will do," Katie said, turning and heading for the door. "I'll see you tomorrow."

"Text me to tell me how things go with the Council. It might not be pretty with Rachel leaving so recently."

"It won't be pretty. You should probably come. It's a public meeting. You can watch them chew my ass. It'll make you feel better."

"I just might do that," Tom said.

"Bye," Katie called, then she exited out the front door, heading for Ashley's office.

Once outside, she issued a heavy sigh of relief. Tom had taken the news far better than she had hoped. She must have been showing more signs of discontent with her position than she had thought. Part of her hoped that it would go just as smoothly with City Council, but Tom was probably right. She was in for an unpleasant afternoon.

7

ASHLEY

Katie was waiting for Ashley in the small, outdated waiting room area of the Public Defender's Office. She jumped up, an expression of sheer joy on her face as Ashley walked through the door. Ashley had not seen Katie so excited in quite some time. She was exhausted and overwhelmed after her meeting with Judge Ahrenson, but Katie's smile was contagious. Now that she was standing, she was practically bouncing on the balls of her feet.

"Did you win the lottery or something?" Ashley asked.

"No, better."

"Better?"

"You know I'd be bored with all that money. I need purpose, not cash."

"I could help you spend it. I don't need a purpose, I'm all cash."

"Bullshit."

"Okay, you're right. Come on back," Ashley said, motioning for Katie to follow her. "So, what has you grinning like a Girl Scout who just sold all her cookies?"

"That's an odd analogy."

"Have you looked in the mirror? You're glowing. It better not be a new guy. Men really shouldn't affect your wellbeing like that."

"No, no, nothing like that," Katie said.

Ashley led Katie past the empty reception desk, back to the

employee section of the office. "Hey, Elena," Ashley said, waving as they passed the office manager who was busy typing at her computer.

Elena lifted a hand in greeting, but she didn't look away from her computer screen. She was truly an excellent hire. She'd been young, barely eighteen, when Ashley had hired her, but she'd worked tirelessly ever since. She had no formal legal training, but this job was an education of its own. If Elena could practice law, she'd be a better lawyer than most in the area.

Ashley continued walking a long hallway, stopping at the very last office, her office, and motioning for Katie to enter first.

"Sit," Ashley said, indicating two beat-up leather chairs across from a flimsy looking, faux wood executive desk.

The leather chair hissed under Katie's weight, losing volume with the loss of air.

"Sorry about the chair," Ashley said. "I'd like new ones, but, budget," she said, shrugging in a *what can I do* kind of way.

"I don't mind. I'm going to be roughing it soon anyway."

That was interesting. It was common knowledge that MHRT was well funded by the Arkman family foundation. Sure, Rachel had left, but Stephanie would not pull funding merely because her niece had decided to go become a full-time college student. Or would she?

Ashley leaned forward, her elbows on her desk and her hands on her chin. "Explain."

"I'm quitting."

"You're quitting? Why?" It wasn't a complete surprise. Katie hadn't been excited about her work for quite some time. Katie seemed to think it was some big, protected secret, but she had no poker face. Anyone with eyes could see she was unhappy and her days working for MHRT were numbered.

"I'm going to work with my dad."

"Doing..."

Katie's father had a financial background, but he ended up losing a lot of other people's money, robbing Peter to pay Paul, and that had led to a lengthy prison sentence for Michael Michello. There was no way he'd be doing that kind of work again. He couldn't be trusted. Plus, Katie knew nothing about investing.

"Private investigations."

Ashley's heart leaped, bounding inside her chest. It felt too good to be true. She'd just been thinking that she needed to hire an investigator to help with Lucas's case, someone as detail oriented and career driven as Katie, but she had doubted that she would ever find someone in her small town of Brine who would have all the qualities that she needed. Katie was a diamond in the rough. And here she was, telling Ashley that she was going into business as an investigator.

"Are you fucking with me?" Ashley said, giving Katie a sidelong look. "Because if you are, I don't think it's funny. I'm going to be legit pissed if you get my hopes up just to dash them later."

"Nope. It's the truth. Cross my heart," Katie said, making a crossing motion with her index finger across her chest. "I'm going to tell City Council after lunch."

"Forest Parker isn't going to like it."

"Yeah, well, this may be news to him, but my life does not revolve around Forest Parker."

"I would love to see his face when you tell them. To be a fly on the wall..."

Forest Parker was the only liberal on Brine City Council, so he was the only one with any kind of tolerance for the public defender's office. Ashley and Forest were friendly most of the time, but he was from one of the rich agricultural families who'd almost all turned political. His politics were usually in line with Ashley's, but he toed a party line, which Ashley thought was bullshit. If anyone really thought deeply about either party's full spectrum of political views, they would realize how contrary some are to others. Yet they accepted them as a package deal without any push back, and that annoyed Ashley. She never accepted anything without fully thinking it through.

"You can come with me," Katie said, sitting up straighter. "Their meetings are open to the public. You can sit in one of the chairs in the gallery."

"I don't know. They aren't going to be happy with you, and my presence will rile them up. Bill Roberts and Tucker Caine hate me."

Bill Roberts and Tucker Caine were the other two city councilmen. Ashley was constantly butting heads with them. Every now and then, when she felt like having a little bit of fun, she'd pop into a city council meeting and start causing problems, asking questions that she knew were contrary to their positions. Just to piss them off.

"Please," Katie said. "I need your emotional support. Don't make me beg. I will."

"I'll do it on one condition."

"That is..."

"You agree to be the investigator for Lucas Campbell's case."

"Done."

"Done? Really?" A smile tugged at the corners of her lips. "But we haven't even discussed compensation. The head office in Des Moines has cleared the use of an investigator in this case—why I even have to ask is another rant better left for a different day—but they don't pay a lot. The rate is $20.00 per hour, and they won't pay until after you do all the work and submit your bill to them."

"That's fine."

Ashley narrowed her eyes. "Don't you need to discuss it with your business partner first?"

"Michael has a lot of making up to do. This can be his first attempt to get back into my good graces. Besides, we're just opening our doors. We've got to start somewhere. Working on a murder case will help us get noticed, especially if Lucas is acquitted."

"Whoa," Ashley put her hands up. "Slow your roll. This isn't going to be an easy case. The allegation is that Lucas walked to his neighbor's house with a shotgun. And that isn't just down the road, it's a mile walk. They lived out in the country."

"So, there was plenty of time for him to turn around and change his mind."

Ashley nodded. "Allegedly, Lucas then knocked on the door, and when Gerald Mock answered, he shot him right in the face."

"Was anyone else home?"

"Not that I've learned, but it is still early. The allegation is that it was just Gerald and Lucas, but Lucas walked home covered in Gerald's blood. He must have been pretty close to him when he fired the gun—"

"Oh," Katie said.

"The complaint filed by the sheriff's department said that deputies followed the blood trail all the way from Gerald's front door back to Lucas's house. They found a shotgun, too. The prosecutor hasn't given us any discovery yet, so I don't know about the ballistics for the gun, but I'm guessing it's going to be bad for us."

"Yeah. That does sound like an uphill battle."

"Yeah..."

There was a long silence, then Katie clapped her hands on her knees and stood. "Well, then, we'll have to come up with a different defense. That's all."

That's all, Ashley thought. It sounded so positive, like they'd inevitably figure it out together, but Ashley knew from experience that not all cases had defenses. Sometimes she had to go into trial waving her hands and banging her fists, hoping in vain to shake something up, to distract the jury from the obvious. Yet, Katie's words didn't feel disingenuous. They felt more like a promise than a wish.

"I like your attitude." Ashley stood and offered her hand. "Welcome aboard."

Katie took her hand. A firm and familiar handshake. Ashley was more than overjoyed to have Katie back on her team. Lucas's case was going to be a challenge. They could easily lose at trial. But Ashley wasn't alone anymore. Katie would be at her side, and she wouldn't have to shoulder quite so much of the burden.

8

KATIE

City Council met in a small room tucked into the farthest end of the courthouse, as if it was more of an afterthought than a space intended for public meetings. Katie always thought its positioning was to discourage the public from attending. To perpetuate the old way of doing things, the good ol' boys club. Usually, it worked, and they could sift through that week's calendar of city issues without interruption. This week, however, Katie and Ashley were about to wreck that peace with their presence.

"Council people," Katie said, knocking on the doorframe and striding into the room.

Even though all three members of city council were men, Katie used the term "council people" because she hoped that one day that would change. That there would be at least one woman sitting amongst them. Maybe someday it would be her. She wasn't political, but she would do her part to initiate progress.

"Katie," Forest said, looking up from the document sitting in front of him. All three council people held what looked like the same document, so Katie assumed that it was the agenda for the meeting. "To what do we owe the pleasure?"

All three councilmen sat at a long table with their backs to a wall of windows, and their faces looking out toward the doorway. There was a small gallery between the doorway and council table, consisting of only two rows of benches with an aisle between them. The men were all seated in a row with Forest farthest to Katie's left, Bill Roberts in the middle, and Tucker Cain to Katie's far right.

"I need to talk to you."

Forest carefully placed the agenda on the desk in front of him. "Can't that wait?" His eyes cut toward Ashley, who was standing behind Katie.

"Don't mind me," Ashley said, selecting a bench to the back left and dropping into it. "I'm just here as a spectator."

Forest looked pointedly around the room to all the empty spaces that rarely held the weight of even one human body, let alone the amount they were designed to hold. "Now?"

"Yes, now," Ashley said.

Ashley looked down at her nails, picking at her cuticles as though she didn't have a care in the world. It was an act. Katie could see the irritation in the set of Ashley's shoulders, but she was not going to back down. Katie had always admired that about Ashley, her gumption. It was clear that the council people did not want Ashley around, but she had a right to be present, and she was not going to let anyone discourage her. Even Forest Parker, who was usually an ally to Ashley, seemed annoyed.

"This will be quick," Katie said, pulling the attention back to herself. "I just came to tell you that I will be resigning as the MHRT lead. You're going to have to hire someone else."

"What? Why?" Forest said, rising out of his seat.

MHRT was his pet project, his replacement for defunding the police department. He'd hand selected Katie as the leader of the team, and she'd done an excellent job. She'd given a year of her life employed in her position, and another year helping with the initial formation of the team. That was two years of her life dedicated to Forest Parker's pet project. An idea he had dreamt up but expected others to carry out for him.

"I'm not sure that's any of your business, but I will be opening a private investigation firm with my father."

"I think that's a splendid idea," Bill Roberts said. He was seated at the center of the table. The longest serving member, and thus the most powerful and influential of the three. He was an elderly man with a thin white fluff for hair. Skin hung from his chin and neck, jiggling as he talked.

"I'm sure *you* think it's a wonderful idea," Forest said. "You were against MHRT from the beginning. If you had it your way, all mentally ill people would be in prison."

"I would not, and I take offense to your statement, Mr. Parker. I'll have you know that my maternal aunt suffers from depression."

"I think we are getting a little off topic here," Katie said, her voice rising to catch the arguing men's attention.

"Quite right," said the last city council person, Tucker Caine.

Katie considered Tucker, trying to decipher his endgame. He was not one to support anyone, in any large or small way, for altruistic reasons. Tucker had been the deciding vote for the creation of MHRT, but Katie had always known that he'd never been a true proponent. He'd ultimately agreed because Forest Parker had promised him something in return. Katie had never learned exactly what had been promised, but she had a strong suspicion it had something to do with the land sale that took place between Forest and Tucker a few months after the vote.

Forest's family had a good deal of farmland throughout Brine County, and they'd held fast to it. Tucker's property abutted some of Forest's. Tucker had done well in the farming world, and it was well known that he was chomping at the bit to expand. After the vote, Forest had made the sale that allowed that to happen.

"I can't help but notice that you've brought Ms. Montgomery here with you today," Tucker continued, his gaze darting back to Ashley. Katie didn't know Tucker's exact age, but she guessed that he was at least ten years younger than Bill Roberts. He had light brown hair that was thinning at the crown, and a sharp pointed nose with eyes set close together.

"Ashley came, yes, but I'm not sure why that concerns you."

"It concerns me because I know what you are up to."

"I'm not sure I know what you mean," Katie said, changing her posture so her body was angled to include Ashley into the conversation.

"I know who Ashley's representing, and I am warning you that you don't want to be involved in that mess."

Ashley perked up, leaning forward, suddenly interested. "I'm curious, Tucker. What do you mean?"

"It's political."

"Oh, poppycock," Bill interjected. "It's not political. It's personal."

It was well known that Bill and Tucker were thick as thieves. They were aligned politically and almost always voted the same way. They'd never argued publicly. Never. But something had changed between them, a rift that seemed to be widening by the minute.

"It's not personal. It's financial," Tucker replied.

"Oh, first it's political, and now it's financial. I don't care what you call it. Those windmills are an eyesore. I bought my acreage and built my very expensive house on a beautiful hill that overlooks much of Brine County's pristine farmland. And then you idiots decided you were going to sell out to that Texas company and put a bunch of iron giants in my backyard."

"It's not *your* backyard seeing that *I* own the property."

"Gentlemen," Forest cut in, casting Katie an apologetic smile. "Don't you think this is a conversation better left for privacy?"

"Oh, no, Forest," Ashley said, laughter in her voice. "Don't ruin my fun. I'm enjoying myself."

"None of this has anything to do with Katie's resignation. Katie," Forest turned toward her, and waited for everyone else to do the same. "We reluctantly accept your resignation. We will not meddle with your future plans, and we wish you the best, don't we?" His eyes settled on Tucker and Bill.

"Absolutely," Tucker agreed.

"Certainly," Bill added. "And I'd like to add, off the record, of course, that I completely understand why Lucas shot Gerald."

"Allegedly," Ashley called out.

"Whatever," Bill waved a dismissive hand. "We all know Lucas did it."

"And I will never understand," Tucker said, crossing his arms and glaring at his mentor whom he had recently idolized.

"Well, gentlemen," Ashley said rising from her seat. "Thank you for your input. You have truly given us lots to think about."

"Yes, thank you," Katie agreed, but she did not quite understand the conversation. What did the allegation against Lucas have to do with windmills? There was a big chunk of information she was missing. Ideas rolled around in her brain as she followed Ashley out of city council chambers and into the courthouse's wide, open atrium.

"What was that all about?" Katie asked.

"We'll talk about it when we get back to my office." Ashley nodded toward the high ceilings that opened up to three separate floors. "You never can tell who is listening in here."

Katie agreed, and they walked side by side back to Ashley's office. A team, once again. Working on a case that originally seemed so cut and dried, but now, after hearing city council arguing about it, it didn't seem quite so clear. Katie couldn't wait to start digging.

9

ASHLEY

"Well, that was interesting," Ashley said as she and Katie walked through the front door of the public defender's office.

"No kidding," Katie said. "What do you think—"

"Ashley, Katie," came a voice that sounded a little familiar, but Ashley couldn't quite place it. She turned to see Michael Michello rising from the battered couch in the waiting area.

"Dad," Katie said with surprise. "How did you know I'd be here?"

"Oh, come on, Katie. I don't need to hire a private investigator to know Ashley would be one of the first people you'd tell about your employment changes."

"Fair enough," Katie said, but she looked irritated. Almost like a teenager embarrassed by a parent picking them up at school, waving too eagerly while calling their name in a packed schoolyard.

"Mr. Michello," Ashley said, intervening and coming toward Michael. She extended her hand to shake. "I hear that I have you to thank for bringing Katie back to me as an investigator."

He took her hand, his grip firm in the way taught to all men in his generation. He caught and maintained eye contact. "I hear I have you to thank for our office arrangements."

There were three empty offices inside the Public Defender's Office.

Ashley had hoped to one day hire a full-time investigator and a few more attorneys, but she'd never had the budget for it. Nobody would be using them in the near future, so she didn't see a downside to offering them to Michael and Katie—at least while they were helping her with Lucas's case.

"They're temporary. Or temporarily free," Ashley amended. "If you like it here, I'll talk to the head public defender's office about an office share situation."

Office sharing was a common practice for many small law firms in rural Iowa. Most firms had only one or two attorneys, but office buildings usually contained three to four separate offices. Nobody wanted to rent space they didn't need. Their budgets were already tight enough, so the solution was to office share. One firm would take two or three offices, the other would take the rest, and they'd put both firms' names on the outside of the door.

Ashley had never office shared, and she'd never heard of anyone doing it with someone other than another lawyer, but she didn't see why the arrangement wouldn't work with investigators. Besides, she planned to hire Katie for every case the head office in Des Moines would allow. This was an opportunity for everyone.

"Let's see how things go for the next month or two, and then I'll make a decision," Michael said.

"We," Katie said. "Then *we* will make a decision. My opinion matters, too."

"Right, right," Michael said, flashing his daughter an apologetic smile.

In that moment, Ashley could see the sad defeated person peeking through Michael's blustery exterior. He feigned confidence as a shield. He was the type of man who could bluff his way through just about anything, but Katie was his weakness. When she was angry, he shrank, becoming something far smaller and far less intimidating than the man he must have been before he'd seen the inside of a prison cell all those years earlier.

"Should we get you two settled?" Ashley said, her words cutting through the tension. If these two wanted their business to succeed, they were going to have to learn how to communicate. Ashley needed them to thrive, so she'd do her best to at least keep them from arguing.

"That's a good idea," Katie said.

Ashley led them back behind the reception counter, pointing out items in the office that they may need. The copier. Pens and extra paper. Legal pads. Katie knew where everything was since nothing had changed from when she last worked in the office, but it was all new to Michael. Elena was at her desk, looking at her computer. Ashley could see her screen and recognized the website as the electronic filing system. Elena was going through new filings, and she was laser focused on something, so Ashley didn't bother her. Elena gave no indication that she'd noticed their presence, but she had. She would turn around when she was ready to chat.

"What's up, boss?" Elena said after a few more moments of Ashley discussing the day-to-day running of the office.

"These are our new office mates," Ashley said, gesturing to Katie and Michael.

Elena knew Katie well. They'd worked together for a full year, and Katie was always stopping by, but she'd only met Michael a time or two. Elena greeted Katie and Michael, and then she turned to Ashley.

"Are they going to help us with Lucas's case?"

"Yes."

"Good," Elena swung around in her chair, her long, dark ponytail swishing through the air. She pressed a few buttons on her computer, then turned back around. "The prosecutor just sent over some of the police reports. I'm printing them now. I thought you might want to get a jump on things."

"You know me too well," Ashley said.

"Just well enough."

The printer whirred to life and spat out three packets, double sided and already stapled. Ashley grabbed them off the copier, the paper still warm from printing, and motioned for Katie and Michael to follow her. She led them past two empty offices.

"You can set up shop here," she gestured as they walked. "Both have desks and chairs already. They aren't fancy, but they'll do the trick." She stopped outside a large room across from the breakroom area. "This is our conference room. Also not fancy, but there's a table and some chairs, so it works."

They all funneled into the room and sat down, Katie and Ashley on one side of the table and Michael on the other. Ashley handed out the packets she'd grabbed from the printer, and they all began to read.

I, Deputy Frankie Pitch, was dispatched to Gerald Mock's farm in reference to a call of shots fired. Gerald lives on the far west side of the county, so it took me fifteen minutes to get to his property. I immediately noticed a trail of blood leading down the long, gravel driveway and out onto the road. I stopped my cruiser to avoid disturbing the evidence and ran up to the house to see if anyone was home.

The driveway to Gerald Mock's residence is approximately a quarter mile long. When I reached the front door, I noticed it was wide open and someone was lying in the doorframe. I did not immediately recognize the individual as his face was unrecognizable. At first, I thought he'd been severely beaten, but then I saw the shotgun shell and realized the person had been shot in the face at close range. I called for an ambulance, but there was no movement, and I could tell that he was already dead.

I called for backup, and I waited with the body until the ambulance and several other deputies arrived. Deputy George Thomanson was the second deputy to arrive on scene. I directed him to secure the scene and start taking photographs while I followed the blood trail. It started out as footprints. Photographs were taken of the prints. They were made from a large shoe, likely a man's.

The shoeprints grew lighter as I followed the trail down the driveway and into the road. After the first half mile, there were only a few splatters here and there, but I was still able to follow them a full mile and right up to the nearest neighbor's door, a house belonging to Lucas Campbell. There was a drop of blood immediately outside Lucas's door.

I radioed to inform Deputy Thomanson of the situation, then knocked on Lucas's door. It took a few moments, but Lucas answered. He was covered in blood and flakes of a grey matter that I later discovered was brain matter.

"Jesus Christ," Ashley said, setting the police report down. "This is bad. Really freaking bad."

"Yeah. It's pretty bad," Katie agreed.

Michael said nothing, but his face had turned a pale shade of green. He'd been to prison, but his crime was white collar. Nothing like this. He was far less used to the gruesome cases than Katie and Ashley, who had been dealing with them for years.

I asked Lucas if he was willing to talk to me, and he agreed. He came outside rather than inviting me into his home, which I found suspicious. I radioed Deputy Thomanson and told him to start working on a search warrant because it didn't look like Lucas was going to let us inside the home without one.

I spoke with Lucas while we waited for Deputy Thomanson to return with the warrant. The conversation was recorded on my body camera. During the entire conversation, Lucas was unemotional. When asked where the blood came from, he feigned surprise that it was there. He then proceeded to pat different parts of his body as though checking to see if he was injured. Then he claimed that the blood was from an animal.

This was precisely why she didn't want her clients talking to cops. Lucas had already given three differing stories about the blood alone—he didn't know about it, it was probably his, and it came from an animal—and the prosecution would make good use of every one of those stories. They'd twist them to make it appear that Lucas was guilty and spinning stories to weasel his way out of the consequences.

Ashley sighed heavily and rubbed her hands against her face. "I'll bring this to Lucas so he can review it. It's pretty horrific. I don't see a great defense. There's no search warrant issue. The idiot answered the door covered in his neighbor's brain matter, and they were smart enough to get a warrant rather than search the house. What the fuck are we going to do?"

"We're going to do what we always do," Katie said calmly. "We're going to look for an angle and then exploit it. What about this windmill stuff that the city council was talking about earlier this morning? That could be a possibility."

"Yeah, maybe," Ashley said, but she doubted it would get them anywhere.

She'd felt like it was a possible angle when she was listening to Tucker Caine and Bill Roberts arguing during the city council meeting, but that was before she saw these details. Bill had said that Gerald had it coming to him, and that Lucas was justified, but that was only because he didn't know the gory details of the case. If the information in the deputy's narrative was correct, even Bill would not hesitate to convict.

"You go talk to Lucas, and I'll go check out the two properties—Gerald's and Lucas's. I'll take some pictures, so we can see if it is even an option."

"Good plan," Ashley said, but she was dreading her conversation with

Lucas. It would be hard to keep her mind from picturing him sitting there on his front porch covered in blood and part of Gerald's brain while chatting it up with Deputy Pitch.

"I'll stay here and start getting things set up," Michael said.

"You sure you don't want to come with me?" A flash of disappointment passed Katie's features.

"No, no, you go on. I need to get things around here organized anyway."

"Suit yourself," Katie said, rising out of her seat.

Ashley followed Katie out of the room, leaving Michael seated at the table. She looked back just before they turned the corner and saw Michael place his hands over his face. He wasn't emotionally prepared for the details of cases like Lucas's. Nobody really was, not until they'd gone through it a time or two. For Katie's sake, Ashley hoped that Michael could handle this kind of work. It wasn't for the faint of heart.

10

KATIE

Lucas Campbell's property had been easy to find. It was only a mile off U.S. Highway 30, which stretched across the center of Iowa, severing it into two nearly equally sized pieces. Katie parked at the end of the long driveway and got out.

The first thing she noticed was the absolute silence. There were no artificial sounds. No honks from cars. No slamming of doors. No tolling of church bells. It should be peaceful, but its absolute completeness created the opposite effect. It was unsettling. It felt utterly deserted of all living things. There were no birds chirping. No cows mooing. No roosters crowing. Nothing but supreme quiet. The only sound came from the whipping of the wind.

She took her camera out, unscrewed the lens cap, and set it to record video footage. Then she did a slow sweep, turning around in a complete circle, documenting her surroundings. She did not speak. She wanted the stillness to dominate the video. There was something almost sinister about it, which felt important to her in that moment. If asked, she couldn't pinpoint exactly why that was, only that it was a feeling, and Ashley had taught her long ago to document, document, document. They didn't *have* to use her recordings at trial, but they couldn't use them if they didn't exist.

Once she finished with that, she started making her way up the driveway. The heels of her boots crunched against gravel with each step she took. The house was approximately a quarter mile from the street, and she'd almost made it there when a figure emerged from the front door of the weather-beaten old farmhouse. A large man in a full set of overalls stood there holding a shotgun trained on her. Katie's mouth went dry.

"No reporters," the man said.

"I'm not a reporter," Katie said. Her hands were so slick with sweat that she was having trouble keeping a grip on her camera.

He nodded toward Katie's large Nikon camera. "No photographers sent here by reporters."

"I'm not a photographer either. I'm a private investigator hired by Ashley Montgomery."

"Ashley Montgomery, you say," the man lowered the gun a little. "That Lucas's lawyer?"

"Yes," Katie said, almost bursting with relief. "I'm here to gather evidence the police officers missed. Anything that could possibly help in Lucas's defense."

"That boy has no defense. Not one that is going to stick," the man said, lowering his gun so the barrel was pointed at the ground beneath him. "And all the evidence you are going to need is straight that way." He pointed off to the east.

"Is that where Gerald Mock lived?"

The man nodded. He was older than she'd originally thought, with a balding head and skin hanging from both his cheeks like jowls. His eyes were light colored, possibly blue, and rimmed in skin that was lighter than the rest of his face, like the opposite of a raccoon. In that moment, he suddenly seemed like a sad old man to be pitied rather than someone who had just been threatening her with a firearm.

"I might have a hard time getting onto his property."

"You don't have to. The problem is easily seen from here." He gestured in the same direction again, this time using the gun. He swept the metal along the horizon where large windmills dotted the landscape, and then he looked through and began sighting each windmill one by one before turning back to Katie. "Get my drift?"

"Yeah. I think so," Katie said, raising her camera and taking several photos of the windmills. There had been a lot of discussion over these windmills. Too much for it to be coincidence or brushed off as unimportant. When she finished and lowered the camera, she turned back to the man. "You must be Lucas's dad."

"I'm Albert Campbell. And you are?"

"Katie Mickey."

"I've heard of you. You used to be a police officer, right?"

"That's me."

"Well, go ahead and have a look around. Take any pictures you need. I don't know if my boy can be helped at this point, but if anyone can do it, it'll be that Ashley Montgomery."

"Thank you."

"Come on in for some coffee once you're finished. I don't get a lot of visitors these days."

"Sure," Katie said, flashing a smile.

He waved, then closed the wooden front door. She didn't blame him for going back inside. February was the worst month out of the year. There were days that it was so cold that frostbite could set in in as few as ten minutes. Thankfully, it wasn't one of those days, but it was still below freezing.

Time to get to work, Katie thought, turning around and taking in her surroundings.

She started by focusing on the house, taking photographs from the outside. It was a traditional farmhouse, two-story and square shaped with a large covered front porch. An old porch swing hung from the far corner of the porch, its hinges creaking as it swayed in the breeze. The windows were old, likely original to the structure, and the white exterior paint was peeling in places, but, other than that, the house appeared to be in decent condition.

Making her way around to the back of the property, she counted and photographed three outbuildings. One was a lean-to type of barn that looked like it could cave in at any moment. There were only three walls to the structure with one side held up by a single pole in the middle. The building was empty aside from some old hay and a couple of large rats. She took a few photographs anyway and continued to the next structure.

It was an old pig barn, boarded up from the outside. There were metal poles on the outside that had once been individual stalls for the pigs, but they were old and corroded. Judging by the exterior, Katie guessed the building had been in disuse since at least the 1980's. Still, she took a couple of pictures, focusing on the sagging roof and places where the wood was rotting.

The final outbuilding was almost a house-like structure. It had the same tin outer frame to it as the other buildings, but it wasn't in the same state of disrepair. This building appeared to be well cared for, even more so than the actual house. Katie made her way toward it, peering in through one of the small windows. It was dark inside, but she thought she could see the outline of a large workbench taking up most of the middle of the room.

Curious, she made her way around to the front door. She twisted the doorknob and was surprised to find that it was unlocked. The door swung open on well-oiled hinges and the interior of the building smelled of wood chips. Feeling around on the wall to her left, she found a light switch and flipped it on. A long light mounted above the work bench burst into life, illuminating every inch of the one room shop.

It was immaculately clean with tools hung along the walls. Katie took several photos as she made her way around the workbench. When she reached the far side of the shop, she noticed an old desktop computer set back in the corner. It was the large blocky kind built in the early to mid 2000's. The screen was off, and there was nothing significant about the computer itself. But it was the photograph taped to the bottom of the screen that caught Katie's attention.

It was a family photograph, taken during what looked like a picnic. Katie instantly recognized Lucas's face. It had been plastered all over the news ever since his arrest. In this image he was much younger with fewer worry lines cutting their way through his face. There were two other individuals in the picture, a woman and a young girl. Katie didn't recognize either of them. She didn't know Lucas had a family. She took a close-up photo of the picture. They weren't around anymore, she felt sure of that. The reason, whether disappearance or divorce, was something Katie intended to learn.

Beside the computer there was a small, round trash can. It was empty aside from some documents stapled together at the top left corner. Katie leaned down and picked them up. There were approximately ten pages in the stack and the very top one read REAL ESTATE PURCHASE AGREEMENT.

Purchase agreement, Katie wondered, *to what land?* Katie started reading the document. As she did, her heartrate started to pick up speed. When she got to the property description and the price, she knew she'd struck gold. This couldn't wait. She reached into her pocket and pulled out her phone. Her hands shook as she dialed.

"Can this wait? I'm on my way to see Lucas," Ashley said by way of greeting. "I got hung up on another client's drama and I haven't made it over there yet."

"No, you've got to hear this."

"What? Why?"

"I think I just found a purchase agreement in Lucas's trash can. It seems that Gerald Mock bought a bunch of land from Lucas a few years ago for pennies on the dollar."

"I'm not sure why that's so important—"

"You haven't heard the best part. I think it is the exact same land that now has all fifteen of Gerald's windmills on it."

"What?"

"It's the windmill property. I'm telling you the windmills are the key to this case."

Ashley was silent for a long moment. When she responded, it wasn't with the excitement Katie had expected. "It's motive. Which is the opposite of a defense. The prosecutor will spin it as buyer's remorse. Jealous and enraged over the amount of money Gerald was making off of Lucas's land, Lucas decided to get revenge. That's what they'll say."

"Oh," Katie said, her heart sinking.

"You know you don't work for the prosecution anymore, right Katie?" Ashley said in a teasing tone. "We don't want to prove motive. That's bad for us."

"Ha," Katie enunciated the word slowly and deliberately. "I know that. But I also think there's more to this. We need to keep digging. Ask Lucas about it. I'm going to go inside and talk to Lucas's father. He's been here holding down the fort, I guess."

"Okay. Fine. I'll ask Lucas. But I'm telling you that it isn't going to get us anywhere."

"Humor me," Katie said. "On a side note, do you know anything about Lucas having a wife and child?"

Ashley sighed heavily. "That's a long story. We can talk about it when you get back to the office."

Ashley was growing impatient; Katie could hear it in the sharp briskness of her tone. It was time to end the call. "Okay. See you soon," Katie said.

Katie hung up without saying goodbye. Ashley wasn't big on pleasantries, hellos or goodbyes. She thought they were a waste of time. Over the years Katie had spent hanging around with Ashley, she'd begun to agree. There was too much to do, and never enough time.

11

ASHLEY

Ashley scrolled through the document on her computer screen, carefully checking for errors. There could be none. This was an application for a judgeship. There was no room for mistakes. She'd been through it at least five times already. Just when she thought she was ready to submit it, she thought, *a sixth review couldn't hurt.* After the sixth time, she finally forced herself to press the small rectangular "submit" button. Then she leaned back and issued a heavy sigh.

It wasn't a sigh of relief, for this was only the beginning of the process. There would be meetings with members of the judicial nominating committee. Gladhanding with local attorneys. Emails sent out urging for support from bar members. She was going to hate every last second of the process. Of that, she could be sure. But at least her decision was made. She was applying for the position. That part was out of her hands now.

She shoved back from her seat and stood, stretching. Then she glanced at the clock. *Shit,* she thought, *it's already one o'clock.* She had tried to visit Lucas earlier in the day, but the jail had turned her away, saying they were preparing to serve lunch. They'd told her to come back. That's why she'd spent the last hour reviewing her application. Now it was time to get back to regular business.

Ashley grabbed her coat off the coat hanger in the corner of her office, shoving her arms into the sleeves as she hurried down the long hallway toward the front of the office. Her coat was a dark red color, long with a faux fur lined hood. A necessity in the frigid Iowa winter. And this time of year, February, was the coldest, most forlorn month of the year.

"Where are you off to?" Elena asked as Ashley emerged into the front area of the office.

"I lost track of time. I need to go see Lucas."

"Judge Ahrenson just called for you."

Ashley stopped, turning to face her office assistant. "What did he want?"

"He said he wants you to stop by. Something about coaching? It didn't make much sense to me, but who am I to judge a judge, right?" She chuckled at her joke.

Ashley knew exactly what he meant. Somehow, he had already heard that she'd submitted her application for his soon-to-be vacant position. Existing judges often coached those who were applying on how to get through the second step of the process, the judicial nominating committee. The committee was a gatekeeper. Only two applicants would come out of committee, and of those two, the Governor would choose one.

"Will you call him back and let him know that I have a meeting at the jail and then I'll be over?"

She was annoyed that news was already getting around about the application she had literally submitted minutes earlier. She also knew that she needed to play the game. This was politics, and she had a judge in her corner. She needed to keep her cool, accept his advice, and do what was necessary to get past this next hurdle. Otherwise, she could kiss her chances goodbye.

"Sure thing, boss," Elena said, saluting.

Ashley forced a smile, and then she turned and hurried out the front door, heading toward the jail. The walk across the street to the law enforcement center usually took close to five minutes. With the bitter cold, Ashley moved faster than usual, and made it in just under three.

"Are you here to see Lucas?" The jailer at the front desk asked.

"Yes."

This jailer was a middle-aged woman with tired eyes, yet she carried herself with confidence. The nametag above the sheriff star on her brown button-up shirt read Theresa. "He's been asking for you. I told him you were here earlier. I thought that would appease him. But that only irritated him further. He's been nagging every jailer that walks by ever since, wondering when you're coming back."

"Well, I'm here. He can stop complaining now."

"Let's hope so." Theresa pressed a button. There was a momentary pause, then the heavy steel door dividing them clicked as the lock disengaged. "Come on back."

Ashley pulled the door open and stepped into the hallway. The door slammed behind her, causing Ashley to jump. She would never get used to that sound. The boom of steel against steel, locks engaging. It symbolized a complete loss of control over her movements. Behind these doors, she couldn't go anywhere, do anything, without permission. That weighed heavily upon her, even now, years after she'd been wrongfully incarcerated.

"Which room do you want?" Theresa asked, pulling Ashley out of her thoughts.

"No partitions, thanks."

"I think you're the only one who uses that meeting room anymore," Theresa said.

"Really? Nobody else trusts their clients enough to be alone with them. Nobody?" There was a sadness creeping into her words, mostly because these people, these defendants, often had few on their side. Their attorney was the one person wholly on their team. At least they were supposed to be. If their attorney had already deemed them too dangerous to be around, then what hope did they have at getting a fair shot with a jury? Not much.

"I guess they aren't bad asses like you." Theresa stopped outside the meeting room and said something into the radio clipped to her shoulder. A moment passed, then a lock clicked, and she opened the door to the meeting room. "Go on inside. I'll bring Lucas through the other way in a few minutes."

"Thank you," Ashley said, stepping into the room.

The door closed behind Theresa, and Ashley fought the momentary urge to panic. She forced herself not to think about the tons of cement and steel separating her from the outside world. She sat in the plastic chair closest to her, with her back facing the door she'd entered. In front of her was the desk, another flimsy plastic chair, and a second door. This one led deep into the bowels of the jail, where the inmates resided. Lucas would enter through that door.

While she waited, she pulled out a stack of files. All pertained to other clients. Each had some form of paperwork that needed reviewing. There was no telling how long it would take the jailer to bring Lucas. If there were no interruptions, it would be moments. If something went wrong with an inmate, and it often did because caging people does not bring out the best in them, then it could be more than thirty minutes. Either way, she had no control over the situation, so all she could do was wait.

She had just settled into the first file when the lock clicked and the back door swung open. Lucas wore a green jumpsuit and bright orange slip-on shoes. Chains encircled his hands and his legs, limiting his steps to little more than shuffles. Ashley set her pen down and closed the file in front of her. Reaching into her bag, she exchanged that file with a far larger one, the one that belonged to Lucas's case.

"Hello, Lucas," she said.

"Hey," he gave her a half wave. The best he could do with his hand restraints.

"Can you remove the chains?" Ashley said to the jailer.

"Sorry, no. It's jail policy now. When they meet with attorneys in this room, they have to keep them on the whole time." She shrugged. "Safety."

The rule was nonsense. There was nothing safe about heavy steel chains. They were effective when it came to preventing escape. Nobody could properly run with both feet chained together. But those hand shackles, they were heavy, and they were steel. A weapon if Ashley ever saw one. Yet Ashley said nothing to the jailer. Theresa didn't make the rules. That was above her paygrade. Ashley would have to bitch about it to the jail administrator later. For now, she needed to focus on her client.

"Unless you two need anything else, I'll leave you in peace." The jailer looked to Lucas, who shook his head, then to Ashley.

"No, thank you."

Ashley truly did appreciate this jailer. Not because Theresa was kind to her, but for the way that she looked at Lucas and her mannerisms toward him. She saw him as a human being, with faults and flaws, but goodness, too. Many jailers treated the inmates like wild, unpredictable animals. Theresa left through the door she'd used for Lucas. It slammed closed behind her, causing both Ashley and her client to wince.

"How are you today, Lucas?" Ashley asked, trying to keep her words light, conversational. The last time she had met with him, he'd been a mess. The picture of depression. A rounded back, darting eyes, and a flat affect. Today, some of that still existed, but he seemed to be coming out of it.

"I'm fine. I mean, as fine as I can be, considering," he lifted his hands, jingling the heavy chains.

"Right. Yeah. I'm probably one of the few attorneys who can say this, but I know how you feel. I've actually been in your shoes. It's not fun. It's not easy. But we'll get through this."

Lucas nodded, his gaze cast downward. For a moment she thought she'd seen the glimmer of a tear forming at the corner of his eye, but it never fell.

"I brought you some discovery." Ashley opened the file and took out two large stacks of files. "I brought you the Trial Information, which is the formal charging document. Unsurprisingly, it charges you with murder in the first degree, premeditated and deliberated."

Lucas nodded, looking at the document as Ashley slid it across the table. The caption read *State of Iowa v. Lucas Mitchell Campbell, Case Number FECR098314*. A small rectangular photograph filled the space between the case number and the words *Trial Information*. It was Lucas's booking photo, a broken man staring at the camera with haunted eyes. When Lucas's gaze came to the photo, he turned away, unable to look at himself.

"I've also brought the Minutes of Testimony." Ashley slid a second document across the table to him. "The prosecutor has listed each witness that he intends to call as a witness at trial. The Rules of Criminal Procedure require him to also provide what's called a "minute" of expected testimony. I want to point out that this is what the prosecutor *believes* these people will say at trial. But people cannot be easily controlled. These statements are in the prosecutor's words, not the witnesses." She tapped the front of the *Minutes of Testimony* with her index finger. "Prosecutors have been known to embellish. That's why we take depositions. It will give us an opportunity to get face to face with these people and hear what they have to say under oath."

"Okay. When will these depositions take place?"

"I don't know. I've got to set them up. As soon as possible since we are demanding a speedy trial. Do you still want to do that? Or do you want to waive that demand and give the investigation more time?"

Lucas shook his head. "I don't see time making anything better for me. They've got me—"

"Nope. None of that. I don't want to hear what you were about to say. I already told you. No confessions. No admissions. Nothing like that until I've completed my investigation. We need a defense strategy and admissions certainly aren't going to help us form that."

"Okay."

"Now, my investigator, Katie Mickey, was out at your property earlier today. She was taking pictures. She says she found some documents in a trash can. A purchase agreement executed between you and your neighbor, Gerald Mock. Do you want to tell me what that's all about?"

Lucas shrugged, his big shoulders rising and falling in an exaggerated way that appeared as heavy as the chains around his hands and feet. "I sold him some of my land. I didn't want to, but I had to do something to tread water. We had a gentleman's agreement. Then he violated it."

"Whoa," Ashley said, putting up a hand. "I'm not sure that I want to hear about all that yet. I just wanted to see if the land sale had actually gone through. It sounds as though it did."

"Yeah, and he—"

"Stop talking or I'm going to leave. I don't want the details of your feud just yet."

"Okay."

"Tell me about your wife. My investigator also told me that there is a photo of your family together—you, your daughter, and your wife—out there in the shop."

"My ex-wife, you mean. Kristy. Haven't you heard this story already? I thought for sure the gossip mongers down at Genie's Diner would have their teeth into it by now."

"Gossip isn't fact." Sure, Ashley had heard plenty about the divorce.

Some said there was abuse. Others claimed Lucas had taken to the bottle. Still others said Kristy had run off with some rich guy from Des Moines, taking their daughter with her.

"They're gone. That's all that matters."

"You better not mean buried in the backyard gone, because that's going to seriously hurt your defense."

"No," he said, forcing a dark laugh. "I don't mean that. Although, I suppose they might as well be. I'll never see either of them ever again. Not after this. God, I wish I could go back in time. Do you ever think that?" He looked up, his hazel eyes intense and sparkling with tears. "Hop into a time machine and return to the moment where you fucked it all up."

"What moment was that for you, Lucas?"

"I know what you are thinking. That I'd like to go back to the moment I got my gun and started walking—"

"No! I don't want to hear it," Ashley shoved to her feet. "I already told you. No admissions. At least not yet."

Lucas continued as though he hadn't heard Ashley's protest. "My moment would be way before that. It was years ago."

Satisfied he was done with case facts, Ashley slowly returned to her seat.

"Back when the farm started hemorrhaging money and I made a choice. My land or my family. Kristy could see the writing on the wall. She knew we were in a hole so deep that we'd never get out of it. But I refused to see it. I just thought if I could sell off a little here and a little there, I'd find a way to catch traction. I was obsessed. I stopped eating. I stopped sleeping. I was a complete mess. A lousy husband and an absent father. Sure, I was physically there, but I wasn't *there*. You know what I mean?"

"Yes," Ashley said.

"I gave Kristy no choice. She left before I could burn through all the money, taking what she could to start anew with Amy. That's what happened. There were no affairs, no violence. Just one delusional father with backward priorities. That land. It has been in my family for generations. I thought it would break me to lose it. So, I clung to it, even tighter after Kristy left with Amy."

"I think that's enough for one day," Ashley said, patting Lucas on the hand and rising to her feet. He was getting too emotional. There was real risk he might say something that would hurt their defense. He needed someone to talk to, she knew that, but she also couldn't allow him to destroy the small sliver of hope she held that she'd somehow find a way to free him.

Lucas nodded, rubbing his eyes with the heels of his hands.

"Read through the documents I gave you. Here is the initial report as well." She handed him Deputy Pitch's narrative. "I'll work on setting up depositions. I'll be back as soon as I can."

"Thank you," Lucas said, his voice smaller, more defeated than it had been at the start of their meeting.

"Hang in there," Ashley said, heading toward the door and pressing the small silver button that told the jailers the meeting was over. "I can't promise things will get better, but I can promise that I'll try."

Lucas nodded.

A few moments later, the door behind Ashley swung open and the jailer led her out. Ashley cast one last look back at her client. His head was in his hands, and he was sobbing, his shoulders shaking, shackles jangling. This was the heartbreaking part of her job. One event, or perhaps a series of events, had ruined so many lives. Gerald was dead, Lucas locked up, Kristy packed up and gone.

But what had led to all this destruction? What was the triggering factor? Gerald and Lucas had grown up together. They'd been neighbors. They'd never been known to be besties, but they'd always gotten along. And Kristy, she'd been Lucas's high school sweetheart. What had finally driven her to the edge? Lucas's answer had been satisfactory, but Ashley felt there had to be more to it. There was more to this story, and she needed to uncover it before she could decide how to best defend Lucas.

12

KATIE

After ending her call with Ashley, Katie left Lucas's shop, looking over her shoulder one last time before flipping the light off and pulling the door shut behind her. There was something calming about the place with its soft scent of wood shavings lingering in the air. Lucas had spent a lot of time in this small building, Katie could see that in the way the tools were well used. She wondered if he would ever make it back.

As she made her way toward the main house, she couldn't get the image of Lucas's family out of her mind. Katie wasn't married. She had no kids, although she hoped that might change one day. Yet it was photos like that, the ones where everyone seemed so genuinely happy, that gave her pause. Was it all a farce? Or had Lucas once been a family man, surrounded by love? If so, why had it changed?

The answer to these questions might not matter when it came to Lucas's defense, but they also might make all the difference in the world. Katie had learned long ago that investigations were unpredictable. She could be following one thread of evidence, expecting one result, when things would take a sharp turn, sending her in an entirely different direction. It was impossible to tell what information was important and what wasn't, at least not at the beginning stages of the process.

She walked around the old house, heading for the front door. The only sound was her feet crunching against the frozen ground, and the occasional caw of a crow somewhere off in the distance. Snow was coming. She could feel it in the stillness of the air. When she reached the front porch, she removed a glove and knocked on the door with her bare knuckles. Her hands were dry, and the skin of her third knuckle split on the third wrap against the cold, solid wood of the door.

The door swung open. "Hello, again, young lady," Albert Campbell said. This time, he greeted her with a smile rather than a shotgun.

"Hello," Katie said, unable to keep from grinning back. She was nearly thirty now. Few people called her *young* anymore. The years in the criminal justice system had made her tough, so few ever called her a lady, either.

"Come on in, come on in," Albert gestured with one gnarled hand. "It's colder than the dickens out there."

"Thank you," Katie said as she stepped inside. "It's about to snow."

"It is." Albert gazed out the door for one fleeting moment before closing it behind them.

The entryway was small, and it split into two separate directions. To the right was a narrow staircase leading to the second floor, and to the left was a small living room. The place looked barren, devoid of life. There were no pictures hanging on the walls or furniture in the living room. Just cold emptiness. It made Katie shiver.

"You must be freezing down to your bones, little missy," Albert said, leading her down a long, creaky hallway toward the back of the house. He moved stiffly with a pronounced limp on his left side.

"I'm alright."

"Do you drink coffee? I've got a fresh pot brewing."

"Yes. Thank you."

"Milk or sugar?" He asked as he shuffled over to an old Mr. Coffee coffeemaker.

"Black is fine."

"Good," he chuckled. "Because I haven't been to the store. That milk in there's probably three weeks old." He nodded toward the refrigerator. "It's well past sour by now."

"Why haven't you been to the store?"

"Nobody to take me. I'd walk, but these old knees don't get me very far anymore."

"Walk? That's crazy. The nearest grocery store is at least fifteen miles away. Don't you have anyone to take you? Any relatives in the area?"

"Lucas is my only child. Everyone else has gone to the good Lord," he paused and cast his gaze upward. "I get by, though. Don't be getting any worry lines in that pretty face on my account."

If Albert was ten years younger, she would have been offended by the comment. But he was a man from a different generation. One where all businesses were owned by men, and they were allowed to give their secretaries a little pat on the butt every now again. The world had changed, but the men Albert's age were too old, too set in their ways, to change along with it.

"Do you have an internet connection?"

"Lucas got me one of those fancy phones a few years back. It does all that internet hub-bub-baloo. It was a Christmas present. That was before he fell on all these hard times, you see."

"Can I see it?"

Albert handed her a steaming cup of coffee and took the phone out of his back pocket, placing it on the small, rickety dining table. She picked it up and the screen sprang to life. There was no passcode protection.

"What are you doing?" Albert asked, taking a seat across from her at the table.

"Setting up an online grocery account for you. You can order food through this app and have it delivered to your door."

"Thank you, but I don't have the money for that. I'm barely making ends meet as it is."

Katie lowered the phone, setting it down and sliding it across the table to Albert. "It's a free service. So long as you spend more than fifty dollars. You can do that, right?"

"With the price of groceries these days? Sure." He paused, staring down at the little screen. "And thank you. There aren't a lot of folks around here willing to help me anymore. Not after what happened between Lucas and Gerald."

"If you don't mind me asking, I have a few questions about your son."

"Fire away. I've got nothin' to hide. That's what I've been telling the sheriff's office every time I call them. I want to tell them what I know, but they won't hear any of it."

"I'm here now. I'm not a deputy, but I am an investigator. I'd love to hear your story."

"Okay. What do you want to know?"

"Do you mind if I record this conversation?" She set a small recording device at the center of the table.

"Not at all. Like I said, I've got nothin' to hide."

Katie pressed the record button and spoke directly to the machine. "This is Katie Mickey, investigator. I am here with Albert Campbell, Lucas Campbell's father." Then she turned and met Albert's wary gaze. "Okay, Albert, here's your chance to tell your side of things."

"Alright, well, as you can tell, we've fallen on some hard times." Albert's voice started out shaky, but it gained strength as he continued. "I'm retired, you see, and my son Lucas has taken over the farm. This land, this farm, has been in our family for generations. It's what you call a century farm. We used to have a lot more land, but with each turn of hands, the plot grew a little smaller. The weather has been finicky these last five years. That, plus a few bad investments, has Lucas on the brink of bankruptcy."

"I saw a contract to sell land in the shop outside. Was Lucas thinking about selling the property?"

"No. Not all of it. Only a few acres here and there. Gerald Mock, the neighbor, wasn't having the troubles that we did. He's got animals over there. Or at least his farm was mostly animals. He wasn't so dependent on the weather, not like us land farmers. When money was tight for us, he was just fine. That's how he ended up buying our land piece by piece."

"Wouldn't the price of animal feed go up if crops are suffering?" Katie asked.

He chuckled. "That's true. I honestly don't know where Gerald gets his money. I assume animals are faring better than crops, but I don't know that for a fact. I don't follow the markets closely. I'm too old for all that. I'll just say that it seems that Gerald was doin' just fine because he always seemed to have plenty of cash. Just take a gander at his property compared to this place. We can barely keep up with repairs and maintenance, while his sparkles like it's owned by the Queen of England."

"If things were so bad, why didn't Lucas sell everything and go?"

"That's my fault, I'm afraid." His gaze dropped to his coffee mug. "I couldn't bear the thought of giving it up. Our family has farmed this land for over a century. That's why they call it a century farm. There have been Campbells here for one hundred years. I didn't want my son to be the Campbell to give that up. Now that I look back, my boy didn't have a choice. We were out of money. I shouldn't have put so much pressure on him to save the land."

"That contract for sale. The one I found in the trash. What land did that cover?"

Albert's eyes drifted up, focusing on the wall behind Katie. If they had been outdoors, he would have been facing the northeast, where the windmills stood. "The land that houses those giant monstrosities."

"The windmills?"

"Yup. And they had an agreement. A gentleman's agreement that Lucas would sell the property to Gerald, but Gerald would not lease it for windmills. That was a mistake."

"Gerald went back on his promise," Katie said. That much was obvious.

"Yes. There was nothin' my boy could do about it. We checked with a lawyer friend here in town. That wasn't part of the written agreement, so we couldn't stop it. Not that we had the money to hire a lawyer anyway. Gerald knew all that, and he took advantage of it."

"Do you know how much those windmills bring in?"

"A lot. I've heard the leases are somewhere in the range of $5,000 to $10,000 per month per windmill."

"So, and I'm just thinking out loud here, if Lucas had kept the land and leased it to the windmill company himself, then his money troubles would have been solved."

"Sure, but my boy would have never agreed to do that. He didn't want the land used in that way. It's farmland. That's how it has been for over one hundred years."

"Lucas wasn't mad about the money, then?"

"No. It was about the land, not money. But it was more than that, too.

Gerald had made a promise knowing that he had every intention of turning around and breaking it. That may be how things are done in the city, but not out here in the country. A promise made is a promise kept."

The longer Albert spoke, the more Katie thought that this was not at all helpful for Lucas's defense. Ashley was right. It would prove motive—a reason to kill—rather than an excuse for Lucas's behavior. They needed something like self-defense, defense of another, or evidence that someone else had framed Lucas. At this point, all fingers pointed squarely at Ashley's client. Even when the person telling the story was trying to do the exact opposite.

"You know what," Katie said, glancing at her watch. "I think we should stop there. I hate to cut you short, but the time has gotten away from me. It's nearly four o'clock. It's about time I start making my way back to the office."

"Sure, sure," Albert said, waving a gnarled hand. "You come back anytime, young lady. Anytime at all."

"Thank you," Katie said, rising to her feet. "I can show myself out," she said as Albert struggled to stand. "Don't get up on my account."

"Are you sure?" he asked, but he was already lowering back down into his seat. Katie guessed his knees gave him a bit more trouble than he cared to let on.

"Absolutely. It truly was a pleasure meeting you. I will be in touch if I have any more questions."

Katie waved one last time and stepped back out into the blustering Iowa cold. Snow was falling freely from the sky, large, fat snowdrops, that made Katie think of frozen tears. As she made her way back to her car, she wondered if she would be back with more questions. She doubted it. Yet, she also felt as though someone needed to check up on this old man living all alone out in the countryside. If his neighbors had all turned against him, she could be his only option for survival through the remainder of the winter, which, in Iowa, could be months away in early May.

13

ASHLEY

After her meeting with Lucas, Ashley ducked out of the jail and into the courthouse. The two buildings were side by side, so she only had to brave a few minutes of the cold. It had begun to snow while she was meeting with Lucas. It was falling from the sky in torrents, a virtual whiteout. She wondered if it was snowing that hard out in the country. She hoped not. Katie's little Impala was no match for the untreated, countryside gravel roads.

Once inside the warmth of the courthouse, Ashley pulled out her phone and dialed Katie's number.

"I'm on my way back," Katie said by way of greeting.

"Is it snowing out there?"

"Yup. Not too bad, though."

"It's going to get worse as you come this direction. It's blizzard-like downtown."

"Wonderful."

"You'll be fine," Ashley said with more confidence than she actually felt. "Just take it slow."

"Easy for you to say."

"I'll see you in a bit," Ashley said.

"Good. I've got some information for you, but it's not the kind you are going to want to hear."

"Great," Ashley said sarcastically. "That'll be the cherry on the top of this truly shitty day. I'm on my way to see Judge Ahrenson right now. So he can talk me through the judgeship application process."

"You applied for that?" Katie sounded surprised and perhaps a little disappointed.

"Yeah. Don't worry, I've got little hope of getting it. Judge Ahrenson just won't get off my ass about it, so I'm appeasing him."

As the words tumbled from her mouth, Ashley wondered how true they actually were. Part of her did feel like she was appeasing the judge, especially if he was going to take senior status and continue judging some of her cases. It was always best to stay on the right side of judges. But that was only a portion of her motivation because part of her truly did want the position. She knew she would be an excellent fit. The question was whether she could convince the judicial nominating committee of that.

"Alright. See you back at the office," Katie said.

They both hung up without saying goodbye, and Ashley made her way up to the third floor of the courthouse, where the judges' personal offices were located. She took the stairs and was not even winded when she reached the top. In her adult life, she had taken to running as a form of stress management. She headed down the hallway, passed four closed doors, and stopped at the last door, which was also closed. A placard next to it read, "The Honorable Judge Ahrenson." Ashley knocked.

"Come in," Judge Ahrenson called.

Ashley opened the door and stepped inside. "Hello, Judge," Ashley said, waving a hand.

Judge Ahrenson was seated at a large, mahogany desk, looking down at a stack of documents. His readers were perched at the end of his hawk-like nose, and he snatched them off as Ashley stepped further into the office and placed them gingerly on the desk in front of him.

"Come to talk politics, I presume," Judge Ahrenson said.

"Something like that."

"Well, let's not waste time. I was just reviewing your application. Nice job. It was very carefully crafted. I appreciate the time you put into it. You'd be surprised at some of the mistakes and grammatical errors some of the other applicants have made." He said the word *applicants* like it was something distasteful.

"Umm, thanks."

"Now, on to the next step." He picked up a document at the end of his desk and handed it to her. "This is a list of all the members of the judicial nominating committee. There are ten in all, and I'm the Judge."

Every judicial nominating committee consisted of five elected members and five members appointed by the Governor. The elected members were all lawyers, and those appointed were laypeople. There was always one judge who would lead the committee through the meeting. Luckily, Judge Ahrenson was the judge selected for this round.

"I have made notes beside each of the names, apart from my own. You already have my vote, obviously, so let's not waste any time on me."

Ashley scanned the piece of paper. Of the five lawyers, she only recognized one name, David Dirkman. He was a private practice attorney, but they'd worked together on a recent case. The case had been complicated, and they hadn't parted ways on the best of terms. Of the five laypeople, two were people she'd seen earlier that morning, Bill Roberts and Tucker Caine, two of the three city council people.

"I only know three of the ten, and they aren't my biggest fans," Ashley said.

"Well, then, we'll have to find a way to change that."

"I'm open to ideas, but I think that's going to be a bigger challenge than you think."

"Do you see the first thing I've written by each name?" Judge Ahrenson said, ignoring her last comment.

Ashley looked down. The first thing written beside each name was one word written in red. It said either *for* or *against*. "Yes. I see it, but I don't know what it means."

"It indicates who is for and who is against the installation of windmill farms."

"Okay," Ashley said slowly. "I don't see what that has to do with—"

"It's politics, Ashley. It has everything to do with it. I know you are representing that Campbell kid."

Lucas Campbell was far from a child. He was older than Ashley, but she didn't correct Judge Ahrenson. To him, they were both kids. "I'm not sure what I can do about that."

"Are windmills going to be part of your defense?"

"I'm not sure how they could be."

"If you're trying to hang the jury, it could be."

"How so?" Ashley was intrigued.

"Politics are growing more and more polarized. I'm sure you've noticed that, even though you don't follow all the nonsense closely."

"It would be hard not to notice it."

"Well, you may end up with someone on that jury who is so against windmills that they will refuse to convict the Campbell kid out of principle."

"You have a point," Ashley said.

All jury verdicts had to be unanimous. Any one holdout would result in a hung jury and a mistrial. That would mean that the prosecutor would have to start all over with a new jury, which would cost a lot of money, time, and effort, or drop the charges.

"But I don't see that as a viable strategy. Charles Hanson is not going to give up on this prosecution, especially when he, too, is applying for the judgeship. It would make him look bad. Even if I get a hung jury, he'll try Lucas until he gets a verdict. And all that time Lucas remains locked up."

"Good," Judge Ahrenson said, nodding his head. "That will help."

But as the conversation continued, Ashley grew more uncomfortable with the idea. A hung jury was infinitely better than a conviction, even if it resulted in Lucas remaining in jail for longer. It meant he would still have a chance. Sure, the prosecution could retry him, but how many times? After two or three trials, they might give up. Trials were expensive, and like so many things, money had a very real presence within the criminal justice system. The county paid for the jury's time unless the prosecution got a conviction. A hung jury was not a conviction.

Murder was a serious crime, so it was possible that the prosecution would never give up, but they also might. There were plenty of cold murder cases out there gathering dust in a police storage closet. This wasn't a cold case, but it was possible the prosecution could give up on it, placing the file in that same storage closet. It wouldn't be the same thing as an acquittal, but it would be a dismissal with prejudice, which was just as good. It meant that the prosecution could never recharge Lucas with Gerald's murder.

"Ashley, yoo-hoo," Judge Ahrenson waved a hand in front of her face. "Are you listening to me?"

"Sorry," Ashley said, blinking hard and focusing back on the Judge.

He nodded and continued going back through the list of the judicial nominating committee members, their likes, dislikes, and other helpful hints. Ashley was only half listening. She needed to get out of there and talk to Katie. Despite what she'd said only moments earlier, Judge Ahrenson might have unwittingly handed her a viable defense strategy.

14

KATIE

Katie had considered stopping by Gerald's property to take a few photographs, but Ashley's phone call and warning about the weather changed her mind. Yet, the drive back to the Public Defender's Office was uneventful, right up until she was about five miles outside of the Brine city limits.

There, the wind picked up and snow began dumping from the sky, creating blizzard-like conditions. It was frightening, but there was little to do aside from slow her speed to a crawl and proceed forward, hands clenched around the wheel, eyes peeled. It took her a full thirty minutes to drive those last five miles. By the time she pulled into the office parking lot, she had a pounding headache from constant squinting and sore hands from gripping the wheel so tightly.

Ashley was waiting at the back door when Katie made her way inside. "There you are," Ashley said. "I've been worried."

"I'm alive," Katie said, stomping the snow from her boots. "But it was definitely dicey." She paused, looking around. "Is my dad still here?"

Ashley shook her head. "He left for city hall to file some paperwork. Business formation stuff."

"Oh, okay." She wasn't worried about him. City hall was just down the street, and all parking was pay-by-the-hour meter parking, so he would have walked. "We've got some things to discuss," Katie said with a sigh.

"Yes, yes," Ashley seemed unexpectedly excited, almost giddy. It threw Katie off guard. "Come into my office."

Katie followed Ashley into her small, windowless office. It was at the very back of the building near the parking lot entrance. Files were strewn across the floor in what seemed like complete chaos, but there was also a pattern that indicated a method to Ashley's madness. The furniture was worn, but sturdy, built in a time when things were meant to last well past fashion.

When they were both seated and comfortable, their gazes met. Eagerness radiated off Ashley in a way Katie hadn't seen in quite some time.

"What has you all worked up?" Katie was almost afraid to ask.

"You were right."

"Right?" Katie repeated the word cautiously, as though it might lead her into a trap. Ashley wasn't one to freely admit when she'd been wrong. "Right about what?"

"The windmills. They might just be a viable defense strategy. They won't get us to a win, but we don't need to shoot for a win. All we need to do is hang the jury enough times that the prosecution dismisses charges."

"And how many times do you think that would be?"

"Considering the cost of bringing a jury in—the state will have to pay for their time unless they get a conviction—the time the prosecutor will have to spend in trial preparation, and the political backlash of a hung jury, I wouldn't think we would need to try it more than five times."

"Five times," Katie said, her tone incredulous. "You have time to try a murder case that will likely last a couple weeks each trial five separate times?"

"Well, no, but I'll have to find a way to make time."

Katie shook her head slowly. "That feels like a longshot."

"Not a longer shot than throwing up all potential defenses and hoping something will stick. That's where we are otherwise." She paused, chewing on her lip. "I don't love the plan either, honestly, but it is Lucas's best shot at freedom."

"I just...I was about to tell you the same thing."

"To shoot for a mistrial?"

"No. That you were right. But I was going to say that after meeting with Lucas's dad, the windmill thing doesn't seem like a good defense."

"Why?"

"Well, for several reasons. The first being that Albert Campbell is out there on that property all on his own. He has no food to eat, and nobody has checked on him since Lucas's arrest. If there are so many people in this community hard core against the windmills, then why isn't one of them helping Albert? When I asked him about friends, he said that nobody will have anything to do with him anymore."

"That's concerning."

"And then there is the motive thing. You were right, the windmills prove motive, and it's one of the oldest motives in the book. Money."

"Why do you say that?"

"Albert swears it's about the land alone, and I'm sure Lucas would do the same if asked, but it's hard to believe that. Lucas was hard up for cash. So hard up that his wife left with his child, divorcing him to eke whatever she could out of the estate before it was all gone. Lucas was selling off parts of the land to make ends meet. That purchase contract I found in Lucas's trash can was between Lucas and Gerald. Gerald bought Lucas's land for a pittance and then leased it for windmills. There are fifteen there now—I counted as I passed—and each windmill brings in between $5,000 and $10,000 per month."

Ashley leaned back in her chair, groaning and scrubbing her face with the palms of her hands. "Back to square one, eh."

"Sorry."

"Don't be sorry. This is your purpose. To find these things out so I don't end up going into that courtroom and making an ass out of myself while accidentally screwing Lucas over."

"What do we do now?"

"Same thing we always do. We keep working. It's not a complete wash as a strategy. It's better than nothing, but we do need something better. I guess I should set up depositions."

"Are you sure you want to do that?"

Depositions were part of the court process. They were technically court proceedings, but judges weren't involved unless a dispute arose between the parties. It was an opportunity for the defense team to question every prosecution witness under oath prior to trial. Witnesses were often unpredictable. They didn't always testify as the State expected, and that was why depositions were so important. Defense could learn exactly what they planned to say and use it against them if they testified differently at trial, even if it was a minor difference.

There was a downside to depositions, though. While the State was legally required to list all their witnesses in every case, the defense did not have to unless they took depositions of the State's witnesses. Once depositions started, defense would have to list every potential witness and allow the State to depose them as well. That wouldn't matter so long as the defense had no witnesses because the defendant couldn't be deposed even if he intended to ultimately testify. But it would matter if there were potential surprise witnesses.

"I can't think of what else to do," Ashley said, "And we are up against speedy trial. Ninety days seems like a long time until you try to fit a murder trial into it, and then it passes in the blink of an eye. There isn't a lot of time to twiddle our thumbs doing nothing."

"Alright."

Ashley grabbed her planner and started flipping through the pages. "We are going to need a full day. My next completely open day is April sixteenth."

Katie wrote the date down on a notepad. She wouldn't be present at depositions. As Ashley's investigator, she was a potential witness herself. It didn't matter, though. A court reporter would be taking down every word, and Ashley would set up a video camera to catch mannerisms and other nuances found in human behavior that might lend additional meaning to their words.

"I'll have Elena draft the subpoenas. Can you serve them?" Ashley asked.

"I'd rather have my dad do it. He needs to start pulling his weight in this investigation anyway."

"Good point."

"How many witnesses are there?"

Ashley flipped open Lucas's file and picked up the indictment. A complete witness list was always listed at the bottom. "Deputies Frankie Pitch and George Thomanson."

Both were individuals that Katie knew well. George was a friend, Frankie was not.

"A medical examiner. The criminalist who tested samples taken from the blood trail leading from Gerald's house to Lucas's. A ballistics expert to testify about the gun found at Lucas's house and the bullets retrieved from Gerald's body."

These were all technical witnesses. Ashley would depose them, but their testimony was based on science, not emotion. Their testimony was not likely to change.

"The last witness is Nikki Nelson."

"Who is that?"

"Gerald's daughter. I'm assuming the sole inheritor of Gerald's estate. If we can find a way to point the finger at her, we should. She had plenty to gain from her dad's death, and she found his body."

It felt like a lofty goal to Katie, one that was likely out of reach, but it was an avenue to explore and that was something. "Do you want me to try to interview her before her deposition?"

"If you can. She's probably going to be hostile, but we don't know if we don't try."

"True," Katie said, writing Nikki's name down on her notepad and circling it. "I'll start with a background check on her. Once I've got that compiled, I'll try to contact her and schedule an interview."

"You've got until April sixteenth. If, for some shocking reason, she's sympathetic to Lucas or if you can find a way to point the finger at her, we'll cancel depositions. No sense tipping the prosecutor off to our strategy if we don't have to."

"Got it," Katie said, standing up. She would leave Ashley alone to focus on some of her other clients. Time did not come in infinite quantities, and every client needed some of Ashley's. There wasn't a moment to waste.

As Katie headed down the hallway toward the front of the office, she wondered how the Brine community would react to Lucas's trial. Every case was different, but the public was almost universally on the prosecution's side. Innocent until proven guilty was the legal standard, but it meant nothing outside the courtroom. The court of public opinion was already in the process of rendering a verdict, and it was Katie's job to figure out how many had already decided to ship Lucas off to prison and throw away the key.

15

ASHLEY

March 10
A month and a half before trial

Ashley took a deep breath, steadying herself. She was outside the office of David Dirkman, Attorney at Law. He was a private practice attorney in the area, specializing in civil litigation, and he was also a member of the judicial nominating committee. She'd scheduled an appointment with him a week ago, and she'd been dreading it ever since.

Go inside, she urged herself. *Get it over with. You're wasting time standing here staring at the front door.* Time was not a commodity she could afford to waste. She didn't even have time for this meeting, but it was the lunch hour, so she had chosen to get it out of the way rather than eating lunch. She'd instead have to eat an energy bar on her way to the courthouse for an afternoon hearing followed by a visit with Lucas at the jail.

Finally, after a few additional beats of silence, she twisted the doorknob and stepped inside.

"Hello, there," said a middle-aged woman sitting at the front desk. She had short, curly hair and round, rosy cheeks. A placard in front of her said "Rhonda."

"Hello," Ashley said.

"I saw you standing out there and I was wondering if you were ever going to come inside. It's freezing out there. You'll catch your death."

Great, just great. Ashley thought. *Rhonda saw me hesitating. She'll tell David and he'll have a good laugh. Ashley Montgomery too afraid to talk to him.*

"Are you a potential client?" Rhonda asked, breaking through Ashley's thoughts. "If so, we'll have to schedule you in for another day. Mr. Dirkman is booked solid." She leaned forward, lowering her voice and placing a hand around her mouth, "He is meeting with a judicial candidate here in a few minutes." She said this like her boss was the most important person in the world.

"I'm the judicial candidate," Ashley said, extending her hand. "I'm Ashley Montgomery."

"You?" Rhonda said with horrified confusion. "But you're a woman and so young..."

"Well, I'm not *that* young. I've been practicing for fifteen years. And, yes, I do happen to be a woman. Is that a problem?"

"No, no, sorry, no," Rhonda said, shaking her head in a quick motion that made her cheeks jiggle. A beat of silence passed, then she seemed to regain her composure. She stood and motioned to a small waiting area. "Please have a seat. I'll let Mr. Dirkman know you are here."

"Thank you," Ashley said.

Rhonda turned on short, stubby legs and disappeared down a long hallway. Ashley did not sit, despite the invitation. She was far too anxious for that. Instead, she paced, walking back and forth across the office entryway. She made four revolutions before a familiar voice called her name.

"Speak of the Devil."

Ashley paused and looked up. "David Dirkman," she said with a forced smile. "It's been a while." It actually hadn't been *that* long. The last time she'd seen him was in December.

"It sure has," he said, flashing a row of perfectly straight, overly white teeth. "Come on back. Let's have a chat." He didn't wait for an answer, and Ashley was fine with that. Instead, he turned and led her down the same hallway that Rhonda had disappeared down.

"This is my Brine office," David said, chattering to fill the empty silence as they walked. "It is small, but it does the trick. The Des Moines Office is much bigger. Sometimes I wonder why I keep this one at all. Most of my clients are in the city, you know, but then I remind myself that this is where I got my start. There's something nostalgic about it."

"And you'd lose your spot on the judicial nominating committee," Ashley said.

"Pardon?" David cast a look over his shoulder before continuing down the hallway.

"If you closed your office here. You'd be leaving this district, and you'd no longer be eligible to be a member of the judicial nominating committee here."

"Ohhh. Right, right." He said this as though he didn't care in the least, but Ashley knew the committee was the primary reason he kept his office in Brine. He had power over the judiciary here. Des Moines was a much, much larger city with hordes of lawyers. All of whom were as hungry for power as David. There was little chance he'd obtain a coveted spot on a judicial nominating committee in the bigger city.

"Here we are." David stopped outside the door to a large office.

She stood there, unable to stop herself from comparing it to her own office. It was easily three times the size with expensive furniture. A mahogany desk. Deep leather chairs. Large bookshelves full of Iowa Code books. And then there were the windows. They were on the second floor, and the entire back wall was windows, all facing the courthouse.

"It's a nice space, isn't it?" David said, straightening his back and puffing out his chest.

"Yeah."

"Ladies first," he said, motioning for her to enter.

Ashley bristled at the antiquated phrase. She was no parasol carrying, girdle wearing lady. She was a candidate for a judgeship. Yet she held her tongue and walked past David, sitting in one of the high-backed leather chairs across from his giant, executive-style desk. The leather was soft and comfortable, cradling her body and surrounding her with its expensive scent.

David closed the door and walked around his desk, lowering himself into his own chair. He leaned forward, threaded both hands together, and placed them on the desk in front of him. "So, you want to be a judge."

"That's the application I submitted." The words popped out of her mouth, automatic, and she silently reminded herself to cut the sarcasm. She was meant to be encouraging his support, not alienating him.

"So, it is."

Was that a mocking smile, or was it just in Ashley's head? "Yes."

"I hear you are representing Lucas Campbell."

"Yes." The seemingly sharp shift in subjects gave her brain whiplash as she tried to keep up and determine where he was going with it.

"Is there any way to get out of that?"

"Get out of it?" Ashley repeated. The answer was "no" and as a lawyer, he should have known that. "A judge appointed me as Lucas's counsel and withdrawal would require a judge's approval and good reasoning."

"Like..." He motioned her to keep talking.

"Breakdown of the attorney-client relationship. Conflict of interest—"

"That one," David said, snapping his fingers. "Use conflict to withdraw."

"What is my conflict? There are no co-defendants, so I can't be representing one of them. Gerald Mock was never one of my clients, so I don't have a conflict with the victim."

"It is a conflict with your own interests. Representing him will hurt your chances at becoming a judge."

Ashley fought the urge to pinch the bridge of her nose and groan. His suggestion would not work, and even if it did, it would be unethical. She could not put her personal interests before her client's. Yet she was also intrigued as to why David thought Lucas's case would have any impact at all. "How?"

"Pardon?"

"How will defending Lucas hurt my chances at becoming a judge?"

"It'll remind everyone of the distasteful work you do. Think about the people you have represented. They are all scumbags. Druggies, alcoholics, psychopaths. That's not exactly a political platform people can get behind."

Ashley bristled. "Silly me. Here I thought I was ethically obligated to provide my clients a zealous defense, and all the while I was apparently doing it as a political platform."

"You know what I mean. That isn't easily explained to the general public."

"Then try. That's what I've been doing all these years."

"Listen, Ashley," his tone had grown sharp, irritated. "I've got my own aspirations. I'm not going to chain my wagon to your train if it's going nowhere. And I'm telling you right now, unless you make some very real changes, this train is barely going to get out of the station."

"You seemed to have no problem hitching up to my train six months ago when you needed help with Noah Scott's representation. Or did you already forget about that?"

David Dirkman had been hired by one of Ashley's former clients, Noah Scott. Noah was charged with murdering his girlfriend, but he had come into some money so he didn't qualify for the public defender anymore. Once charges were filed, David had come begging, groveling for her help. That case had ended badly, and they hadn't spoken since. Now, he seemed intent on distancing himself from her.

"I didn't forget about that, but I'd like to," David said.

"Touché." Noah had ended up threatening Ashley's life. She'd like to pretend it didn't happen either, but memories like that were not easily suppressed.

"You're demanding a speedy trial in Lucas's case. Is that true?"

"Yes." Once again, Ashley's brain was racing to decipher the meaning of this sharp change in direction.

"Then waive. Push the trial out to a date way after the decision for Judge Ahrenson's position is made. Six months should be plenty of time."

Ashley shook her head, and there was a touch of sadness burrowing its way into her chest. Not sadness for this idiot sitting across from her, but a genuine concern that if an attorney couldn't understand her ethical obligations, then there was little chance society ever would. "My client is in jail. I can't put my interests over his."

"Then you're not getting this position. The committee will be meeting right around the trial date, and nobody will vote for you."

"You're wrong there," Ashley said, a ball of fire forming in her chest. "I know I have Judge Ahrenson's vote, so that's not nobody. That's one." She stood and started making her way toward the door. "But thank you for your very helpful advice," she used air quotes around the world helpful.

He probably responded, but she didn't wait to hear it. She headed straight for the front door of his office and out into the gusty spring air. The sharp Iowa wind whipped at her hair, tangling it, as she made her way down the street toward her own office. She couldn't wait to get back to her world where she was surrounded by things that made sense. What was she doing applying for this judgeship anyway? She was no politician, and nothing would ever change that. Yes, it was time for a woman to be on the bench, but she was starting to wonder why Judge Ahrenson thought she would ever make it through committee. At this point, it seemed hopeless.

16

KATIE

March 20

Nikki Nelson was a ghost. There was very little public information about her. Born Nikki Lee Mock to Gerald and Malinda Mock, her birth certificate named Brine County Hospital as her place of birth and aged her at thirty-nine. That meant Nikki was close to Lucas Campbell's age and would have been in his class or a year behind him.

Unlike Lucas, who had been a star football player in high school, Nikki's name did not publicly exist anywhere aside from one birth announcement. She had no social media accounts and was not mentioned as an employee on any business page that Katie could find, and she thought it was all quite odd considering the massive amount of information most people dumped onto the internet these days.

Katie sighed, leaned back in her chair, and rubbed her eyes. They were dry and gritty, as if they'd been covered in sand. It was allergy season again and staring at her damned computer for hours on end was not helping. She was at her and her father's makeshift office inside the public defender's office. This was perhaps the hundredth search she'd done, looking for information on Nikki, thinking once again that she was missing something. Apparently not.

"How's it going?" Ashley's voice came from the doorway.

Katie had an L-shaped desk with her computer facing the side wall and the writing portion of her desk facing forward, toward the door. She startled and turned to see Ashley in the doorway, leaning casually on the doorframe, eating an apple.

"Honestly?"

"That's how I like all my answers, honest."

"Like shit. I cannot find this woman. It's crazy. It's like she doesn't exist. I mean, her last name is Nelson, right? But she was born Mock. So, when did she change her name? Why did she change her name? There is no record of a name change—at least not that I can find—and no indication she's been married. It's all very strange."

"Why don't you just ask her?" Ashley said, taking a bite of her apple.

"You say that like it's simple, but it's not. Lucas's Minutes of Testimony list her address as the same as Gerald's, next door to Lucas and Albert Campbell. I've been out there four times, pounding on the door, and there was no indication that anyone was home. Not once. My dad hasn't even been able to serve her the subpoena for depositions."

"That's not good." Ashley took another bite of her apple.

It wasn't good. If they couldn't serve Nikki her subpoena, she wouldn't be required to appear for depositions. And then they'd really have no idea what she was planning to say at trial.

"Why don't you go out there one more time," Ashley said, pushing off the doorframe. "If you don't find her, then you can call over to your buddy George Thomanson at the Sheriff's Department. Give him the subpoena and have him do it."

As investigators, Katie and her father would normally be the ones serving all the subpoenas for Ashley. In a pinch, and they were certainly in one of those, they could pay the Sheriff's Department to complete the service. That was expensive, though, and their defense team wasn't flush with cash.

"Okay," Katie said, rising to her feet and stretching. "I'll do that now."

The wind battered Katie's Impala as she drove toward Gerald Mock's property, causing her to hold fast to the steering wheel just to stay on the road. Spring was Katie's least favorite time of year. To her, it was far worse than January and February's biting cold because she expected the cold in those months. But spring in Iowa was unpredictable, at best. The thermometer might read sixty degrees, but the wind made it feel more like thirty.

Aside from the weather, the long drive to the farm was uneventful. Katie continued to wrack her brain, trying to come up with a reason Nikki was so content to stay in the shadows. She could have been in criminal trouble, but that would have entered the gossip mills or police records. By all accounts from townspeople, Nikki had been a shy, quiet girl. Nobody knew her in adulthood. Few people had even seen her. A Nikki Nelson sighting seemed almost like spotting a rare, nearly extinct animal, especially now that so much attention had been focused on Gerald Mock as Lucas's victim.

When she arrived at the residence, Katie drove all the way down the driveway and parked near the front door. In the past, she'd parked by the street and walked, but it was a long walk, and she doubted this attempt would produce different results from the last four. After a brief pause, she once again grabbed the subpoena meant for Nikki, got out, and walked up to the front door, her boots crunching against gravel.

The house was two stories with a covered, wraparound porch made out of durable and expensive composite material. The porch roof was angled away from the house everywhere other than the front door, where it rose to a peak. The front door was an imposing double wide door structure with large windows occupying the entire front half.

Katie stepped onto the porch and pressed the doorbell while holding Nikki's subpoena clutched in her other hand. It was her fifth time doing this, and she couldn't shake the strong sense of *deja vu*. She stood there in complete silence, the wind whipping at her hair. *Five minutes*, she told herself. *You took the trouble to drive all the way out here, so give it five minutes.*

She looked down at her watch. It was late morning, ten twenty-nine exactly. She'd give it until ten thirty-five and ring the doorbell every minute. If Nikki was inside, perhaps she would be annoyed enough to come outside. After the third ring of the doorbell, Katie thought she heard movement inside.

"Hello?" She called. "Nikki. Is that you? I don't mean you any harm. I just want to talk to you."

"What is in your hand?" A soft, barely audible voice said from inside.

Katie leaned forward, looking through the large windows, but she couldn't see anyone. The speaker was outside Katie's line of sight, presumably tucked against the wall.

"Nikki? Is that you?"

"What is in your hand?" The voice repeated.

"It's a subpoena. To testify."

"I don't want to testify."

"Is this Nikki?"

"Yes."

Katie issued a heavy sigh of relief. She had found the elusive Nikki Nelson, and she'd been out here all along. "Will you open the door? I need to talk to you."

"No!" Nikki shouted, her voice quick and sharp.

Katie was at a loss. What was she supposed to do? A subpoena was not officially "served" until the paper physically touched some part of Nikki's body. A conversation through the door was not sufficient to establish personal service.

"Okay, well, then, can you step out onto the porch for a few minutes?"

"No!" This time she shouted even louder. She was starting to sound deranged.

"Is it the questions? I don't have to ask you anything. I just need to—"

"I said no."

Frustration blossomed within Katie. She didn't understand what was happening. Sure, people dodged subpoenas—nobody wanted to be dragged into a court battle—but most would simply hide until Katie had gone. Presumably, that was what Nikki had done the other four times Katie had tried to serve her. So, what made this time different?

"But you can come inside," Nikki said with a sigh.

"Oh, okay," Katie said.

There was the click of not one, but four deadbolts sliding out of the door frame. *Click. Click. Click. Click.* Katie couldn't help thinking of bullets sliding into the chamber of a gun. As the door started to swing open, Katie took one last look over her shoulder, out at the deserted countryside. If Nikki was as unhinged as Katie was starting to suspect, she was on her own. There would be no backup coming or assistance rendered.

17

ASHLEY

After Ashley's disastrous meeting with David Dirkman, one of the lawyer members of the judicial nominating committee, she hadn't wanted to continue with the process. She'd been inclined to withdraw her name from the running and continue her life as she knew it, but then she'd spoken to Judge Ahrenson, and he'd convinced her otherwise. Which was why she'd scheduled a meeting with Tucker Caine and Bill Roberts, two non-lawyers of the judicial nominating committee, over the lunch hour.

The morning had passed in a blur as Ashley kept busy and tried to keep her mind from wandering to the eventual meeting. She had no idea how it would go. Neither man seemed to like her much, and she'd done nothing to cultivate any relationship with them over the years. Now, she was scheduled to meet with them both at the same time, which was convenient because it killed two birds with one stone, but it also made it two against one.

She was dreading it. Every few moments she found herself watching the clock as its hands moved toward alignment at the twelve, wishing for them to move slower. Then, at eleven thirty, her office phone started ringing.

"Yes?" Ashley said, picking up the receiver.

"You've got a call from Tucker Caine's office," Elena, Ashley's office manager said.

Ashley's heart leaped. Maybe he was cancelling the appointment. Then it fell for the same reason. If he refused to meet with her, she'd have no opportunity to explain herself aside from the actual committee meeting, and Judge Ahrenson said that would be too late. She needed to have a number of committee members on her side or at least willing to be on her side before even entering that room.

"Do you want to take the call?" Elena's kind, sweet voice cut through Ashley's bitter thoughts.

"Want and should are two very different things," Ashley said with a heavy sigh. "But, yeah, patch him through."

"Okey dokie," Elena said. "He'll be there when I hang up."

Ashley waited a beat, then said, "This is Ashley Montgomery."

"Ashley, Tucker Caine here," he said in his smooth, liquid voice.

"Oh." Ashley was taken aback. She'd expected someone from his office staff would be calling to inform her that she'd been shunned. Perhaps he disliked her enough to personally deliver the news, giddy as he cancelled the appointment.

"We've got a meeting today at noon."

Here it comes, Ashley thought, bracing herself for whatever insult he was bound to sling at her.

"Can you meet with me at one o'clock instead?"

"You? As in you alone? I thought I was meeting with you and Bill Roberts together."

"Yes, well, Bill and I have hit a bit of a," he paused, "A rough patch these last couple of days. We aren't seeing eye to eye, and I think it would be more productive to have our discussions separate."

"Umm, okay," Ashley said, glancing at her paper calendar. "I have a meeting set for that time, but I can reschedule."

"That's a good girl."

Ashley winced. *Girl.* She wasn't a fucking girl. She was a lawyer in her mid-thirties who handled very serious cases. Cases that mattered in the lives of her clients, but also affected the community. To call her a *girl*—a child—was an insult, but she forced herself not to respond in kind.

"Right, well, I'd better start working on rescheduling that appointment. I don't have a lot of time before I meet with Mr. Roberts."

It was already eleven forty-five. She was going to have to ask Elena to reschedule her appointment because there was not a lot of time to walk over to Bill's office, and Bill was of the generation that felt like early was on time and on time was late.

"Sure," Tucker said, "But keep an open mind. Bill isn't right all the time."

"Okay," Ashley said, trying to puzzle out the undertone of the statement. Tucker had once followed Bill's words as though they were gospel, and he was living in the Bible Belt. Yet, here he was giving her a caveat, trying to nudge her into one way of thinking. About what, she had no idea. Maybe Bill Roberts planned to insult her, tell her she had no business even applying for a spot on the bench. It was fair to assume it had something to do with her, since the meeting was about her. "I'll keep that in mind."

"That's all I can ask. I'll see you at one."

Ashley said goodbye, then hung up the phone. Grabbing her laptop bag, she shoved her computer, some pens, and a couple of notepads into it before rushing out the door and toward the front of the office.

"I have to meet with Tucker and Bill separately now," Ashley said when she reached Elena in the open, reception area of the office. "Can you call my one o'clock appointment and move him to later this afternoon?"

"Sure. What if he can't come then?"

"Just fit him in wherever you can."

"Sure thing," Elena said, giving Ashley a fake salute. "Good luck with Bill Roberts."

"I think I'm going to need it." Ashley pulled on her jacket and headed out the front door.

Aside from his work on the city council, Bill Roberts worked in insurance. He had an insurance office a few blocks away, but as a city council person he also had an office inside the courthouse. They had agreed to meet at the courthouse. Ashley dashed across the street and into the building where she'd spent many of her days, heading down the long, winding first-floor corridors to Bill's office.

The door was shut. She'd never been inside it before—she and Bill weren't exactly buddies—but she knew it was the right office because the door had a nameplate bearing the name *William Roberts*. Below it hung a large, white poster with a thick, blue line running across the middle of it with the words *Backing our Boys in Blue*.

It was signs like this one that annoyed the ever-living shit out of Ashley. Boys? She didn't even like law enforcement, and she understood referring to them as *boys* rather than men was an insult. And what about the girls? There were women in law enforcement. Katie had once been one of them. None of this mattered in Brine, of course, since there was no longer a police department. All law enforcement wore the brown of the Sheriff's Department. But still, the poster stood for something. It signified Bill's way of thinking.

The very thought of that sign had Ashley's blood boiling. She took a moment to settle her nerves, breathing in a few calming, steadying breaths before knocking on the door.

"Come in," came Bill Robert's sharp, almost high-pitched voice.

Ashley opened the door and stepped inside. It was a one-room office. Not large by traditional standards, but it was twice the size of Ashley's. The furniture wasn't extravagant, but it was newer, sturdy, and in good condition.

"You're late."

Ashley glanced at a clock hanging on the wall. It read eleven fifty-six. She was exactly four minutes early. In any other situation, she would have called him out, but she kept her mouth shut. She had applied for a political position, and that meant biting her tongue sometimes. Even if it meant drawing blood.

"Sit," Bill nodded to the chairs across from his executive-style desk.

Ashley followed his directive.

"You want a spot on the bench," Bill said.

Ashley was not one for small talk. She saw no point in discussing the weather. Yet she also knew it was important, especially to political types. It was probably not a good sign that he was cutting right to the chase.

"Yes," she said, slowly, cautiously.

"I could ask you about your credentials and all that, but I already know who you are, what you do. I know you've been toiling over there at the public defender's office for fifteen years now. You've tried some big cases, and you've caused me quite a lot of hell when it came to that deal with

Forest Parker and his plan to defund the police and replace it with the mental health response team."

Ashley was willing to put up with some shit in exchange for a judgeship, but she was not going to tolerate insults against the MHRT project. That project had done more for the community than anything else. She could rage at him, hurling crime statistics that show without a doubt that mental health is a huge factor contributing to crime rates. But she knew that wouldn't gain her any ground with him. She needed to speak in terms that mattered to him.

"Yeah, well, that saved the city some money, didn't it? There are still the same number of officers, but they are all employed by the Sheriff's Department. That means the county has to foot that bill. Not you. Sure, you contribute to the MHRT team, but barely. That's almost completely funded by private donations and Stephanie Arkman."

Bill looked up, his eyes flashing with something like anger, but it was gone in an instant. "You have a point there. I sure do like to save the taxpayers some money when I can."

It has nothing to do with saving taxpayers' money and everything to do with retaining your position on the city council, Ashley thought.

"I don't want to talk about all that," Bill said, waving a dismissive hand. "That's in the past."

"Okay." Ashley had come to this meeting prepared to defend her work, her past. If he didn't want to talk about the past, what did he want to discuss?

"You have property in the county."

"Umm, yeah. An acreage about twenty miles south of town."

"How many acres?"

"Ten."

"Have you spoken with Mr. Larson yet?"

"Mr. Larson?" Ashley repeated. "The realtor?"

The man was not originally from Brine, but he had become infamous over the past year, convincing people to sell or lease their land to a Texas oil company, allowing them to build windmills on their property. Ashley had not heard from the man, but she assumed that one day he would come knocking on her door, making the same request posed to so many others.

"Yes, the realtor."

"I grew up on that property, Mr. Roberts, I don't intend to sell it. Not to anyone."

A smile spread across Bill's lips. "That's precisely what I was hoping to hear. You stick to that position, and you have my vote."

"Wait, what?"

"You heard me. You help to keep those giant metal monstrosities out of our county, and I'll back you one hundred percent, your soon-to-be honor."

Ashley blinked several times. Was it really that simple?

"Are we on the same page?"

"Yeah," Ashley said with a nod.

As they ended their meeting and Ashley rose to her feet, she had a strange sense that she'd just made a deal with the devil. She had never been on the same page with Bill Roberts on anything. Yet they'd somehow found common ground with this windmill thing. She didn't share his position that no windmills should be anywhere in Brine, but he didn't ask so he didn't need to know. Surprisingly, she'd been able to keep her mouth shut. Maybe this politics stuff wouldn't be as difficult as she'd previously thought.

18

KATIE

The first thing Katie registered as she stepped inside Gerald Mock's former house was the smell. Heavy duty cleaning products, a scent so powerful it made her sneeze.

"Sorry about that," Nikki said. She closed the door the moment Katie crossed the threshold and locked all four deadbolts with methodical precision. "That's where I found him with blood everywhere. I spend hours cleaning every day, but I still can't seem to get rid of the smell of it."

"Blood?"

"No, death."

"Okay." Katie didn't think death had a smell. Decomposition certainly did, but not death alone.

"You don't believe me."

"I believe blood has a smell, and your father lost quite a lot of it in this spot."

Nikki shook her head. Her hair was short, shorn nearly to the roots. It didn't move even with the violent jostling of her head. Katie would call it a pixie cut, but there was no style to it. It looked like Nikki had cut it on her own, chopping locks of hair off in large chunks near the base of her skull.

"I'm not talking about blood. I'm talking about death. My mother died a few years ago. Cancer. But I could smell it on her, death. She'd been sick for a long time, but I knew when the end was near. I knew it before the doctors. And that was because of the smell."

Katie blinked several times. She didn't know what to say. It was obvious that this woman had been through quite a lot of tragedy over the past few years, and her mental health was suffering.

"I smelled it on my father, too. Right before he died. I told him that death was coming for him. I told him to watch out, but he didn't listen. Nobody listens to me. They always think that I'm crazy. Crazy. Crazy. *Crazy.* Dad answered the door when I told him not to, and *boom*, just like that," she snapped her fingers, "He was gone."

"Wait, wait, wait. Can we back up a bit?" Katie asked. "That's a lot to process, and I'm, well, before I forget, I need to give you this." She grabbed Nikki's wrist, turning her hand over and pressing the subpoena into it. "You've been served."

Nikki didn't close her hand around the document. She just stood there, frozen to the spot, letting it flutter to the floor while wearing a blank expression. This wasn't Katie's first time serving subpoenas. She'd done it regularly during that year she worked with Ashley as an investigator, but this was by far the strangest one.

There were several beats of silence, and then Katie said, "Are you going to pick that up?"

Nikki shrugged. "Not right now."

"Don't you want to know what it says?"

Nikki shrugged again. "Would you like some tea?"

"Umm, sure," Katie said. Nikki's behavior had been so odd that part of Katie wanted to refuse and get out of there, but there was a larger, more curious part of Katie's brain that made the decision to stay.

Nikki led the way down an ornate hallway toward the back of the house. It opened up into a large, open concept kitchen and great room. A wall of windows covered the entire back side of the house, giving a stunning view of the rolling countryside. Everything in the kitchen looked expensive, state of the art, and new within the past five years. It couldn't be more different from Lucas's battered old country house.

"Your dad had cows?" Katie said, looking out the back window. She didn't see any animals on the property.

"They were on the land across the street, but yes. He had cows." Nikki filled an ornate, traditional Japanese tea kettle with water from the tap.

"Do you take care of them now?"

"No. I don't leave the house." She flipped the switch, turning one of the stove's gas burners on, and placed the teapot on top of it.

"You don't leave the house," Katie paused, "Like ever?"

"No."

"For how long."

"It started when mom died. I didn't like to leave, but I would go outside, wander this property." She gestured toward the large row of windows. "I've never liked animals much, so I stayed away from the animals, but I kept a little garden outside."

"So, you do leave the house."

"No. Not since dad died. I don't go outside anymore."

"Oh, so who takes care of the animals? I presume your dad gave them to you in his will."

"You presume wrong," Nikki said. The teapot started to squeal. "Have a seat." She nodded to a long table situated near the windows in an open-concept dining area as she removed two mugs from a cabinet and placed a tea bag into each of them.

Katie remained rooted to her spot, watching the entire process. Nikki had been more than a little strange throughout this interaction, and Katie was not going to drink something she hadn't seen prepared. It could be poisoned.

"Who got the animals?"

"A friend of my dad's. He came out here with a big trailer and took them all away a couple days ago. I watched them through the window."

"Why wouldn't he give them to you?"

"Because I don't like big animals. I already told you that." Nikki handed Katie her mug of tea. "Cream or sugar?"

"No, thank you."

Nikki removed some cream from the refrigerator and poured a generous amount into her mug. Then she added a heaping spoonful of sugar. She then led Katie over to the dining table and they sat on opposite sides.

"If you don't leave, how do you get groceries?"

"Like anyone else. Amazon. And food delivery services."

"Okay."

It wasn't a full answer because it didn't explain where the money for the food came from, but Katie assumed that Gerald had left some money for his daughter.

Nikki nodded, smiling as she took a sip of tea. It was the kind of grin that put Katie on edge. One that held no humor. The stretching of the lips in an almost maniacal mimicking of true mirth.

"I have a lot of questions for you, Nikki. I'm here to serve you a subpoena, but I'm also a private investigator hired by Lucas Campbell's attorney."

"I figured that."

Katie was a little taken aback by this comment. Most people would not want to discuss their father's murder with an agent of the person accused of perpetrating the crime. Yet Nikki seemed to have no qualms about it. "Do you mind if I record our conversation?"

"Nope."

Katie placed a black recording device on the table between them, and pressed play. "This is Katie Mickey, and today's date is March 20. I'm sitting here with Nikki Nelson, and she has agreed to answer a few questions, isn't that right, Nikki?"

"Yes."

"Okay, I want to start with some background."

"Sure."

"Your name is Nikki Nelson, yet your father's name was Gerald Mock. Are you currently married?"

"I was married briefly. It was about a year before mom got sick. Then, when I learned about mom's cancer, I moved back in here to help out. My husband refused to come. And that was that. He filed for divorce within six months after I moved, and it was over."

"But you never changed your name back?"

"No. Mom got really sick really quickly. I was wholly focused on her. Then, after she died, I stopped leaving the property at all. She was the first person I smelled death on. After that, I didn't want to be around people. I didn't want to know who would die and who would live."

Smelled death, Katie thought. It wasn't the first time Nikki had made that statement, and it made her sound deranged. She could dig deeper into that topic, and she probably would, but first she needed to know if Nikki would be helpful to the defense in other ways.

"You grew up with Lucas Campbell, right?"

"Sure did. He was a year older than me, but we were in high school together. He was always nice to me, but we didn't hang out. He was an athlete. One of the popular guys. And I was, well, I was nothing."

"Did you maintain a friendship with him after graduation?"

"I moved to Kansas with my husband. I didn't hear from Lucas during that period of time. He was married himself and seemed happy. It wasn't until I came back when I started realizing that things weren't all sunshine and roses over on the Campbell farm."

"What do you mean?"

"They were bleeding money. Within five years, Lucas had sold nearly everything, and his wife and daughter, they were both gone. The poor guy had nothing left."

Katie blinked several times, trying to understand Nikki. This was the man that was accused of shooting her father in the face, yet she'd just expressed sympathy for *him*.

"Wasn't your father one of the people who purchased some of Lucas's property?"

"Yes. The first plot of land dad bought from Lucas was before mom was even sick."

"Did you know of any agreement about windmills?"

"Yes and no."

"Can you elaborate?"

"I didn't know about it at the time. When dad purchased the property, I think he was genuinely trying to help Lucas see the light. It was time to move on. Farming might have been in his family, but it wasn't in his blood anymore."

"But was there an agreement that your dad would not lease the land for windmills?"

"I didn't know it, but yes, there was. It wasn't in writing, and it wasn't binding. Or at least that's what the lawyer for the oil company said."

"You spoke to a lawyer from the oil company?"

"I didn't. I overhead my dad talking to him. I had a tough time after mom died. Like I said, I couldn't leave the property, and I was getting worse, not better. Then that realtor started coming around. Mr. Larson was his name. He apparently lives in town, but he's not from Brine originally."

"What do you mean by 'coming around?'"

"He would stop by. He would call. He would email my dad. He seemed to be everywhere, constantly talking to dad about the property."

"What did he want?"

"He wanted dad to lease the land to that Texas windmill company."

"Exactly what your father promised not to do."

"True. And he told Mr. Larson that. He said, 'I promised not to put windmills on the property. I can't go back on that promise.'"

"So why did he?"

"Because of me."

"I don't follow."

"I've told you several times that I cannot leave the property. That's not an exaggeration. I do not, I cannot leave. I have panic attacks, or at least that's what my virtual psychologist tells me. To me, it just feels like dying. Either way, I can't work. Dad knew that. The realtor, Mr. Larson, must have eventually noticed it as well. One time he showed up with a lawyer, they told dad that the handshake with Lucas wasn't binding, and he needed to think about my future. How I was going to survive if something happened to him."

"And the answer they proposed to him was windmill money," Katie finished for her.

"Yup."

"So, you cannot leave at all?"

"No. I can't."

"Didn't you go to your father's funeral?"

"I didn't. They streamed it virtually for me. In that sense, I attended. But, no, I didn't go."

"Wow," Katie sat back in her chair, trying to process the information. "So, you don't blame Lucas for being angry?"

"Lucas wasn't angry."

"What?"

"He was hurt."

There had been quite a few odd twists in the conversation, but this one seemed the most bizarre of them all. "Do you believe Lucas shot your father?"

"Yes."

"Yet you sound like you are excusing the behavior. Do I have that right?"

"I'm not excusing it. Lucas didn't have a choice."

"He didn't *choose* to kill your dad?"

"No. The universe did. Like I said, dad smelled like death before Lucas got to our front door. I told him not to open it. I told him he would die. He didn't listen. By then, the universe had decided that he would die. There was nothing that anyone, including Lucas or even me, could do to stop it."

Again, Katie was stunned into silence. This was not a defense, *the universe decided, not Lucas*, but she felt as though it was a concept that she needed to spend more time pondering. A jury would never go for that kind of hippie mumbo jumbo. They were country folks. They believed in God, not the universe, and they certainly did not believe in the smell of death. Yet there could be something here. A way Ashley could spin it to her advantage.

"Well, I think that's all the questions I have for you." Katie reached over and switched the recorder off. "Thank you for the tea."

"Come back any time. It gets lonely out here."

Katie stood and stretched. "Your neighbor, Albert Campbell is awfully lonely, too."

"Tell him to stop by sometime."

"Really?"

Nikki nodded. "I've got a huge house and nobody to share it with. I've known Albert all my life. He was like a second father to me. It would be nice to have someone around again. Someone I can take care of."

Katie had been worried about Albert, all alone out here in the country. His house was practically falling down, and he had very little money. If he stayed with Nikki, it could solve all his problems. Then again, Nikki was quite odd. She could be putting on an act, but to what end? She didn't know.

"I'll talk it over with Ashley, Lucas's attorney. If she's okay with Albert spending time with you, then I'll pose the arrangement to him. How does that sound?"

"Wonderful."

Katie left the house with a strange buoyancy, like a weighted down buoy on a windy day, bobbing up and down in the water. There were some positives that came out of the conversation with Nikki, but plenty of drawbacks as well. She could help the defense, yet she wouldn't show up to trial or even depositions. Even if they did find a way for her to appear, her testimony probably wouldn't sway a jury. Katie didn't know what it all added up to, and she would need to sit down with Ashley to do the calculations. Did Nikki help or hurt their case?

19

ASHLEY

The meeting with Bill Roberts shook Ashley's confidence. She was qualified to take Judge Ahrenson's place, of that she had no doubt, but she didn't know if she could withstand the politics required to get there. Everything was so polarized these days. There was no middle ground anymore. People took positions and expected everyone else to fall into line, refusing to even listen to those with even slightly differing opinions.

Yet she also felt a sense of responsibility to women everywhere to give it her best shot. Judge Ahrenson had been right. There were no women on the bench in her district, and it was time for that to change. She couldn't give up now, despite the draining nature of the process. She forced herself to walk down the street to Tucker Caine's office inside First Iowa Bank.

A hushed silence descended upon her as she entered through the front door of the bank. Tellers stood stoically behind the counter, but they were as quiet and still as the English Queen's Guard. There was no music playing softly over the sound system, only the sound of her heels clicking against marble. When she reached the middle of the large, open lobby, she looked left and then right. There were offices in both directions, but, to her right, a sign on the door read, *Tucker Caine, Regional Manager*.

She headed for the door and knocked several times, wincing as the sound reverberated off the high ceilings. Then she stood there, waiting for

Tucker to come to the door. She shoved her hands into her pants pockets to keep from fidgeting. It was unsettling, this atmosphere inside the bank. The intent was reverence, like a church, but Ashley had never felt comfortable inside churches, either, despite her Catholic upbringing.

A few moments passed, and then a sharp click sounded as Tucker opened his door. A man exited first. He was tall and thin with dark hair, greying at the temples. A carefully maintained goatee snaked its way around his mouth.

"Ashley," Tucker said as he joined the man in the doorway, "You're early." He smiled, but there was something forced about it.

"Ashley." The man with Tucker repeated her name, slowing its pronunciation with a southern drawl. "You wouldn't happen to be Ashley Montgomery, would you?"

"The one and only," Ashley's gaze darted from Tucker to the man. "And you are?"

"Matthew Larson." They shook hands, and then he reached into his pocket, producing a business card and presenting it with the flourish of a magician. "Realtor."

She'd never seen his face, but she recognized the name immediately. This was the realtor who had been working with the oil company, trying to buy and lease property for the windmills.

"Okay," Ashley said. The proper response would be to say *nice to meet you*, but it wasn't nice to meet him. She didn't want any part of his business.

"I've been trying to track you down. You're a busy one. I was starting to think you were a phantom."

"Nope. I exist." She gestured to herself as if to say *I'm here in the flesh*, but she didn't ask why he had been looking for her. That answer was obvious. He wanted to discuss leasing part of her property. She hadn't been avoiding him. She truly was busy and difficult to catch, but she was also eager to avoid the windmill conversation.

"Do you have a card or something?" He nodded toward his card that he had thrust into Ashley's hands. "So I know where to reach you."

Ashley blinked several times. "I'm the public defender. I don't have a card." And even if she did, she would have made a show of checking her pockets and shrugging, saying she was out of them even if her pockets were stuffed full.

"Oh, right, right," Matthew said, snapping his long, bony fingers as though her profession had only slipped his mind.

He was not local; he had no reason to know her. This gesture made her feel like he'd been stalking her. "I'm here to meet with Mr. Caine," Ashley said, nodding toward Tucker, who was standing behind Matthew, almost as though he was hiding. "So, if you don't mind, I'd like to get to that."

"Right, right. Of course, Ms. Montgomery," Matthew said with a bow. He moved past Ashley into the hallway, then turned back to Tucker. "I'll be in touch with you tomorrow." Then he turned and strode out of the building, his expensive leather shoes silent as the bank around him as they struck against the opulent flooring.

"Sorry about that," Tucker said, ushering Ashley into his spacious office.

She came in and stood in the middle of the room, shifting her weight awkwardly as he looked left and then right down each hallway before closing the door and turning back to her.

"Have a seat, have a seat," he said gesturing to the large leather chairs opposite his desk.

Questions swirled around in Ashley's mind. What was that man, that realtor, doing in Tucker's office? Had they been discussing her? She hoped not. She had no intention of getting roped into the local debate over wind-mills. She understood that she would have to play a certain level of politics, but that was A-team stuff, and she had no intention of putting more than C-team effort into it.

"How was your meeting with Bill?"

"Roberts?" Ashley asked.

"Yes." Tucker sat in his high-backed chair, threading his fingers together and placing them on the desk in front of him. "Did he mention me?"

"Umm, no. We discussed the job. The judgeship that I'm applying for. You are both on the nominating committee. That's the reason I'm here."

"Yes, yes, I know," he said with a forced chuckle. "I was just checking to see what kind of lies that man was spreading."

That man. The words caught in Ashley's mind like flies in honey. Tucker and Bill had been friends for as long as Ashley could remember. It was Bill who had secured Tucker's position on City Council. Bill's son, Jonnie, had been Tucker's best friend. When Jonnie was killed in a car accident at the age of nineteen, Tucker and Bill grew even closer. Like father and son.

"He's telling everyone that the windmills are bad," Tucker continued, pulling Ashley out of her thoughts. "But he is wrong. Wind energy is the way of the future. The Democrats aren't right about much of anything, but they are right about our reliance on oil. We cannot keep getting it from places like Russia and the Middle East."

"Okay." Ashley had thought the goal was more of an environmental, climate change thing, but she supposed she could consider the two major parties agreeing on *anything,* no matter the reasoning behind it, was a win.

"Would you put any on your property?" Tucker asked.

"Any...what?"

"Windmills."

"No."

"So, you agree with Bill. That we shouldn't allow windmill farms in Brine County."

"I wouldn't go that far."

"Then how far would you go?"

Everyone had their tolerance limits. Judgeship or no judgeship, Ashley was nearly at max capacity with Tucker. "Why is everything so extreme? So, what? I have to be either for or against windmills entirely? I can't just say that I don't want to put any on my property? I don't personally need the money, maybe someone else does. Because that's the true reason. I understand the benefits, both financial, political, and environmental, but I don't like the way they look, so I don't intend to put one smack dab in the middle of my backyard. Is that okay with you?" She had spoken so quickly, so forcefully, that she had to stop to catch her breath.

Tucker was momentarily shocked by her outburst, but then he regained his composure. Then he said, "Everyone needs a little extra padding in the bank."

"Not me."

"You have all the money in the world? I guess the public defender pays you pretty well."

"I have a decent salary, state retirement benefits, no children, and my home was an inheritance from my mother. So, no. I don't need more money. But I appreciate your concern for my financial condition." Ashley said that last bit with more than a little sarcasm.

"Everyone has their price, Ms. Montgomery."

"I don't know what you mean by that exactly, but I assure you that I do not."

"You want this judgeship, don't you?"

"That's why I'm here," Ashley said calmly, but all the while her mind was trying to determine what the hell was happening here. They hadn't spent a moment focused on her merits for the position. Only her political alignment with one issue within the county.

"This isn't the last you are going to hear of this windmill thing," Tucker said.

"I'm sure it isn't."

"If you want my support when the judicial nominating committee meets on May 1, you'll need to get on the right side of this windmill thing."

"I thought I already told you that I wasn't picking a side. I'm not for or against. I'm in the middle."

"Then get out of the middle. That's the only way you will see my support. Do you understand?"

"Yeah, I think I do."

Ashley understood wholly and completely. Tucker would not support her without her vocal support of the windmills. But she couldn't do that, not personally or professionally. The windmills were going to be an undercurrent issue in Lucas's trial. Ashley's plan was to use the debate to nudge the jury toward jury nullification or to at least get them to hang. It would blow his defense if she came out in support of windmills.

"Thank you for your time, Mr. Caine," Ashley said through clenched teeth. She rose from her seat and headed out the door.

He said something more to her, probably some bullshit platitudes, but she wasn't listening. All she wanted to do was get the hell out of there and back to her office, back to life as she knew it.

20

KATIE

It was nearly one thirty when Katie returned to the office. Ashley wasn't there, but she found her father in one of the empty offices on his hands and knees crawling around on the floor.

"What are you doing?" Katie asked.

Michael startled and sat back, banging his head on the bottom of the desk. He issued a groan and Katie winced. That had to hurt.

"I didn't mean to scare you."

"Not scared," Michael said, rubbing his head as he rose to his feet. "Just trying to get things set up around here."

"And that involves tummy time?"

"No. It involves plugging in a scanner. The plug-ins in this building just happened to be super low and behind desks."

"I see. Well, ask me to help you next time. You shouldn't be doing all that at your age."

"I'm not even sixty-five yet. I've got plenty of gas left in this engine." He patted his belly. "Speaking of fuel, have you eaten lunch yet?"

Katie fought the juvenile urge to roll her eyes at her father's lame joke. "No. I haven't. But I've got a lot of work to do, and I need to talk to Ashley." A bell jingled from the front of the office. "That's probably her now."

"I'll order something in. Does that Genie's place deliver?"

"Genie's Diner?"

"Yeah."

"No. But they do takeout."

"We can do that," Michael said, following Katie as she walked down the hallway and into the front of the office.

As she suspected, Ashley had returned.

"Bullshit. Bullshit. Bullshit," Ashley mumbled as she walked around the reception desk and into the employee area of the office.

Only Ashley, Katie, and Michael were present. Elena was out for a late lunch.

"Your meeting with Bill and Tucker went well, I take it?"

"No. Horrible. Absolutely horrible."

"So, you can't count on either of their votes when the committee meets?"

"Not necessarily. Bill says he will support me so long as I refuse to allow windmills on my property."

Katie raised an eyebrow. Windmills again. They seemed to be sucking up all the political oxygen in every room. No matter where she was or who she spoke to, the conversation always seemed to steer back to windmill farms. People were fired up about them.

"What about Tucker?" Katie asked.

"He won't support me unless I come out publicly praising windmill farms."

"You can't do that."

"I'm aware," Ashley said with a groan. "That's why I think it is bullshit, bullshit, bullshit."

"I see."

Just then, the bell above the front door of the public defender's office jangled, announcing someone's entry into the office. Michael, Katie, and Ashley all turned in unison, but it was Ashley who spoke.

"Oh, no. Not you. I don't want anything to do with you right now."

The man was tall and thin and wearing an expensive-looking suit, charcoal grey with a light blue pocket square. Katie didn't recognize him, but based on his clothing, she knew he wasn't a current or former client of Ashley's.

"I just need a moment of your time." He spoke with a Southern drawl.

"No. Absolutely not. You get out of here before I call the cops."

Katie leaned toward her father. "Who is that?" She whispered.

"Sir," Michael Michello said, striding toward the reception desk. "I'm Michael Michello. I don't believe we've met."

"Matthew Larson," he said, looking down at Michael's extended hand with disdain. "This won't take long, Ashley."

Katie realized he was the realtor working for the Texas oil company. An infamous man if one could believe the whispers around town. Nobody liked him. Not even those who supported the windmill farms. Most people categorized him as "pushy," but Katie would say he was a downright asshole, based on what she'd heard.

"It'll take plenty long," Ashley spat, "Because you'll be waiting all day if you think you are going to take one second of my time. Now get out of here." She pointed at the door.

"I'll walk you out," Michael said. "I was going to go pick up some lunch anyway." He turned to Ashley and Katie. "I'll ask Genie to make an order you like. You two go there often enough. She should know what you'd want, right?"

"Yes," Ashley and Katie said in unison.

"I'll be back in a flash."

Michael stepped around the reception desk and stood next to Matthew Larson, crossing his arms. He was a good twenty years older than Matthew, but he had at least fifty pounds on him and a prison background. If Katie were a betting person, she'd bet on her father winning a physical fight with this fancy skinny boy any day.

"Ready?" Michael said, cocking an eyebrow. "It's time to go."

"Fine," Matthew said, directing his words toward Ashley. "But I'm not giving up. If you don't talk to me now, I'll find a way to make you talk to me."

"Is that a threat?" Ashley said.

"No. It's a promise."

Katie almost laughed. This guy would resort to an overused platitude to make a point.

"Just go," Katie said.

Matthew shot Ashley one more intense look, and then he turned on his heel and marched out with Katie's father following close behind. Ashley and Katie watched in silence as the two men left, but the moment the door closed behind them Katie turned to her friend.

"What was that about?"

"I'm not 100 percent sure, but I think he wants me to put some windmills out on my property. I ran into him outside Tucker Caine's office. He said he had been looking for me. Apparently, he found me."

"Apparently. What was he doing with Tucker Caine? I thought his property was maxed out with windmills already."

"Who the fuck knows? Probably trying to track me down. Anyway," Ashley said, clapping her hands together. "How was your morning? Did you find little Miss Nikki Nelson?"

"I did, actually."

"Did you learn anything helpful?" Ashley said, rubbing her hands together.

"I think so?"

Ashley leaned forward with interest.

"Nikki is an agoraphobic."

"As in *Woman in the Window,* can't go outside, agoraphobic?"

"Yes. That kind."

"Diagnosed?"

"She didn't give me her medical history, but it seemed pretty clear to me. She can't go outside, and if she does, she has panic attacks."

"For how long?"

"It started a few years back when her mother died from cancer. Nikki was her caretaker. She took it hard and stopped leaving the property."

"She could go outside then?"

"Sounds like it. I think that changed with her father's murder. Her condition grew more pronounced."

"And you see it as a good thing because she won't testify at trial."

"Not exactly."

"Oh?" Ashley said, lifting an eyebrow.

"Nikki is sympathetic to Lucas."

"She's what?"

"This is going to sound strange, but she claims she can smell death."

"Everyone can smell death. That's the decomposition process."

"No," Katie said, shaking her head. "She thinks she can smell death on someone *before* they die. She said she could smell it on her dad before he answered the door. She knew he would die. She couldn't predict how it would happen, only that it would happen. That's why she doesn't blame Lucas. She believes there was no avoiding it."

"Huh," Ashley said, crossing her arms.

"What are you thinking?"

"I'm thinking that I have no idea what to do with that information."

"Same here."

"Did you learn anything else?"

Katie shook her head. "Not really. I taped the interview so you could listen to it, but I don't think so."

"Okay," Ashley said, issuing a heavy sigh. "We aren't getting anywhere with this defense. I feel like we are going round and round in circles. It's probably time for me to pop over and have a conversation with Lucas. See if he has some suggestions."

"Now? But dad should be back any minute with your lunch."

"Put it in the fridge. I'll eat it later. I don't want to be here anyway just in case that realtor creep shows back up."

"Okay," Katie said.

Katie watched her friend's thin frame as she exited out the front door. Ashley was carrying herself a little differently these days, with less confidence. This case was starting to get to her. It was starting to get to all of them.

21

ASHLEY

March 27

Ashley had intended to visit Lucas right away, but a crisis had come up with another client, derailing her plans. Then it seemed like fire after fire continued cropping up with multiple clients. But that was the way of it. Shit ran downhill. When it rained, it poured. There were only so many hours in a day. So, it wasn't until the next week before Ashley had a long enough break in her schedule to visit Lucas.

She arrived at the jail at eight o'clock sharp, intending to spend a full two hours with Lucas. She had to black it out on her calendar to remind herself not to schedule anything in that block of time.

"You're here bright and early this morning," the jailer behind the counter said. It was Theresa again.

"Yes. I need to see Lucas Campbell."

"Lucas, huh? Hopefully your visit will help."

"Help with what?"

Theresa typed something into a computer. Then she slid an electronic signature pad through the gap in the glass. "I'll need you to sign here."

Ashley signed her name and slid it back. "Help with what?" she repeated.

"He's been a bit down," Theresa said with a heavy sigh. "He isn't eating much, and he's lost some weight. You might be shocked by his appearance."

"Okay."

Theresa pressed a button, unlocking the heavy steel door leading back to the jail. Ashley pulled it open and met her on the other side.

"I suggested that we put him on suicide watch," Theresa said, "But the powers that be won't." She gestured toward the ceiling. "They said they won't unless he starts making suicidal threats. The problem is that he isn't talking to anyone."

They were walking down a hallway and stopped outside the row of meeting rooms. "Do you want the room without the partition again?"

"Yes."

She pressed a button on a radio clipped to her shoulder and said something into it. The sound of the heavy lock disengaging followed a few moments later. Theresa gestured to the door. "Go on in. Make yourself comfortable, or as comfortable as you can, and I'll bring Lucas over in a few."

"Okay," Ashley said, pulling the door open and stepping inside. She sat down in a flimsy, plastic chair and waited.

As promised, Theresa brought Lucas in within minutes. Ashley had to fight the urge to gasp when she saw him. The man before her was not the same person she remembered. He still wore the jail jumpsuit, but it now hung from his frame, a few sizes too big. A scraggly beard had formed on his chin, and his hair was unbrushed and wild. Large bags hung beneath his eyes, clinging on like great purple ticks.

While these were bothersome changes, these weren't the most disturbing of them all. That was in his eyes. They were blank. They had never held a spark of happiness or joy or anything like that, at least not since he'd been arrested, but at least there had been something. Now there was nothing. He stared at her with a dull expression. One that conveyed no emotion, no thought.

"Have a seat, Lucas," Ashley said, regaining her composure after a long beat of silence.

Lucas stepped forward, his ankle and wrist chains jangling with each step. They were the same chains he'd worn during other meetings, but this time he seemed to struggle under their weight.

"I'll leave you two," Theresa said. When Lucas was fully in front of her with his back to her, she gestured to him and mouthed, *see what I mean?*

Ashley nodded. She couldn't imagine who wouldn't or couldn't see it. Lucas was a complete and total wreck. They remained silent until the heavy door slammed closed behind Theresa, then Ashley focused her full attention on Lucas.

"What happened to you?"

Lucas shook his head. "I don't know what you mean."

"You look like hell. Is that intentional? Are you trying to garner sympathy? Because this new look of yours makes you seem more like a deranged serial killer than a farm boy born and raised in Brine."

"Aren't I a deranged killer? That's what they've accused me of, at least."

Ashley shook her head.

"I know, I know," Lucas raised his chained hands. "No admissions."

"Seriously? What the hell is going on with you?"

Lucas shook his head. "It's everything. Losing my family. My freedom. Now the farm." A tear slid down his cheek. "The bank is repossessing it. Where is my dad going to go? Nobody will help him."

"Oh, Lucas," Ashley said with a sigh. He had enough problems from the legal system, losing what was left of the farm must have been the final blow.

"And on top of all that, I can't sleep."

"I know it's hard to sleep in here." Ashley understood better than most.

"That's not what I mean. I've always had trouble sleeping, even at home. I have to take sleeping pills, and they won't give them to me in here."

"Why not?"

Lucas shrugged. "They want me to see a doctor first."

"That's bullshit. Where are your pills?"

"They are still out at the farm."

"I'll send Katie out there today. She can check on your dad and bring the pills to the jail. I will make sure they give them to you. It's your prescription, you have a right to have it."

"Thank you." A tiny spark lit behind his eyes. Just this tiny favor was enough to give him hope.

"And I think I have a potential solution for your father. It's a bit odd, though."

"Okay..."

"Nikki Nelson. Do you remember her?"

"Yeah. She's Gerald's daughter."

"She has invited your father to come stay with her. She has her own mental health issues, and she's afraid to leave the house. His presence will do her some good and taking care of him will give her something to do."

He looked up, his eyes filling with tears. "She would do that for my father? After what I did to her—"

"Allegedly," Ashley interrupted.

"After I allegedly killed her father?"

Ashley shrugged. "Apparently."

"Well, I think it's a good idea. Nikki always was a kind soul. Even in high school when everyone was so self-absorbed and boastful. She was always herself."

"I'll let Katie know," Ashley said. "You've met her, right?"

"Katie? Yeah. She stopped by and introduced herself a couple days ago."

"She's a damn good investigator, and she's been looking out for your father. She has been ever since she met him and realized he was on his own. She pretends to be tough, but she's as soft hearted as Nikki Nelson. She'll be happy to hear the situation with Albert is sorted."

Lucas wiped away a tear and pressed the heels of his hands into his eyes.

"When does Albert need to be out of the house?"

"The land auction is April twenty-eighth."

That was the day before depositions. "That should get us plenty of time to arrange to move your stuff out of the house."

"I'll call Kristy. She can have it all. Dad won't need it living with Nikki."

It saddened Ashley that Lucas was willing to give everything he had left in the world to his ex-wife. "Has she come to visit you?"

"Who? Kristy?"

"Yeah."

"No." Lucas shook his head. "She's got Amy with her full-time, and I don't want her to see her father caged like an animal."

"Fair enough." Ashley glanced at her watch. It was already nine-thirty, and she had a ten o'clock hearing. "I probably better be going."

"When will you be back?"

"As soon as I can. I don't know that I'll have time to sit down and have a chat with you, but I will definitely send Katie over with your medications. Hopefully before this evening."

"Thank you," he said with wide, tired eyes. "For everything. You probably don't hear that enough, but this work you do, it's important."

"Thank you," she said, and she meant it. She didn't hear it enough. Nobody ever thanked her, and it sometimes made her feel small. It was nice to feel seen, truly seen by at least one of her clients. "That means a lot to me."

Within a few minutes, she was out of the jail. She called Katie on the walk over to the Courthouse doors and told her about the medications and arrangements for Albert. Katie sounded relieved, and said she'd head out to the Lucas farm sometime that afternoon.

They ended their call as Ashley stepped inside the courthouse to focus on another hearing completely unrelated to Lucas. Because that was the way of it as a public defender. Even if a case came along like Lucas's, one that was all consuming, she still had other clients to attend to. She headed up the stairs and was shocked to see who waited for her outside the district court courtrooms. Matthew Larson.

He was true to his word. He wasn't giving up.

22

KATIE

After ending her call with Ashley, Katie immediately left for the Campbell farm. There was no time to waste, especially if she wanted to get Albert settled into Nikki's house and back in time for Lucas to take his medications and get a good night's sleep.

The weather was typical for March, yo-yoing up and down from freezing temperatures to seventy-degree days. Today, the weather was mild, in the mid-fifties with an overcast sky. A tad gloomy, but a nice break from the miserable February temperatures. The radio was on, and her mind was blank as she drove for perhaps the final time to the property while it was still owned by the Campbell family.

When she arrived, she pulled all the way up the driveway, parking right in front of the deck. Albert came to the door holding his shotgun, but he kept it at his side, smiling and waving at her.

"Howdy-do, little lady," Albert said.

"Hello there," she said as she came up onto the rickety porch.

"To what do I owe the pleasure?"

"I've come for a couple reasons. We've solved your living situation. Nikki Nelson would like you to move in with her."

"She does? I thought she was mad at me. She never visits anymore."

"That has nothing to do with you. Or Lucas. She's got some problems of her own, Albert, but I'll let her explain those to you. It's not my place."

He nodded.

"Let's get packing up your stuff."

"What about the furniture?"

"Kristy is coming for that. I spoke to her earlier today. She said you should take whatever you want, and she'll come get what remains before the auction."

"I don't want any of this stuff. What's an old man to do with a couch when he has no home?"

Katie didn't know what to say to that. It was a valid point. Instead of dwelling on it, she switched topics.

"Ashley mentioned Lucas had some sleeping medications. Do you know where he would keep those?"

Albert's bushy eyebrows shot up in surprise. "He wants them?"

"Umm, yeah. Is that a problem?"

He shook his head, a sharp snap back and forth. "He said he wasn't goin' to take them anymore."

"I guess he changed his mind. Ashley went to see him today, and she said he looks terrible. He hasn't been sleeping. He's under a lot of stress. Why did he stop taking them?"

Albert shrugged. "They worked too well, I guess. Sure, he slept like the dead, but it didn't help none when he could barely wake up the next morning to get his chores done."

"They made him groggy the next day?"

"More than that. He'd wake up and not only his mind would be tired, but his body, too. He'd move around like he was as old as me, complaining about sore muscles and stiff joints."

"I see. Well, I think he's desperate at this point. He needs some sleep if he is going to be any assistance in his defense. He can't face a jury looking like he does now. They'll convict him based on that."

Albert shook his head, slowly, sadly, because he knew it was true. First impressions were important. "Pills are in the cabinet behind the mirror in the hall bathroom." Albert pointed a finger down a dark hallway. "I'll run upstairs and pack my things."

He turned and made his way up the stairs. His movements were slow, but steady. Definitely not a run, but the closest he could probably get to a run. Katie flipped a light switch that looked like it would illuminate the hallway, but nothing happened. *Power company must have shut off service,* she thought. Albert couldn't even pay for electricity, and that saddened her.

It was also ironic because it, too, went back to the windmill issue. If Lucas had agreed to put windmills on his property, they would have plenty of money and more than enough electricity. Shutting the energy off now felt almost like a power move, a punishment for not falling in line with the big oil companies.

Katie turned on the flashlight application on her phone and made her way down the hallway and into the bathroom. She approached the mirror and pulled on it. The front opened, moving stiffly on creaky hinges. Inside the cabinet, she found a toothbrush, toothpaste, an array of over-the-counter medications, and one prescription pill bottle. She picked it up and turned it around. The script was for Lucas Campbell. Zolozien 12.5mg.

Bingo.

She grabbed the pill bottle and made her way back down the hallway to wait for Albert at the front door. Albert was still moving around upstairs. She could tell from the way the floorboards creaked overhead. After a few minutes, Albert reappeared at the top of the stairs. He carried one small bag, and that was all. She did not comment, because she knew he didn't have much. This was probably the last of his belongings. She met him at the top of the stairs and helped him bring it down. They paused in the doorway.

"Ready to go?" Katie asked.

Albert turned and looked around one last time. A tear slid down his cheek, but he wiped it away. "As ready as I'll ever be."

He held out his arm, and she hooked hers around it, leading him out of the home he had lived in all his life. The home where he was born, and where he thought he would die. It was the only place he knew, and he was leaving for the very last time.

23

ASHLEY

April 14

Depositions were two days away, and Ashley still didn't know where she was going with Lucas's defense. Usually, she had a fully formed strategy by now. Something better than jury nullification. It might be self-defense or alibi. A missing element of the offense charged. Faulty search warrant. Miranda violation. Anything would do.

She'd stared at the police reports for hours on end. Reading and rereading until her eyes tired and her mind grew fuzzy, willing herself to see something that she'd missed before. But it wasn't there. She was going to have to admit defeat. She had nothing other than the hope that someone on the empaneled jury hated windmills enough to excuse murder. It was a longshot. A very long shot. A mere chance.

The office phone rang, causing her to jump. She stared at it for a long moment, reorienting herself, then picked up. "Hey, Elena." It was always Elena, the office manager, when she first picked up the line. Direct calls didn't come to Ashley's office.

"Hey-ya. How's it going back there?"

"Frustratingly."

"That's too bad. Listen, I have Theresa from the jail on the line. She's asking to speak with you. Do you want to talk to her?"

"Yeah, sure. Patch her through." Ashley was intrigued.

This was a rare occurrence. In the fifteen years she'd been practicing law, she could count the number of times a jailer called her office on one hand. It simply didn't happen, and when it did, it was usually bad news. Inmate suicides, injuries, or jail breaks.

Ashley paused a beat, mentally bracing herself for a crisis, then she said, "This is Ashley."

"Hi, Ashley, this is Theresa."

"Yes, hello, Theresa."

She didn't add the obligatory *how are you* because it was a superficial question. People asked it, but they never actually cared to hear the answer. They expected *good* or *fine* and the same question posed back to them with the same response. It was a waste of words.

"I'm probably not supposed to be doing this, but I need to talk to you." She kept her voice low, hushed.

"Okay. Let's talk."

"No, no. Not over the phone. In person."

"Is everything alright?" Ashley was growing alarmed. The conversation felt very Deep Throat-ish. Like something was very, very wrong.

"I don't know."

"Are my clients safe?"

"Yes, yes, it's nothing like that. It's just. There's something with Lucas."

"Is Lucas okay?"

"Sorta."

These were all non-answers, and Ashley was growing frustrated. Yet she couldn't blame Theresa. "When does your shift end?"

"Ten o'clock."

Ashley glanced at the wall clock. It was already nine thirty. "Why don't you swing by my office before you head home for the day. Will that work?"

"Yes. I'll be there as soon as I can."

After Theresa hung up, Ashley cradled the phone and sat there, staring blankly at the wall, dissecting the conversation. What was going on with Lucas? And why all the secrecy?

"Hey, boss," Katie said, knocking on the outside of the door.

Ashley looked up.

"Penny for your thoughts," Katie said, tossing a penny to Ashley.

Ashley caught it and set it down on her desk. "Are you saying my thoughts are worthless?"

Katie cocked her head, confused.

"Pennies are worthless these days."

"Not that one. It's copper. If you melt that sucker down, you could get a good three cents from it."

"Ohhh," Ashley said, a smile flicking into the corners of her mouth. "I stand corrected. It is mostly worthless."

Katie flopped into one of the chairs across from Ashley's desk. "Seriously, what's on your mind?"

"One of the jailers just called. There's something going on with Lucas."

"What is it?" Katie leaned forward.

"She wouldn't say over the phone. She's going to stop by when she gets off work at ten."

"That's weird."

"I know."

"Are you ready for Lucas's depositions?"

"Nope. You don't happen to have some new information that could blow this case wide open, do you?"

"Sorry, no," Katie said with a heavy sigh. "I have spoken to just about everyone in town who is willing to talk to me, but I keep getting the same information. The oil company and their cronies are greedy vampires and Lucas is a good dude, but that doesn't excuse murder."

"I thought as much. That realtor, Matthew Larson, might actually be a vampire. I don't think he sleeps. He keeps popping up everywhere, asking if I've reconsidered placing windmills on my property. I swear to you, he's driving me mad. If he keeps this up, and there's no reason to believe he will stop, I'm going to start having nightmares about it."

"Do you think depositions will help?"

Ashley rubbed her hands over her face. "At this point, it couldn't hurt. I know we will have to file notice of our own witnesses after we take depositions, but we don't have any right now and that doesn't seem likely to change. So, might as well. There's nothing to lose. It'll be a fishing expedition," she shrugged. "But sometimes that's the way of things."

"That sounds hopeless."

"It's about like this penny here." Ashley picked the penny up off the desk, pinching it between her thumb and index finger. "Not hopeless, but practically hopeless."

24

KATIE

The phone rang and Ashley gave Katie the *one moment* sign, then she picked up the receiver. "What's up, Elena?" There was a short pause, and then she said. "Send her back."

Katie started to rise from her seat, assuming it was a client there for an appointment, but Ashley gestured for her to sit back down.

"Who is it?" Katie asked.

"Theresa," Ashley said, cradling the phone. "I want you to be a second set of ears. I have a feeling that whatever she has to say is important."

"Okay."

Ashley's office was cramped. It was only slightly larger than a good-sized walk-in closet. With all the furniture and the piles of files on the floor, it was not easy to get around. Katie moved to the chair closest to the corner and farthest away from the door, allowing easier access for Theresa. Then they both sat quietly, staring at the door. A few moments passed, then Elena's smiling face filled the doorway.

"This is it," Elena said, stepping aside and allowing a tired looking middle-aged woman to step into the room. "Let me know if you need anything." This question was posed to Ashley, then she flashed one last smile before leaving and closing the door behind her.

"Hello, Theresa," Ashley said. "Thank you for stopping by."

Theresa stood in the small room, blinking.

"I know my office isn't much, but it does the trick. Would you like to have a seat?" Ashley motioned to the chair next to Katie.

Theresa nodded and sat down.

"This is Katie Mickey. She's with Michello & Mickey's Investigative Services. She's the private investigator I have hired to work on Lucas's case. Do you mind if she stays?"

"Ummm..."

"I will afford you the same amount of discretion as Ashley," Katie said, trying to match Ashley's delicate tone, but failing miserably.

Ashley was not a gentle person by any stretch of the imagination, but she had always been able to soften her edges when needed. And Theresa needed it. Her eyes were so wide, she made Katie think of a raccoon caught in a trap. Wild, skittish, and ready to bite.

"Okay," Theresa said after a long moment. "She can stay."

"I don't want to waste anyone's time, so I'm going to cut right to the chase," Ashley said. "What's this all about?"

"Lucas."

"What about Lucas?"

Theresa took a deep steadying breath, then slowly released it. "I am not supposed to be telling you any of this. I'm probably going to lose my job."

Both Ashley and Katie remained silent. It was Theresa's time to speak. They'd get to their questions later.

"But I can't hold my tongue. There is more to this story, and it seems like everyone on the prosecution side knows it. Charles Hanson called me into his office yesterday."

Charles Hanson was the local prosecutor, the elected County Attorney.

"He's never done that before. I've never been inside a lawyer's office in all my life. Now, it's been twice in one week."

Katie had been inside Charles's office, but that had been under the reign of the former County Attorney, Elizabeth Clement. Back when Katie was an officer. It was far roomier and more expensively furnished than Ashley's office. She wondered what Theresa thought about the obvious differences in budget, but she kept the thought to herself. This was not a time to distract from whatever bombshell Theresa was there to drop.

"What was the purpose of your meeting at Charles Hanson's office?" There was a simmering rage boiling below the surface of Ashley's words.

Many prosecutors saw themselves as the good guys and defense counsel as villains. Katie had once thought that way herself, but experience working for the defense side had taught her to think differently. Most prosecutors were career prosecutors who had never done defense work and weren't privy to Katie's enlightened thought process. It wasn't always a problem, but it did become an issue when they thought they needed to win at all costs, that the ends justified the means. Whatever came next, it sounded like Charles was potentially stepping over a line that was not ethical.

"Well, Mr. Hanson just wanted to tell me that what I was seeing at the jail was not related to Lucas's pending case."

Ashley snorted. "Maybe not for him, but he's not able to determine what evidence is relevant to the defense. Last I checked, he was the prosecutor, not the defense attorney."

"Right, well, that's why I'm here." Theresa folded her fingers together, then unfolded them, unable to be still. "It didn't feel right to me. I thought about it through the rest of my shift, and the more I thought about it, the more I knew I needed to tell you. You have a right to know."

Katie removed a small recording device from her pocket and placed it on the table.

"Do you mind if I record this conversation?" Katie asked.

She didn't have to get Theresa's permission. In Iowa, it was legal to record someone else so long as one party privy to the conversation was aware that it was being recorded. That was ridiculous, of course, since she would always know if she was recording someone else without their knowledge. Her knowledge of the recording didn't make the choice to do so less sneaky. All the same, there were times that she did resort to such measures. But that was only with uncooperative, combative witnesses. Theresa had come of her own accord. She was trying to do the right thing. Katie was not going to play any tricks.

Theresa's gaze darted from the recorder back up to Katie's face. "Who is going to hear it?"

"Honestly, I don't know." Katie turned to Ashley.

"Potentially nobody. Even if we end up using you as a trial witness, we don't have to disclose our evidence unless we take depositions. And in that case, we won't be using the recording at trial, we'd want your live testimony, so it wouldn't be part of discovery either."

"So, why record it at all?"

"For the same reason Katie is here. For accuracy purposes," Ashley said. "We as people can sometimes hear things differently. Whether that's because we try to hear only what we want to hear, or for some other reason, it seems to be true. Three people can witness a shooting, and all three could have slightly separate versions of the event. One person might say they heard three shots and saw a man with a blue shirt holding a hand-gun. Another might swear the shirt was purple and there were only two shots. A third might say the shooter was shirtless and he had an assault rifle."

"Okay."

"My point is that I don't want to mishear you," Ashley continued. "I don't want to make the mistake of attributing my thoughts to your words. That's the primary purpose of the recording. But, of course, if we do take depositions, we are going to have to disclose you as a witness if we intend to use you, you'll have to be deposed, and we'll have to turn over the recording."

Theresa's eyes widened. A deer in headlights.

"She's not trying to scare you, Theresa," Katie said. "We just want you to be prepared."

A long beat of silence passed, then Theresa nodded. "Okay, you can record it."

Katie pressed the record button, then gave a short narrative of the date, time, location of the meeting, and all persons present. Then she turned to Ashley, signaling that she was ready for the questioning to begin.

"So, Theresa, what did you come here to tell me?"

"It's about Lucas's medications."

"What about them? I hope the jail isn't keeping them from him again."

Theresa sucked in a deep breath. "That's just the thing. I think I've figured out why the jail administrator didn't want Lucas taking the medications."

Ashley leaned forward in her seat, and Katie could feel her body doing the same, as though moving of its own accord.

"Why not?"

Then Theresa launched into a story of events that had been occurring less than a quarter mile away. Information that could make all the difference in the world in Lucas's defense. As she spoke, both Ashley and Katie grew more interested, each poised on the edge of her seat. After a while, Katie's mind kept ticking through potential witnesses, questions to ask, and evidence to gather. More than likely, Ashley was doing the same.

"When I met with him today, Charles Hanson asked for copies of the jail recordings."

Virtually every corner of the jail was under video surveillance. Anything that happened, including incidents with Lucas Campbell, would all be on video. Indisputable evidence.

"He asked for originals. He didn't specifically tell me that I wasn't supposed to make copies, but that's what he wanted. I'm not the best listener, especially when a powerful man is telling me to go against my conscience." She reached into her pocket and slid a thumb drive across the table. "So, here it is. All the same recordings that I gave to Charles Hanson earlier today."

A smile flicked into the corner of Ashley's mouth. "Thank you, Theresa. You did the right thing. Charles Hanson was more than a little wrong. We can most certainly use this information to assist in Lucas's defense." She turned to Katie, excitement flashing in her eyes. "Tell Elena to call off depositions. We've got a case to build, and we don't need depos to do it anymore."

"Sure thing," Katie said, suddenly excited for what was to come.

Lucas's case had been a mess. No defense. No strategy. No direction. But now, everything was about to change.

25

ASHLEY

April 26
Day one of Lucas's trial

The District Court courtroom was packed by the time Ashley arrived, and she was early. Trial didn't technically start until nine o'clock, but the entire courthouse was a chaotic mess of people within ten minutes of the court-house opening its doors at eight o'clock. The people all seemed oddly chip-per, as if they were waiting for entrance into a county fair, not a murder trial.

Katie was not there yet. Ashley had left her at the office, telling her that there was no reason for her presence until eight thirty at the earliest. Now Ashley was starting to wonder if Katie would be able to find a seat. She pulled out her phone, preparing to send Katie a text, but then she saw her red-headed friend and investigator bursting through the crowd.

Ashley released a breath and then set her computer bag down on the defense table and started to unpack it. Katie's presence wasn't technically or legally important, but she was strong emotional support. Someone who would be on Ashley's side no matter what. Even if the crowd of people hated her defense and hated her client, Katie would be there to support her. Everyone needed at least one person in her corner. That was one of the reasons why defense work fit Ashley so well. She was willing to be fully in someone's corner even if they had done something horrible.

She removed her laptop, three legal pads—one for Lucas and two for herself—and a large stack of pens. Then she took out an *Iowa Rules of Court* book and set it next to her computer.

"This place is a zoo," Katie said, finally reaching the front of the courtroom. She'd come through the partition and into the space reserved for legal parties. "Can I sit up here during jury selection?"

Ashley's first inclination was to say *no*, but why not? There were three chairs at the defense table and there was nothing preventing it. "Yeah, sure. I could use an extra set of eyes during selection. The judge will then sequester witnesses, so you'll have to leave the courtroom in case I need you to testify."

The judge typically sequestered witnesses so they couldn't listen to trial testimony and adjust their own testimony based on the things that other people said.

"You can sit in after you testify, though. Most of those people out there in the gallery are in the jury pool. They called in one hundred people. Those that aren't selected for the trial will likely leave, and this place will clear out like a church at the end of mass."

Katie gave Ashley a sidelong look. "You and your Catholic analogies. When are they bringing Lucas?"

"Soon," Ashley said. "I hope."

"Have you talked to Theresa this morning?"

"Briefly. She's nervous."

"Yeah. I thought she was going to have a heart attack when I served her the subpoena. Poor lady thinks she's going to be punished for her testimony."

"She might be right."

Just then a court attendant entered the room through the back doors, shouting for everyone to take their seats. She was a small, flighty woman with shifty eyes and a big bellowing voice. She only had to shout her command three times to get the excited group of people to respond. People instantly grew silent and found the nearest seat in the benches along the gallery.

"Has everyone checked in?" The court attendant asked.

She was asking this question to ensure that everyone summoned for jury duty was considered in the random drawing process. If they were there and they hadn't checked in, they couldn't be chosen for the jury, and it would appear in the court system as though they hadn't responded to their jury summons.

Nobody answered.

The court attendant sighed heavily, then said, "Raise your hand if you haven't checked in."

The courtroom was still, silent.

She turned to leave, and a murmur came up from the crowd as people went back to their gossiping, then she turned back, and they stopped. "This is your last chance."

Nobody responded and the court attendant left the room through the doors leading to a private hallway back to judge's chambers and the Clerk of Court's office, her heels clicking against the marble floor and reverberating around the room. The silence in the room slowly started to abate, and then the back doors swung open and in walked Lucas.

He wore a green, button-down shirt that accentuated the green in his hazel eyes, and a pair of slacks. The clothing fit well, but none of it belonged to Lucas. Katie had borrowed the clothes from Tom Archie, a friend of Katie's and Ashley's former boyfriend. The two men were nearly the same size. As Lucas walked down the aisle toward them, Ashley would have said he looked like any other middle-aged middle-class man except for the two deputies flanking him. They, too, wore slacks and collared shirts, but they were very obviously law enforcement.

A burst of fury blossomed in Ashley's chest. They were parading him in front of the jury. For constitutional fair trial reasons, Lucas was allowed to wear plain clothes and attend trial without chains. To do otherwise would give the jury a visual symbol of guilt. Unfortunately, the way the jail brought him in wasn't much better. They were clearly guarding him, so he might as well be in chains.

"What the hell?" Katie grumbled.

"No shit," Ashley hissed through her teeth. All eyes followed the three men as they walked down the aisle toward the front of the room. "This could have been avoided if they'd brought him over in time."

When the three men reached the front, Ashley pulled the middle chair out and Lucas sat down.

The taller of the two jailers looked around, then said, "Where do we sit?"

Ashley glared at him. "Not my fucking problem. If you were here on time, you would have your pick of the gallery."

"I'll have to ask someone to move," the tall jailer said.

"No. You won't. How do you think you are going to explain that to them? Oh, yes, I'm a *jailer* and I need this seat. Umm, no. Not unless you want the court ordering a mistrial already."

Charles Hanson, must have noticed that there was an issue because he'd risen from his seat and lumbered over.

"What's the problem?"

"They don't have anywhere to sit," Ashley gestured to the two jailers.

Charles looked around, "Well, we can't ask anyone to move."

Ashley gave the tall jailer an *I told you so*, look. Of course, he immediately accepted the prosecutor's words as though they were gospel, but Ashley had been questioned.

"I have two extra chairs at my table. You can pull those back so they are up against the railing and sit there."

The courtroom was separated, gallery from participants, by a short railing. It was only waist high, but it was a physical barrier that lay people did not cross. With the first crisis of the day solved, all parties went back to their respective tables. Lucas sat between Ashley and Katie, with Katie to his right and Ashley to his left.

"Are you ready for this, Lucas?"

Lucas shrugged. "Yes and no. This all feels unreal to me. It's like a bad dream I can't get out of. It's been that way ever since the night before my arrest. I keep thinking I'll wake up, but I don't."

Ashley nodded and patted him on the back. "I understand."

"Are you ready?" Lucas asked, catching Ashley off guard.

The question could have seemed negative but meaning often had nothing to do with the actual words and everything to do with the way they were said. Lucas wasn't challenging Ashley. He wasn't asking her if she was legally prepared for his defense. He was posing the same question to her in the same way she'd posed it to him. It surprised her because in fifteen years of practice, no client had ever asked her that.

Ashley took a deep breath and slowly released it. "I'm always nervous before proceedings start. I wasn't an athlete, at least not on any scale above peewee sports, but I presume this feeling I'm having is a bit like the jitters that come from the moments before the whistle blows and the game starts."

"I remember that feeling. Excitement, anticipation, and a little dose of dread for what could go wrong."

"Exactly. It's like this before every trial, but this feeling will disappear once we get going."

It was Lucas's turn to pat Ashley on the back. "Just like a ballgame. You don't need a pep talk, but you've got this. No matter what happens in the end, I know you've got this."

"Thank you," Ashley said, smiling at Lucas. "Now let's kick some ass."

26

KATIE

"Will the following people step up and take a place in the jury box," the court attendant called in her loud, resounding voice.

This was not Katie's first experience with jury selection, but it was her first time watching it from a position at counsel table. Sitting out in the gallery, it was possible to review the process with partial disinterest, almost even boredom. But up here, where all the action occurred, there was an excitement buzzing in the air.

As the court attendant called name after name of the twenty-nine jurors who would be subject to initial questioning, Ashley wrote their names down on a jury pool map, so she'd know who was seated where when she began her questioning. The number of jurors was far more than the traditional twelve, and that was for good reason.

Once each attorney was finished questioning and passed the jury for cause, they would each exercise seven strikes. Once they were finished making those strikes, the attorneys would choose an alternate by striking one of the final three jurors called to sit. The remaining juror would be an alternate. The courts did it this way so that jurors wouldn't know who the alternate was until the jury went to deliberate and the alternate was excused. People paid closer attention when they thought their opinion would matter.

After living in a small town and working with the public for years, Katie at least vaguely recognized all the names as they were called. Ashley surely knew these people as well or possibly even better since she was a Brine native, and Katie was only a transplant. Yet two names not only stuck out, but they caused Ashley to actually groan. Not loud enough for the jury to hear, but Katie caught it. Those names were Tom Archie, Ashley's ex-boyfriend, and Matthew Larson, the realtor who had been badgering her.

Tom made his way to the jury box, keeping his gaze straight ahead, showing Ashley respect and deference by stoically looking forward and avoiding eye contact. Matthew had been the opposite. He'd stood and strutted his way to his chair, gaze locked on her, baring his overly white teeth in an obnoxiously giddy smile.

Once all potential jurors were situated, Judge Ahrenson went through a few opening remarks, introducing himself, his court reporter, counsel, and the Defendant. He explained the nature of the trial. Then he turned to Charles Hanson and said, "They're all yours."

"Thank you, your honor," Charles said, struggling to his feet.

Charles had always been a bigger boned man, but he'd put on quite a few pounds since he'd tossed his hat into the ring of attorneys jockeying for Judge Ahrenson's soon-to-be vacated position. He took a few steps closer to the jury, then opened his arms wide like a pastor welcoming his congregation.

"Good morning, everyone. I'm sure you are excited to be here on one of the first beautiful days of the year." He chuckled at his joke—nobody wanted jury duty, especially when the weather was just turning warm—and the jury joined in, hesitant at first, but growing bolder when they saw the Judge was also smiling.

"Many of you have probably heard of me, since I am your elected County Attorney." He hooked his thumbs through his lapels and chuckled. "But those of you who thought you could avoid jury duty by not registering to vote, well, to you I'd say, gotcha." He leaned forward, widening his eyes.

This time when the jury laughed, there was a slight twinge of anxiety to it.

"Let's get down to business, shall we?"

Several heads nodded. The remainder of the jury sat still. Katie wrote down the names of individuals who were already nodding along with the prosecutor. While exciting, her seating was not for entertainment alone. She was there to help Lucas and Ashley.

"As Judge Ahrenson told you, we are here for the brutal murder—"

"Objection," Ashley said, her tone almost conversational.

Judge Ahrenson sighed in a *here we go again* sort of way. Everyone knew that he was backing Ashley as his replacement, but that didn't mean he enjoyed her courtroom antics. "What's the objection?"

"Burden shifting. This is an alleged crime. My client, Mr. Campbell, is innocent until a unanimous jury finds him guilty beyond a reasonable doubt."

"Sustained. Watch your words, Mr. Hanson."

The ghost of a smile quirked into the corner of Ashley's mouth, but it was gone as quickly as it had appeared.

"That's a good point. The Defendant," he put extra emphasis on the word *defendant*, "is charged with the heinous crime of murder against his neighbor, Gerald Mock, but he is presumed innocent. Does anyone here know what that means? The presumption of innocence?" Charles Hanson was an expert prosecutor, and he was proving it by using Ashley's objection to segue into his next topic.

Nobody said anything, and Tom's hand slowly rose into the air.

"Mr. Archie," Charles said, calling on Tom, his tone good natured. "Just the man I wanted to talk to."

"Do you, uh, want me to answer your question?" Tom asked.

"What question?"

"The one about the presumption of innocence."

"Umm, sure." By the way Charles uttered these two words, it sounded as though he would rather that Tom didn't answer the question.

"It means that Mr. Campbell over there is a person, just like you and me. He's been accused of committing a crime, but he isn't guilty until a jury of twelve people finds him guilty beyond a reasonable doubt. That means that as we sit here, he is innocent. He remains innocent until you prove otherwise."

"Very good," Charles said. "You must have learned that from your ex-girlfriend."

Tom's face reddened. "I have been around the criminal justice system my whole adult life. I was once the jail administrator, remember? I am also the lead of the local Mental Health Response Team."

"Sure, sure. But peace officers don't always have quite the same kind of grasp on legal concepts as you seem to."

"I guess I'm smart."

"Speaking of your girlfriend, you used to date Ms. Ashley Montgomery, the Defense attorney here, didn't you?"

Tom's face was bright red all the way up to the tips of his ears, but Ashley sat frozen in her chair, betraying nothing.

"Yes, but that relationship ended years ago."

"Are you still friends?"

"I guess. Not like we were before we started dating."

"With benefits?"

Tom's clear, sky-blue eyes flashed with something Katie rarely saw in him. Rage. "No, but even if we were, that would be none of your business."

"Is there anything about your relationship with Ashley that would make you unable to be a fair and impartial juror in this trial?"

"No. I'm not the only person here who knows Ms. Montgomery, as I'm sure there are plenty of people who know and have been friendly with you as well. Even some who I dare say could have voted for you. That doesn't disqualify them, does it?"

Charles took a step back, unaccustomed to having his questions turned around on him. "No, but—"

"Then no. My former relationship with Ashley has nothing to do with Lucas Campbell or the charges you filed against him."

"Alright," Charles Hanson said, giving his head a quick shake before turning to the rest of the gallery. "Is there anyone else here who knows Ms. Montgomery more than just a passing acquaintance?"

"I'm actively trying to buy her property for a client," Matthew Larson said, raising his hand. "I keep giving her offers and she keeps shutting them down."

"That's because you are a coward and a snake," an elderly woman croaked from the back row. She was staring at Matthew Larson with unmitigated hate. "If you ask me, we are here *because* of you and that blasted client of yours. Splitting this town down the middle, and all for what? Money. You should be ashamed of yourselves."

This is a positive turn of events, Katie thought. The prosecution would strike this woman, Katie knew that without a doubt, but not before she opened the door to jury nullification. It may only be a slight nudge, but Katie, Lucas, and Ashley would take anything they could get.

"Oh, you keep your mouth shut, you old goat," a twenty-something man said from the front row of the jury pool. "You've probably been living like a communist off social security longer than I've been alive."

"Don't talk to her like that," growled a middle-aged man with a handlebar mustache and what looked like a sleeve full of prison tattoos. "You respect your elders."

"She's not old, she's ancient."

Within moments, almost every member of the jury pool was talking all at once, their voices growing more agitated with each passing moment. Katie glanced at Ashley, unsure of what to think or do. She was hoping to get some reassurance from her friend, but it was not there. Ashley was staring at the deteriorating situation through wide, shocked eyes. Then the judge started banging his gavel.

"Stop it! Stop it all of you or I will hold you all in contempt of court. Don't think I won't!" Judge Ahrenson shouted over the crowd.

It took several minutes, but, eventually, everyone started to settle down. But even then, the jurors continued to give one another side-eyed suspicious looks.

"We are going to take a recess," Judge Ahrenson said. "Court attendant," he paused, looking around.

The court attendant materialized as though out of thin air. "Yes, your honor."

"Make sure the jury pool remains in this room. And make sure they behave themselves."

The court attendant swallowed hard and looked back at the unruly group of jurors.

"Counsel." Ashley and Charles Hanson both looked up. "I want you and the Defendant all back in my chambers. We are going to have a discussion outside the presence of the jury."

Ashley rose from her seat and motioned for Lucas to do the same. Katie would have given just about anything to be there for whatever discussion was soon to follow, but witnesses were not invited. She'd have to settle for Ashley's rendition of events later that day. She sat back in her chair, reviewing the unruly jury pool. Besides, someone ought to remain in the courtroom in case things took a turn for the worse and went horribly wrong.

27

ASHLEY

Charles Hanson was first to follow Judge Ahrenson back into chambers with Ashley and Lucas close behind. The jailers were not permitted, so they had to stay in the courtroom.

"Mistrial?" Ashley asked once everyone was seated around a long table set up in the corner of Judge Ahrenson's office.

"You would want that, wouldn't you?" Charles snarled.

Ashley coquettishly and exaggeratedly batted her eyelashes. "If you say so." She was messing with him, of course. A mistrial would be great. That was one of her strategies. She wanted a not-guilty verdict or a mistrial. A mistrial wouldn't be as helpful this early in the trial, but it would still be helpful. They'd have to start all over again, and Charles Hanson would not like that.

"I'm not ready to declare a mistrial yet. Neither of you has done anything wrong. It's this jury," Judge Ahrenson gestured toward the doorway in the direction of the courtroom. "I've never seen anything like it. Every once in a while, one or two jury members may get into a verbal disagreement, but the whole jury..." He sighed and shook his head.

"If I may make a suggestion," Charles said.

"Yes, go ahead."

"We excuse the elderly woman who spoke first."

Judge Ahrenson picked up a stack of papers, looking down at it. "That would be Mrs. Donna Carter."

"On what grounds?" Ashley said, her face flushing red. This was the prosecutor's way of getting rid of unwanted jurors without having to waste one of his seven strikes, and it irked her.

"She's obviously made up her mind."

"I didn't hear her say that, did you?" Ashley shot back. "I don't even recall you asking her if she could be a fair and impartial juror."

"That's because I didn't have the chance. She was too busy fighting with everyone."

"Don't blame this on her. It's just like you to blame the woman. What about Matthew Larson? He's basically a stalker. I don't know how he got on this jury pool, but he has been following me everywhere."

Lucas had remained silent, his eyes bouncing back and forth from Ashley to Charles as they argued, but he stiffened when Ashley mentioned the realtor's behavior.

"That's enough," Judge Ahrenson said, drawing all eyes back to him. "I have half a mind to dismiss the whole lot of them and bring in a whole new jury."

"So, a mistrial," Ashley said.

"It wouldn't be a mistrial per se."

"Then what would it be? How do you bring in a whole new pool without first deciding this one is tainted? So far, only a few members of the original twenty-nine have answered questions. Tom Archie." Ashley raised a finger, "Donna Carter." She raised a second finger, "Matthew Larson. And then there's the young guy up front, I guess his name is Freedom Marks. Is that really the guy's first name? Freedom?"

"So it seems," Judge Ahrenson said. "And you have a point. I can't send out the entire jury without calling a mistrial. What's your take on this, Charles?"

"I don't think a mistrial is necessary. We don't even need to dismiss any of the jurors. We know what has them all fired up. It's the windmill farm projects. Why don't we dismiss Matthew Larson for cause since it is his presence that has led to this nonsense."

Ashley liked the sound of that. It would save her a strike, but something told her that she wouldn't like what Charles had to say next.

"Then we can limine out any mention of the windmill farms or windmill projects," Charles finished.

Limine, in trials, simply meant that the judge made a pretrial ruling to keep evidence from ever being mentioned. If Ashley was drinking anything in that moment, she would have spit it out. Because if the judge ruled in the prosecution's favor here, it would cripple her defense. Sure, she had one other trick up her sleeve, but it wasn't a slam dunk, and it would be a far stronger argument with the background of the windmill projects.

"The windmills have nothing to do with murder," Charles added.

"That's preposterous," Ashley said, finally getting over her shock and finding her words. "The windmills have everything to do with this incident."

"I didn't know windmills could kill people," Charles shot back.

"It shows motive."

"Oh, well, I didn't realize *you* cared about motive. Usually, it's the prosecutor who wants that information, and in this case, I'm willing to give up that evidence."

"Sure, it's admissible when *you* want it, but not when I do? It's not an element, but you prosecutors are usually so focused on it. Now when the tables are turned you want to keep it out. Typical, just typical."

"Okay, that's enough you two." Judge Ahrenson rubbed his temples. "Retirement cannot come soon enough. Sometimes I feel like I'm stuck dealing with a bunch of squabbling children, and I'm done raising kids."

Both Charles and Ashley looked up, waiting for his ruling.

"I think you both have a point. Let's dismiss that Larson guy and get him out of here. That should calm things down."

"What about evidence of the windmill farms?" Charles asked.

"I'm going to reserve ruling on that. Neither of you filed a motion in limine within the ten-day timeframe, so I'm not going to decide on that just yet when it comes to the actual trial. Throughout jury selection, though, I don't want windmills brought up again. Is that clear?" His sharp, blue eyes darted from Charles to Ashley.

This was a ruling that Ashley could handle. The information about windmills was already out there, thanks to Mrs. Carter. She didn't need to rehash it again in jury selection. It was most important that she be able to use it at trial. "I think that's fair."

Charles crossed his arms, but he said, "Yes, your honor."

"Now let's get back in there and get this show on the road," Judge Ahrenson said.

Judge Ahrenson hung back as Charles, Ashley, and Lucas funneled back into the courtroom. The packed room was still and silent, not at all the way it had been when they'd left. Everyone seemed to be on edge with anticipation. Katie caught Ashley's eye. There were questions there, but Ashley could explain them to her during one of the breaks. For now, she had a trial to win.

28

KATIE

It was nearing three o'clock in the afternoon, and they still hadn't picked the jury. Ashley was now questioning the group, but it sounded like she was starting to wind down. Originally, Katie had wondered why so many were called in as potential jurors, but it didn't take long before she understood. Both attorneys struck at least twenty people for cause, and the courtroom had slowly emptied as the potential jurors were excused and permitted to leave.

The original three arguing jurors—Donna Carter, Freedom Marks, and Matthew Larson—were all eventually struck for cause. Of the three, Freedom Marks, was the only person who chose to leave the trial. The other two had remained in the gallery to watch. It was a public proceeding. It wasn't uncommon for struck jurors, especially at Mrs. Carter's age, to choose to stay. Children and retirees seemed to be the most curious members of society.

"The defense passes for cause," Ashley finally said, turning around and focusing her comment on the judge.

In the next ten minutes, both attorneys exercised their seven strikes and their one strike for the alternate. Then the court attendant read out the names of those jurors who were chosen. Everyone else was permitted to leave. Few did.

"Now that we've finally selected our lucky thirteen," Judge Ahrenson said, smiling at the jurors. "I will read you your oath, and then we will get into opening statements."

The jurors nodded. There was a collective enthusiasm and dread coming from the group. None of these individuals had ever served on a jury before. It was rare in a small town. Usually, there was at least one person who had been selected in the past, but not this time. They didn't know what to expect, and maybe that was for the best.

Katie had seen plenty of trials, but this one felt as though it was going to be different. Perhaps because there was more at stake here than merely Lucas and Gerald's lives. This whole trial was taking place on a broader canvas than a mere murder. It felt as though the town's soul was on trial here as well.

"Will you all raise your right hand?" Judge Ahrenson said. Then he read a long admonition about juror's duties to faithfully administer justice, to abstain from discussion until after the trial ended, and to withhold judgment until they heard all the evidence. "Do you promise to uphold your duties as a juror?" He finally said.

The group said, "I do," at the same time, and everyone reclaimed their seats.

"Now is the time for opening statements. Is the State ready to proceed?"

The State always went first. This was because they had made the accusation, and it was their burden to prove it beyond a reasonable doubt. Katie had always found that to be backward. They made the accusation, so the Defendant should be given the first chance to refute it, but that wasn't the way of things.

Charles Hanson nodded and slowly rose to his feet.

"Good morning, excuse me afternoon, ladies and gentlemen," Charles said, chuckling.

This time, the jury didn't laugh along with him. Perhaps they had tired of his schtick. Katie certainly had.

"I want to bring your attention back to January 30 of this year," Charles said. "Back when the weather was cold, blustery, inhospitable. That was the day, the morning, rather, when Lucas Campbell, the Defendant, decided to take the law into his own hands. That man," he pointed at Lucas, and Lucas winced, "Shot his neighbor to death."

"Now, some of you may not like Gerald Mock, at least not on a personal or professional level, but that isn't important here. What's important is that Lucas Campbell, the Defendant, took it upon himself to grab his gun, walk a full mile through the frigid cold, knock on Gerald's door, and shoot Gerald point blank in the face. Then he walked home, grabbed a bag of Doritos from the pantry, and sat on the couch, snacking." Here he paused, looking over all the faces of the jurors. "As though nothing had happened."

Several members of the jury glanced furtively in Lucas's direction, their eyes darting toward him and then away again like hungry fish to bread who were then spooked by the presence of the person tossing the food. One or two gazes seemed curious. The others were all accusatory.

"You are going to hear evidence throughout this trial that will prove beyond a reasonable doubt that the Defendant, Lucas Campbell, is guilty of murder in the first degree. You will hear from Deputies Frankie Pitch and George Thomanson. They were the first to arrive on scene. They found the body, then followed the blood all the way back to the Defendant's front door."

"The Defendant was covered in blood and even bits of brain that were later identified as Gerald Mock's. A gun was in the entryway, propped up against the wall. The same gun that criminalists will identify without a doubt as the gun that shot the projectile that killed Gerald Mock."

"And poor Gerald. You are going to see photographs of him. Gruesome pictures that will not be easy to forget. Those of you who knew Gerald in life will not recognize him. Law enforcement had originally thought someone had physically assaulted Mr. Mock, his face was such a mess, but they quickly learned it was a gunshot wound."

"Defense is undoubtedly going to have something to say about this evidence. They'll find a way to twist the truth. They will try to focus your attention elsewhere, but it is important that you remember who is missing in this trial. That person is Gerald Mock. He doesn't get to testify. He won't be here to explain his side of the story. And the reason for that is because that man," he again pointed at Lucas, "Shot him. He did so with malice aforethought. He did so with the specific intent to kill. At the end of this trial, I am going to ask that you render the only verdict justice will allow. That is a guilty verdict for murder in the first degree."

"Thank you," Charles said, then turned his back to the jury and lumbered his way back to his seat.

Katie had seen Charles perform countless opening statements, but this one was more effective than many of the others. It even had Katie wondering somewhere in the back of her mind if a conviction was the rightful outcome here.

"Is the defense ready to deliver an opening statement?" Judge Ahrenson said after a short pause.

"The defense reserves opening," Ashley said. Her tone was conversational, a stark difference from Charles's passionate speech.

"Very well," Judge Ahrenson said. He turned to the jury. "The defense is reserving opening. That means that they will wait until it is their turn to present evidence before Ms. Montgomery makes her opening statement." He glanced at the clock. "It's nearing four o'clock, so we will adjourn for the day. Go home, get some rest. You've got a big day ahead of you tomorrow."

Then the judge stood and everyone stood along with him. The judge remained as the court attendant led the jury out of the courtroom. It was a sign of deference. Throughout the trial, all individuals in the courtroom and within the judicial system would be required to show the jury the same respect. Then the judge left the courtroom and Katie turned to Ashley.

"You really are going to leave them to ponder that opening overnight? You didn't want to respond?"

"I wanted to respond, but it's not in Lucas's best interest. Reserving opening was the lesser of two evils. When I do eventually deliver it, I'm tipping my hat to the defense strategy. I don't want Charles to know that until after he's presented his case."

"Okay," Katie said.

She wasn't convinced, and she could tell that Lucas felt the same, but Ashley was the expert attorney. They had to trust her. If there was any attorney that Katie would blindly follow, it would be Ashley Montgomery. She only hoped that wouldn't be a mistake that cost Lucas the remainder of his freedom.

29

ASHLEY

All trial strategies contained some form of gamble. It was just part of the process. Nothing was guaranteed. Juries were fickle. Witnesses impossible to control. Evidence didn't always come in as expected. Risk was impossible to avoid. Decisions had to be made, and Ashley, as the attorney, was the ultimate decision maker.

With great power comes great responsibility, Ashley reminded herself. She had chosen a career that gave her a degree of power. Not a lot of power, but enough to seriously impact the remainder of many of her clients' lives. Especially when the person was looking at life imprisonment if things went belly up.

Ashley tried not to second guess herself, but in these moments when the jury filtered out while shooting her and Lucas nasty looks, it was impossible to do otherwise. Yes, it was a wager, and it would be easy to say *I knew what I was doing* after the verdict was read. At least so long as the verdict was positive for her client. Yet, in this moment, she still didn't know.

The second the jurors were out of the room, Katie leaned over and said, "You really are going to leave them to ponder that opening overnight? You didn't want to respond?"

Of course, she wanted to react to Charles Hanson's opening. She would have loved to jump up and say, "that's all bullshit, and here's why..." but that would blow their defense strategy. She only had one opening statement. She had to use it wisely.

"I wanted to respond, but it's not in Lucas's best interest. Reserving opening was the lesser of two evils. When I do eventually deliver it, I'm tipping my hat to the defense strategy. I don't want Charles to know about until after he's presented his case," Ashley said.

"Okay."

Katie didn't look convinced, and neither did Lucas. Ashley wasn't convinced either, but the decision had been made. The jury had left. There was no taking it back now.

"I'm going to go back to the office," Ashley said, suddenly annoyed. "I've got more work to do. I'll see you two again in the morning."

"I'll come with you," Katie said.

Ashley almost told her that she shouldn't. That she wasn't interested in spending time with someone who didn't believe in her. But she forced herself to swallow back the emotions. Her real anger wasn't meant for Katie. It was for herself. Katie was only thinking the very same thing that Ashley was thinking internally, and that was, *this could be a mistake.*

"Let's go," Ashley tossed the extra notebooks and pens into her bag and then started walking toward the door. She expected the hallway to be empty, but it wasn't. One person remained. "What are you doing here?"

"Waiting for you," Matthew Larson said. He stood leaning up against a wall near the stairwell. He pushed off it with one foot and came walking toward her and Katie.

"Why?"

"Yeah, why?" Katie asked.

"This is an A to B conversation, you should C your way out of it," Matthew said.

Ashley rolled her eyes.

Katie scoffed. "Nice one. I bet you've been keeping that insult pocketed and ready to produce since grade school."

Ashley barked a laugh. "Probably. He seems like the playground bullying type." He'd certainly been making his rounds bullying the good people of Brine.

"I just came to say that I'll be watching the trial," Matthew said, his gaze intent on Ashley.

"What the fuck is that supposed to mean?"

"Nothing." He raised his hands as a form of surrender. "I only mean to say that I have friends in high places. You should keep that in mind."

"You've got to be kidding me. Are you threatening me?"

"I don't believe I said anything that could possibly be construed as a threat."

"Get out of my way," Ashley said, making a move to step around him.

Matthew caught her arm. "You're making a mistake."

Ashley froze and looked down at his large hand hooked around her bicep. "No. You're making a mistake. And if you don't take your hand off me this very moment, you will come to learn just how big that mistake will be."

He dropped her arm and stepped back, lifting both hands in surrender.

"And I'm not selling my property. Not to you or anyone else. I know your tactics. I am not falling for them."

"My employer is acquiring properties honestly. There is nothing untoward about his behavior."

"Oh, yeah? Does your employer plan to make a bid on the Lucas farm when it goes up for auction?"

He shrugged. "We'll see. That auction isn't until," he paused, tapping a finger against his chin, feigning contemplation. "Well, it's in a couple days now, isn't it?"

"You're disgusting." It was true, so she didn't have to fake or force the vehemence behind the words even though he was playing right into her hands. She had plans and it would help if the oil company bought that property.

He shrugged. "I'm doing my job. Of all people, I thought you would be able to understand."

Ashley shook her head. He was not going to goad her into a drawn-out argument. "Come on, Katie, let's go."

For half a second, Ashley thought that Katie might punch Matthew in the face. She stood stock still, hands balled into fists, glaring at the realtor as if she could think of nothing more satisfying than the crunch of her hand against his nose. Then she turned and moved toward Ashley. They headed down the stairs and into the main atrium of the courthouse.

"Ashley Montgomery, just the person I was hoping to see," came a familiar male voice.

Ashley swung her head to the right. Tucker Caine was striding down the hallway toward her.

"Do you have a moment?" He asked.

No, she did not have a moment. She didn't even have a second. Or a millisecond. But this guy, this man, was so much like so many others. They expected women to be at their beck and call. She would have loved to tell him as much, but she also needed his support if she was going to get through the judicial nominating committee.

"Umm, sure."

Katie looked back, her expression quizzical.

"You go on ahead. I'll be there in a few minutes."

"Wonderful," Tucker said, flashing Katie his politician smile. "I'll have her back to you in a jiffy."

It was Katie's turn to roll her eyes. "Fine. Don't make it long." Her gaze was focused on Tucker. She was speaking solely to him, not to Ashley. "I have some things I need to discuss with her."

"Sure, sure." Tucker turned on his heel and motioned for Ashley to follow, then headed down the hallway that led to his city council office. When they reached his office, he opened the door and waved a hand. "Ladies first."

Ashley cringed. She was not a lady. She didn't even want to be a lady. What was it with men thinking that all women aspired to have the etiquette of a debutante? Still, she kept her mouth shut and entered the room.

"Have a seat," he said as he made his way around the desk and dropped into his chair.

"What's this about? In case you haven't noticed, I'm in the middle of a murder trial. I've got work to do."

"I have noticed, and that's precisely why I wanted to talk to you. I've heard that you reserved your opening statement. What was the purpose behind that? You don't have any tricks up your sleeve, do you?"

Ashley blinked several times. "I must have heard you wrong. You can't possibly be asking me to divulge my defense strategy. Right?"

"Oh, of course not. I mean, if you wanted to, you would certainly have my full attention."

"That's unethical."

"Oh, right. Yes. Ethics." He swatted at the air as if he was chasing away a pesky fly. "Here's the thing, though. My position is a political one. That means I have ties to people who make demands of me. You're asking for political support. Usually that comes with an *I'll pat your back if you pat mine* sort of deal. And the powers above me want Lucas convicted. Ergo, I want Lucas convicted. You need my political support for something you want. Do you see how we can pat each other's backs here?"

Ashley sat there for a long moment, trying to gather her thoughts while simultaneously controlling her rage. He was threatening her. Telling her that she had to choose between Lucas and her future as a judge.

"There is no winning for me in this scenario," she finally said.

"I fail to see why that is."

"You're telling me that I must collude with you, against my client, or you will ensure the judicial nominating committee doesn't allow my name through as one of the judicial candidates sent to the governor. Not now, and probably not ever. Yet, my ethical obligations as an attorney require me to get the best possible outcome for my client. If I collude with you, I've violated a fundamental tenet of my ethics, and I'm subject to the loss of my license to practice law. I must be an attorney to be a judge. Ergo—lose, lose situation for me."

"Oh, who is to know? You don't lose your license unless you get caught. I don't intend for either of us to get caught."

"I assure you that none of my clients intend to get caught either. Yet, they do. Every day, they do."

"We're smarter than them."

"I think we're done here," Ashley said, bolting up from her seat. "I've had enough of this conversation."

"Consider it, please. There is still plenty of time before the committee meets. You still have several days to change your mind and come to the right decision."

Ashley shook her head and walked out. It was complete and total bull-shit, but she supposed that was the way of politics. For all the blustering about constitutional rights, nobody batted an eye when trampling a person like Lucas's constitutional rights. He was poor and he had no power. He wasn't a person to them. He was an object they could use.

Ashley felt certain, in that moment, that Tucker Caine saw her the same way.

30

KATIE

April 27

"Call your first witness," Judge Ahrenson said in that quiet, yet authoritative, way he always spoke.

"The State calls Deputy Frankie Pitch to the stand," Charles Hanson bellowed.

Katie was not sitting at counsel table anymore. She was not needed up there, and Ashley didn't want the visual inequity of three people at the defense table and one on the prosecutor's side. It would make it seem like Lucas had the upper hand, which he didn't.

The deputy entered the courtroom and strode up the aisle, head held high and shoulders back. People were crammed into the pews, shoulder to shoulder, but still and silent enough to hear the deputy's utility belt clicking with every step. He crossed through the partition separating the crowd and the legal parties, pausing briefly to glare at Lucas, before continuing up to the bench and raising his right hand.

"Do you swear to tell the truth, the whole truth, so help you?" Judge Ahrenson asked.

"I swear," Deputy Pitch said before snapping his hand down as quick as a salute and taking his place in the witness chair.

"Good morning, Deputy Pitch," Charles said.

"As good a morning as it can be cooped up indoors on a beautiful day like today."

"Yes, we all would like to be elsewhere, wouldn't we?"

"Yes."

The jury laughed, but this wasn't Katie's first time hearing this kind of banter. It was meant to charm the jury. It didn't always work, but it seemed to be working today.

"How long have you been a deputy?"

"Two years."

"Were you involved in an investigation into the Defendant, Lucas Campbell?"

This was the only time Charles would use Lucas's name. He was establishing that Lucas was the Defendant, and for the rest of the trial, Lucas would simply be "the Defendant." Which was Charles's way of dehumanizing him, making him seem detached. Like something less than. A partial person, an animal, or a nonliving thing. Something that starts with the word "the" instead of a name. The rat. The arm. The prison.

"Yes, I was." Deputy Pitch paused, casting a dark glance at Lucas. "A murder investigation."

"Tell me, how were you notified of this gruesome affair?"

"Objection," Ashley said. The word came quick, bursting forth from Ashley's lungs. She was angry, but her tone sounded as calm as if she was commenting on the weather. "The State is using his questions to testify."

"Sustained."

"Your honor," Charles said, seemingly aghast.

It was an act; he was stepping over the line. Even Katie, a non-lawyer, could see that.

Judge Ahrenson gave Charles a hard look. "I know what you are doing, and I don't like it. Ask your questions, but do so without the flowery descriptions."

All eyes swung back to Deputy Pitch, who sat there, looking dumbfounded. A few beats of silence passed and then he said, "I don't remember the question."

"How did you get involved in the investigation of the Defendant?"

"Oh, yes. It was early in the morning on January 30."

"What time in the morning?"

"Probably around five o'clock. Dispatch had received a call from Gerald Mock's farm."

"Who called 9-1-1?"

"I believe the caller was Gerald's daughter, Nikki Nelson."

"Was Nikki living there with Gerald at the time?"

"Yes."

"What was the nature of the call?"

"The dispatcher didn't have a lot of information. I believe it came in as an accident with a firearm, one potential fatality."

"You responded to the farm, I presume."

"Yes. I did. I got there shortly before the ambulance."

"May I approach, your honor?" Charles said to the judge.

"Yes, you may."

Katie shifted in her seat, and she saw Ashley and Lucas do the same. Charles was already going for the photographs. They would be gruesome, unpalatable to the jury, and Charles would take every advantage of that. He was going to force those pictures into their faces as many times as possible, whether they wanted to see them or not.

"What I am showing you have previously been marked as State's exhibits one through twenty. What are these?" Charles said as he approached the witness stand and handed a stack of enlarged photographs to the deputy.

Deputy Pitch took several long moments flipping through them all. The courtroom was so still that the rustling of the paper could likely be heard all the way in the back. When he got to the end, he looked up. "These are pictures I took after I arrived at Gerald Mock's property."

"Are they clear and accurate depictions of the scene as you remember it on January 30, 2022?"

"They are."

Charles turned to the judge. "Your honor, the State offers State's exhibits one through twenty into evidence."

"Any objection?" Judge Ahrenson asked Ashley.

He was talking about legal objections. There were all kinds of personal objections to the pictures. They were unnecessary and only meant to incite the jury's passions, for Deputy Pitch could easily describe the scene without their aid. Nobody was refuting the fact that Gerald was shot in the face or that Lucas had been the one to pull the trigger. Yet, there was no point in making an objection. The judge was going to let the pictures into evidence, and an objection would only make the jury think that Ashley was trying to hide the ball.

"No objection."

"State's exhibits one through twenty are accepted."

"May I publish to the jury?" Charles asked.

"You may."

Here we go, Katie thought as Charles repositioned a giant TV screen, so it was front and center before the jury.

Ashley got up and moved. She could not see the screen from her angle. Lucas remained seated, his hands in his lap. Katie could not see the screen either, but there was little she could do about that. Attorneys were part of the action, they needed to know what was happening so they could be prepared. They were allowed to move around so long as it was achieving that goal. Onlookers in the gallery were not.

"This is State's exhibit one," Charles said, his slow, almost Southern sounding voice booming through the silent courtroom.

The jury issued an audible gasp as their eyes locked on the screen. Some members looked away immediately, others looked like they were about to be sick.

"Tell the jury what they are seeing, Deputy Pitch."

"This is a photograph of Gerald Mock. He is the victim in this matter."

"How did you identify Gerald Mock as the victim?"

"Umm, he was dead, lying there in the doorway, covered in blood. His face was so messed up that we didn't know who he was at first."

"That's what I mean. How did you identify the person here," he pointed to what was undoubtedly the image of a body, "As Gerald Mock?"

"Several ways. The body build was consistent with that of Gerald Mock, and the body positioning was just inside the door. It was as though he'd answered the door and—"

"Objection, speculation."

"Sustained." Judge Ahrenson turned toward the witness. "Testify to what you *know*, not what you *think* you know."

"I don't understand," Deputy Pitch said, shaking his head.

Katie almost felt sorry for the guy. He was young, heavily muscled, and attractive. He had a good job in a position of power. Yet none of those things could make up for his not quite stellar intelligence.

"Phrases like 'It was as though,' are going to get you in trouble," Judge Ahrenson said.

"How else did you identify the body?" Charles asked.

"The daughter, Nikki Nelson, was home. She said it was her father. It was early, but people out in the country are usually early risers, especially when they have animals to care for. Gerald and Nikki were both awake, both dressed by the time Lucas came knocking around 5:00 a.m."

"Was Nikki the person who called 9-1-1?"

"Yes."

"What I'm showing you is labeled State's exhibit two." Charles pressed a button on his computer.

The jurors expressions grew more somber.

"What are we seeing in this photograph?"

"This is a close-up picture of Gerald Mock's face. Or, what's left of it."

"Do you know how Mr. Mock died?"

"I originally thought he'd been beaten to death. There was so much swelling and so much damage, it seemed like the only option. But then Deputy George Thomanson found the shell casing. That's how we figured out that Gerald had been shot in the face at close range."

"Then what did you do?"

"Well, the ambulance had already come and gone. There was no point in them staying. He was deader than a turkey on Thanksgiving, so they left him there for the medical examiner."

"Okay. What did you do next?"

"I noticed a trail of bloody footprints."

"Footprints? As in shoe prints or footprints?"

"Believe it or not, they were footprints. I could see the individual toes."

"Did that surprise you?"

"Umm, yeah. It was freezing that morning."

"I'm showing you State's exhibit three. Is this a picture of the footprints?"

The jury had no problem looking at State's exhibit three. Bloody footprints were nothing compared to the horrific images they had undoubtedly already seen.

"Yes. It is."

"How about State's exhibits four through ten? What are these photographs showing?"

"This is the bloody trail of footprints, leading from Gerald Mock's front door all the way to the Defendant's house."

"How do you know they start at Gerald's house instead of the other way around?"

Deputy Pitch furrowed his brow. "Because Gerald's house had the dead body."

"Any other ways?"

"Well, the footprints start out dark, saturated in blood, then they grow lighter, like the feet are losing blood as they move along."

"What did you do when you got to the Defendant's home?"

"I knocked on the door."

"Did anyone answer?"

"It took a few moments, but yes."

"Who answered the door?"

"The Defendant."

"Can you describe his appearance?"

"Yes. He was wearing a t-shirt that had once been white and a pair of shorts. The shorts were a shade of blue, I think. I don't know, I didn't pay that close attention to that. My focus was on all the blood. He was covered head to toe in blood and some grey matter that turned out to be part of Gerald's brain."

Katie's gaze cut toward the jury. There was no humor left in them anymore. Their expressions were intent, but horrified. Several people visibly winced at the mention of brain matter.

"Did he say anything to you?"

"No. He just opened the door, saw me, then turned around and walked away, leaving the door wide open."

"Was he holding anything?"

"He had a bag of chips in his hands. A blue bag of Doritos. I think they were Cool Ranch flavored."

"The Defendant was able to eat while covered in someone else's internal organs?"

"Apparently."

A woman, seated in the back corner of the jury box, gagged, but she did not vomit.

"Did he invite you inside?"

"Yes."

"I'm showing you State's exhibit eleven. What does this photograph show?"

"That's the Defendant. You can see the bag of chips there in his hand."

"How about State's exhibit twelve?"

"That's the entryway to the Defendant's house. There is a living room off over to the left there and a stairway upstairs to the right."

"What's that propped up against the side of the stairway?"

"That's a shotgun."

"I'm showing you State's exhibit thirteen. What is the jury seeing here?"

"This is a close-up photograph of the gun. As you can see, it is covered in blood. The blood was later identified as Gerald Mock's blood."

"Did you feel this shotgun was significant?"

"Yes. I believed it was the gun used to kill Gerald Mock."

"What did you do with it?"

"At first, I left it alone. I was more concerned with the Defendant. He was the one that could become a danger to me. But once Deputy Thomanson arrived, he handled the gun. He took this photograph, seized it, and sent it off to the criminalistics laboratory in Ankeny for testing."

"Did you interview the Defendant?"

"I tried to, but he wasn't making a lot of sense."

"What do you mean?"

"I asked him what he had been doing that morning, and he said something about wolves."

"Did you find that to be odd?"

"Yeah. We don't even have wolves in Iowa. At least not in these parts. Coyotes, yes, but not wolves."

"Do you believe he was calling Gerald Mock a wolf?"

"Objection. Speculation," Ashley said.

"Sustained." Judge Ahrenson turned to Charles. "You know better than that. Do not ask the witness what he *believes*. Ask him what he *knows*."

Charles did know better than that, but this was his strategy. Katie had seen attorneys do it often, even Ashley. They'd ask a question that they knew was objectionable, but the point wasn't to get an answer. The point was to put a certain thought in the jury's mind. Here, Charles wanted the jury to think that Lucas had hunted Gerald like a wolf.

"What did you do then?"

"I arrested the Defendant and charged him with the murder of Gerald Mock."

"Thank you, deputy," Charles said, nodding solemnly at his witness. "I have no further questions. The defense might have a few, though."

All eyes swung over to Ashley.

"I do have a few questions," Ashley said, flipping back a few pages on her legal pad. "You mentioned a shell casing, is that right?"

"Yes. Deputy Thomanson found one inside the Mock residence."

"Just one?"

"That's all that's necessary to blow—"

"Thank you," Ashley said with a tight smile. "Please answer my questions directly and do not elaborate. You can do that with the State's questions, but not with mine."

Ashley's use of the words, "the State," was as intentional as Charles's use of "the Defendant." While he was dehumanizing Lucas, she was trying to impart the might and power of a large looming entity. Something so big that it could crush the small and the weak. The King. The monster. The giant.

"Okay."

"That means that only one shot was fired, right?"

"As far as we can tell."

"Well, is there any evidence to the contrary?"

"No."

"So, one shot, then. Right?"

"Yes."

"Where was Gerald's daughter when you arrived?"

"Nikki?"

"Yes."

"She was in the kitchen, seated at the table."

"What was she doing?"

"Eating breakfast."

Ashley paused, waiting for that to sink in for the jury. "She was eating breakfast while her father's body lay in the entryway, covered in blood."

"She was in shock."

"Well, now, you don't have the credentials to make that determination, now do you?"

"Umm."

"You aren't a doctor, are you?"

"No."

"So, you have no way of telling if someone is in shock or not, do you?"

"No."

"Nikki was doing the very same thing as Lucas, wasn't she?"

"She wasn't covered in her father's blood or bits of his brain."

"That wasn't my question."

"Yes. She was doing the same thing as Lucas."

Ashley looked down at her notepad, made a checking motion with a pen a few times, and then looked back up.

"You mentioned footprints. Bare footprints, right? Meaning, without socks."

"Yes."

"Footprints are unique, right?"

"Yes."

"Unique in the same way that fingerprints are unique. Isn't that true?"

"Yes."

"Did you test the footprints to see if they matched Lucas's unique footprint?"

"The defendant was covered in Gerald's blood."

Ashley looked up, her expression stern. "You didn't answer my question."

"No. We didn't test the footprints."

"Does my client, Lucas Campbell, live alone?"

"No. His father, Albert Campbell, was living with him at the time. I'm not sure what that—"

"There's no question pending, deputy," Ashley said, cutting him off mid-statement. "You mentioned that Lucas answered the door in a t-shirt and shorts, right?"

"Yes. Saturated in—"

"Yes, yes. We know. Those shorts, though. They weren't basketball shorts, were they?"

"No."

"They were boxer shorts. Wouldn't you agree?"

"Yes."

"So, Lucas answered the door barefoot and in pajamas."

"Yes."

"You've already mentioned this multiple times, but just to be clear, it was the pajamas that had Gerald's blood on them, right?"

"Yes."

"So, your theory is that Lucas walked barefoot and in pajamas—shorts and a threadbare t-shirt—in negative temperatures over to Gerald's house in order to shoot him?"

"Yes."

"And then he returned home and did nothing to conceal his actions. Am I right?"

"I suppose."

"Don't you think that's odd?"

"Stranger things have happened."

"I'm sure they have. But do you often see murders like this? Ones that happen in front of witnesses, in pajamas, where there is no attempt to cover it up?"

"No two cases are the same."

Ashley shook her head. Katie could see the irritation in the set of her shoulders. She could also tell that Ashley would not get anything more out of this witness. There was no point in questioning him further.

"I have no further questions for this witness."

"I think it is time for our morning break," Judge Ahrenson said. Then he stood and everyone else did the same.

The jury funneled out. Not a single person even glanced in Ashley and Lucas's direction. That was a bad sign. They already believed in Lucas's guilt, and Katie didn't blame them. The morning's testimony had been brutal. Could Ashley turn things around, or was the trial already over?

31

ASHLEY

To say the morning had been a disaster would have been an understatement. It was an absolute train wreck. No, worse than that. An airplane crashed into a train running headlong into a building full of explosives. That kind of morning. And the State was only partly through their testimony.

Only one other witness aside from Deputy Pitch had testified. It was the ballistics expert. Expert testimony was never very exciting. They were driven by science, which meant that their testimony couldn't be swayed or manipulated by emotion. He had testified as expected. The gun seized from Lucas's entryway was the gun that shot the fatal bullet.

Ashley hadn't asked the ballistics expert a single question on cross examination. That was a mistake that many younger attorneys made. They thought they had to ask at least one question. But that wasn't true, and sometimes asking even one question could highlight a fact that would be harmful to the client.

After finishing with that witness, the Judge had broken for lunch. Ashley had been too hyped up to eat. She'd forced down half an energy bar, and was now seated alone at the defense table, looking over notes. Lucas was back at the jail, hopefully getting some sustenance, but she doubted it. He was more stressed than she was, and for good reason.

"Who is up next?" Katie asked.

Ashley startled and spun to see her investigator standing directly behind her chair. "Sorry, I was lost in thought. I'm sure he's going to call the medical examiner or another criminalist, something like that. The middle of the day is almost always reserved for technical testimony, when the jury is tired and only half listening."

"When do you think you'll start putting on evidence?"

Ashley shrugged. "Charles doesn't have a lot of witnesses, so maybe late tomorrow or early the day after that."

Just then, the back doors swung open, and Charles Hanson shuffled down the aisle. Sometime over the lunch break people must have started filing back in, because the courtroom was nearly full. Ashley scanned the crowd, catching sight of Matthew Larson. She'd expected to see him, but she was surprised Tucker Caine was sitting next to him.

"Hold on," Ashley said, shoving out of her seat and marching past the partition, out into the gallery. Tucker and Matthew were near the back. Despite the ever-growing crowd, there still wasn't anyone near them. Matthew saw her coming first and waved.

"What are you doing here?" Ashley asked.

"I thought we discussed this yesterday," Matthew said.

"Not you. You," she nodded to Tucker. "Don't you have better things to do than sit in on jury trials?"

Tucker shrugged. "I'm on the judicial nominating committee, and the two attorneys trying this case have applied for the presiding judge's position. I don't understand why I'm the only committee member here."

"Because you're the only one blackmailing the attorneys."

"Blackmail is a strong word."

"That's why I used it."

Tucker bared his teeth in what to some would pass as a smile. "That's no way to talk to someone who has control over your life."

"Actually, you have no control. I thought I explained this thing about circular logic last night. Your little proposal is a lose-lose scenario for me, so that means that I lose. Since the outcome is a foregone conclusion, there is no point in pandering to you or worrying about the future or your decision-making ability in the future. It's no longer *my* future, so I don't actually care what you think anymore."

Tucker opened his mouth to say something, then closed it again. He sat there for a long moment, long enough that Ashley almost turned on her heel and walked away, but he spoke up just before she did.

"Then lease some of your land to Mr. Larson, here."

Ashley blinked several times. "Excuse me. Are you saying that you'll support me for the judgeship if I sign a land contract with that vile company? You, as a city councilperson, are encouraging, no, baiting me, to get into bed with a company that has ravaged this community? I'm not sure if I can even fathom the right words to explain how fucked up that is."

Tucker shrugged. "It's your call. I'm giving you an out from this whole ethical dilemma that seemed oh so important to you last night."

His flippant regard for the importance of her job had her blood boiling. This was precisely why she never belonged in politics. Even if building windmills would have been the right thing for the town, these political idiots had to find a way to fuck that all up. It wasn't about wind energy anymore. Maybe it never was, but it certainly wasn't now. This was about money and power, plain and simple. Two things that could corrupt the virtually incorruptible.

"Is everyone ready to go?" A voice from the front of the courtroom called.

Ashley looked up. The court reporter had entered from judge's chambers and was looking around. "Where's Miss Montgomery?"

"I'm here," Ashley waved a hand. "I'll be ready to go in a few seconds."

Ashley turned to leave, and as she did, Tucker said, "We'll finish this later."

"No, we won't. It's finished now. You both know my answer on both accounts."

Then she marched back up the aisle and to the front of the courtroom. She was reclaiming her seat when the jailers brought Lucas back in and deposited him next to her. He looked tired and haggard, a shell of the man who she had once seen walking so confidently around town.

"You doing alright?" Ashley asked, placing a hand on his shoulder.

He shrugged. "I don't know how to answer that."

"You don't have to. Just keep your head in the game. It looks bad now, but we haven't had our chance to go."

He nodded and wiped away a tear. "I trust you."

Just like that, Ashley knew exactly why she couldn't be corrupted. It was the Lucas Campbells of the world. Those who needed help. The ones who had few people on their side. Nobody who could share the burden, save for their attorney. She would not take advantage of Lucas's trust. Not for money. Not for power. Not for ambition. Sure, Lucas had shot someone, but he wasn't a murderer, and she had every intent of proving that to the jury.

32

KATIE

"The State calls Nikki Nelson to the stand," Charles Hanson bellowed like he was the town crier for Brine, Iowa.

Ashley wasn't often wrong, but she had been wrong in predicting the timing of witnesses. She had thought the State would call the medical examiner or a blood expert next.

Everyone turned to look at the back of the courtroom, but nothing happened.

"The State calls Nikki Nelson," Charles repeated.

Again, nothing happened.

A small woman scampered up the aisle and whispered something into Charles's ear. His face grew ripe tomato red and then he turned to the judge and said, "Your honor, we have some business we need to take up outside the presence of the jury."

Judge Ahrenson sighed irritably. "We just came back from lunch, Mr. Hanson. Don't you think that would have been a good time to bring up whatever issue you have going on here?"

"Yes, your honor, and I'm sorry." All arrogance had disappeared from his demeanor, replaced by the countenance of a groveling child. "I was unaware of the issue until this very moment."

"Very well. Court attendant, please usher the jury out. I'll let you know when we are ready for them again."

The jury was not pleased with the change in plans. They'd just had lunch and were only starting to settle down when they were having to get back up and march back out of the room. Some of them clucked their tongues disapprovingly while others glared at the doleful, helpless looking prosecutor.

Everyone in the courtroom rose until the last jury member had departed, and then they were allowed to sit back down.

"We are still on the record," Judge Ahrenson said. He was not speaking to the crowd; he was directing his words to the court reporter. This conversation was meant for appeals purposes only. If the case was appealed, the appellate judges would be able to read the transcript and understand what was happening. "The jury has just left, and we are now convened outside their presence, at Mr. Hanson's request. Mr. Hanson, what is the reason for this disruption?"

"It's my witness, Nikki Nelson. She was served a subpoena and commanded to appear. She is not here. My office has contacted her, and she refuses to come. Apparently, her intent is to disregard the subpoena and a direct order by this Court to testify."

"Is that so," Judge Ahrenson's blue eyes flashed with fury. "Well, we can send her an invitation, then."

Katie's shoulders stiffened. They were going to send a sheriff out to Nikki's house to forcibly bring her into trial. That was what he meant by "invitation." It was synonymous with arrest. He might even hold Nikki in contempt of court. Katie's heart quickened. That could not happen. Poor Nikki's mental health was already so frail. She couldn't withstand much more trauma.

"If I may, your honor," Ashley said, rising from her seat.

All eyes in the courtroom swung toward the defense table.

"Nikki Nelson is an agoraphobic. She's terrified of leaving her house. She's been that way since she lost her mother a few years ago. The condition was exacerbated with the loss of her father. I don't think dragging her in here and forcing her to testify is going to benefit anyone."

"Then what do you propose?" Charles growled. "You don't want her to testify at all, do you?"

"On the contrary, I very much would like to hear what she has to say."

"You would?" Charles was visibly shaken by that response. Katie could practically see the wheels turning in his head as he tried to work out why Ashley would want his witness to testify.

"What would you propose?" Judge Ahrenson's tone was soft, and he was looking at Ashley with something akin to pride. "Seeing that you are the only one of the two of you that has taken the time to understand the witness's condition. Maybe you have a thought on a work around."

"I do have an idea. It's not ideal, but we could have her testify virtually. We've got that TV there," she nodded to the giant television Charles had used to traumatize the jurors with crime scene photos. "Her house is internet capable. So is this courtroom. We could hook her up by GoToMeeting or Zoom. That way we have the testimony, and we don't have to harm her in the process."

"That is an idea." By the tone of his voice, it was clear that Judge Ahrenson approved of the plan. "What do you say, Mr. Hanson?"

"I'd prefer she be here."

"Do you intend to go get her?"

"What?"

"I'm not sending sheriff's deputies out to get her. You don't have any authority to do so either without my command. So, what do you intend to do? If I don't grant your request for a pickup order—which I'm not now that I know the full story—then how else are you going to get her here?"

Charles was silent for a long moment, his pale freckled face growing a darker shade of red with each passing second. Finally, after it seemed like his face might actually pop under the pressure, he acquiesced.

"Can you get her on the line?" Judge Ahrenson said to Ashley.

Ashley was already typing furiously on her computer. She whispered something to Charles, and he handed her a long cord. She plugged it into her computer, and, just like magic, there was Nikki Nelson's face, filling the TV screen.

"Well, will you look at that," Judge Ahrenson said. "Technology sure has come a long way." He stared at the screen for a beat, reverence clearly written in his expression, then he turned to the court reporter and said, "Bring the jury back in."

The jurors were interested in the new face right in front of them. They filed into the courtroom, and their eyes locked on the television. They did not look away.

"Are we ready to proceed?" Judge Ahrenson said once everyone was seated and situated.

"Yes, your honor. The State calls Nikki Nelson to the stand."

"Ms. Nelson, can you hear me?" Judge Ahrenson was almost yelling, and speaking in slow, deliberate words like he might to a small child or a non-English speaker. "This is the judge. Can you hear me?"

Katie had to fight the urge to laugh. The older generation was hilarious with technology. They didn't understand it. Try as they might, they probably never would. It simply changed too much, too fast. Those who grew up with computers, they were prepared for the changes. It was their way of life. But this older generation, they remembered a time when there were no computers, there was no internet, and research could only be done through books.

"I can hear you, sir," Nikki said, her voice tenuous but firm.

"Can you raise your right hand?"

"I have it raised."

"Do you swear to tell the truth, the whole truth, so help you?"

"I do."

"Your witness, Mr. Hanson."

"Thank you, your honor," Charles said. "Good afternoon, Nikki."

"Good afternoon."

"Do you know why you've been called here to testify?"

"My father died."

"Your father was killed?"

"Sure."

Several jurors shifted in their seats. It was an odd way to answer the question. Now that Katie had gotten to know Nikki better, she recognized it as Nikki's personality rather than something odd or nefarious.

"Can you walk me through the day? January 30."

"The whole day? Or just up until it happened?"

"Let's start with you waking up. Tell the jury about that."

"I woke up at four-thirty, like I always do. I used to take care of the animals. We have cows and goats, you see. It's my job to feed them and keep the barns clean. Dad used to do all that, but he was getting up there in years, so I started taking over the heavy work."

"Were you living with your father at the time?"

"Yeah. I'm living there now. Lucas's dad moved in with me. He's a right help, he is. Makes my days a whole lot less lonely."

Charles blinked several times, and then he cut an accusatory gaze toward Ashley. A glare that said *you're up to something and I don't like it.* She shrugged in response.

"So, what did you do after waking up?"

"I got dressed and came downstairs. Dad was already up, drinking his morning cup of coffee. He wasn't a very sound sleeper."

"Was your father in good spirits?"

"I wouldn't say that."

"Was something bothering him?"

"Not particularly. At least not until I told him that he was going to die."

"Wait, what?" Charles spluttered, his gaze shifting to the jury, then back to Ashley. Once again, Ashley merely shrugged.

This was one of the primary reasons Ashley didn't want to take depositions. There isn't a second chance for the prosecutor to probe their witnesses for additional information. Katie had known about Nikki's belief she could see and smell death on others, but that was only because she'd taken the time to sit down and chat with Nikki.

The prosecutor wouldn't have been interested in anything other than the facts that law enforcement had provided to him, and law enforcement didn't ask the right questions. They'd been too focused on other things like blood trails and shell casings to worry about Nikki.

"I saw it on him. Death. It's like an aura that hangs around people, bluish green in color. It comes shortly before they die. Dad had it. And there is this smell. I can't explain it, but I'll try. It's slightly rotten yet sweet, like wilting flowers. Dad had that, too."

"Are you saying that you can predict when someone is going to die?"

"No."

Charles sighed with relief, but it was short lived.

"Not exactly. I can't tell when you are going to die. At least not right now. If you develop a greenish blue aura around you and you start to stink, then I can say you're going to die within ten minutes."

"That doesn't sound like a very useful talent."

"It isn't. It causes far more harm than good, because there is no changing fate once the aura comes. I tried to change Dad's fate. I told him not to answer when the doorbell rang, but he didn't listen to me. He told me my foolish girly ideas were not stopping him from doing whatever he wanted in his house. I told him it was a mistake, but he ignored me."

"Did you know who was at the door?"

"No." Nikki furrowed her brow. "How would I know that? I'm not clairvoyant if that's what you are trying to ask."

"I thought you could predict death."

Nikki sighed. "I just told you that I can see death on people. That's all."

"Okay," Charles said, shaking his head. "Can we, umm, take a short break?"

Judge Ahrenson glanced at the clock. "No. We will take our afternoon break in fifteen minutes."

"Okay." Charles turned around in his chair and leaned against the railing so he could talk to one of the assistant county attorneys. A brief, whispered conversation took place, then Charles turned back around. "Your honor, the State has no further questions for this witness."

That was a surprise to Katie. She and Ashley had discussed Nikki's testimony multiple times, and they both expected her to be on the stand for at least an hour. Given her surprise testimony, Charles must have decided she was too unpredictable.

"Cross?" Judge Ahrenson asked Ashley.

"No cross. Defense will recall Ms. Nelson later."

"Why not question her while she's here now?" Charles asked.

Ashley stiffened. "Because I don't want to." Her gaze flicked to the jury. Katie's did the same.

They were looking from one attorney to the next, assessing counsel rather than the trial in front of them. Most frowned when their gazes settled on Charles but settled into something more neutral when looking at

Ashley. That was a positive development. She was starting to gain their trust. That wouldn't change the facts of the case, but it would help when it came time for Ashley to explain how the jury should look at the evidence.

"I don't tell you how to do your job. I don't need you telling me how to do mine," Ashley said.

"Fair enough. You may step down, ma'am," the Judge said to Nikki, "But you should remain beside whatever device you are using for this call. You are still under subpoena."

"I will," Nikki said.

It took a few moments to turn the television off and roll it to the side so that it wasn't in the way. The courtroom overflowed with excited anticipation, everyone likely wondering the same thing as Katie. What would come next?

Then the judge said, "Call your next witness."

33

ASHLEY

They ended the day with the medical examiner's testimony. Charles had used it as another opportunity to accost the jury with gruesome photographs. There was power in adding visual to the auditory testimony. It reminded the jury of their own mortality and how quickly it could end. It had the defense, once again, ending on a low note.

Within seconds after the jury was out of the room, Charles had shifted his focus to Ashley. He was now standing in front of defense table, nostrils flaring.

"Yes?" Ashley said, calmly, almost pleasantly. "How can I help you?"

"What was that?"

"It's called a jury trial."

"Not the trial, that business with Nikki Nelson. You had Albert Campbell move in with her just to throw off my case."

Ashley blinked several times, trying to temper her anger. "Yeah, sure, you're right." She shoved out of her seat, so she was in a standing position, looking him eye to eye. "I moved an agoraphobic, a woman who can't leave the house where she's spent most of her adult life caring for two ailing parents in with a neighbor that she has known all her life who is also in need of her assistance because he's so goddamn old and really should be in a nursing facility but he can't be because he has no money. I did all that to fuck with you? You really are a self-centered bastard, aren't you?"

"I didn't think about it that way."

"Also, why do you think I had anything to do with Albert and Nikki's living situations? I didn't move them in together. I didn't even suggest it. In fact, I didn't know about it until after they'd already decided on that route. I learned of it because my investigator understood their precarious situations and continued checking up on them. So maybe you should take more interest in your witnesses instead of simply *using* them like they are here to serve you as a prosecutor and for no other purpose."

"You knew Nikki was crazy."

"Agoraphobia does not mean she's crazy. It means she's suffered quite a lot of trauma, which is the reason we are all here, right?"

"I'm not talking about that. I'm talking about her seeing death."

"Yeah, I knew about that. Again, that knowledge came with hiring an investigator who behaves like any empathetic human being. But also, that doesn't make Nikki crazy. How do you know what she sees?"

"It's all in her head."

"So, what if it is? It doesn't affect your life or even this case. She claims she saw death on her father. That doesn't change anything about your allegations against my client. It's not like she had said that she'd killed her father. In fact, she'd said the exact opposite. She told the jury that she had tried to save him by warning him. It didn't have to matter to your case, but I guess it has now that you've excused her as a witness. This is the exact problem with you arrogant men. You think that anyone who doesn't think just like you is crazy. Hysterical. Insane. Nikki is none of those things."

Charles rolled his eyes. "You feminists just hate men."

"I don't hate all men. For example, I don't hate Lucas here." She patted her client on the shoulder. He was still seated in his chair, watching the conversation through curious eyes. "I just hate pieces of shit like you."

"Again, you'd choose a murderer over someone who is trying to do the right thing."

"Depends on your definition of *the right thing*. Also, Lucas isn't a murderer. The jury hasn't convicted him yet."

"It's a foregone conclusion."

Lucas stiffened.

"You better leave, Charles, before I say something that might burst that overly-inflated, fragile ego of yours," Ashley said.

"We'll see who is laughing at the end of this trial," Charles said before he turned and lumbered away.

Lucas and Ashley were both silent for a long moment. Enough time for Katie to come up and join them.

"That guy sucks," Katie said.

"Really fucking sucks," Ashley agreed.

"But doesn't he have a point?" Lucas asked, dropping his face into his hands. He rubbed his palms hard against his skin, and then he looked back up. "I'm screwed. Nobody in their right mind sees photographs like that and decides on a *not guilty* verdict. Hell, I want to convict me."

"Have some faith," Katie said, dropping to her knees so she and Lucas were at the same level. "Ashley hasn't had a chance to go yet. That starts tomorrow. Things will look a whole lot better then."

Lucas looked up at Ashley with tired, resigned eyes, but Katie had sparked a tiny glimmer of hope.

Ashley responded in the only way she could. She nodded.

Lucas stood and the deputies led him out of the courtroom. Ashley and Katie watched silently until the doors closed behind him and he was gone.

"Your opening is first up tomorrow, then?" Katie asked.

Ashley sighed and nodded. "It's earlier than I had expected. There are still too many balls in the air at this point. I'm going to have to keep it short. It isn't ideal, but it's probably the best possible scenario."

"You know what's best."

That was the problem. Ashley was taking a lot of risks in this trial. Any one screw-up could end up ruining Lucas's life. It was a crushing amount of pressure, but there was little she could do to alleviate it.

"Let's go," Katie said, motioning toward the door.

Ashley packed up her things and they left the courtroom. She held her breath when they stepped out into the hall, wondering if that damn realtor or Tucker Caine would be waiting to confront her. But the hallway was blissfully empty. They made their way down the stairs and out into the crisp spring air. She started to take a deep breath of the clear, Iowa air, but froze. There, standing only a few yards away, was Matthew Larson.

"Him again," Katie growled.

"So it seems," Ashley said as the lanky realtor approached them.

"Good evening, ladies," Matthew said.

"It was good," Katie grumbled.

"What do you want this time?" Ashley demanded.

"Nothing."

"Why is that so hard for me to believe?"

Matthew shrugged. "I told you I wouldn't give up. I haven't, but I've tried a different angle. I didn't realize you had a sister, Ashley."

Ashley froze. Her sister, Karen, was a few years older than she was. "How did you learn about her?"

Karen's existence wasn't a secret, but few people remembered her. She was from Brine, but she didn't have many friends when she was in school. She was exceptionally shy and a little awkward, with wild, bushy hair. She'd graduated in Lucas's class and moved away immediately. She couldn't get away from the county faster.

"Land records."

"What?"

"You didn't tell me that Karen had a partial interest in the twenty acres on the Montgomery property."

The property had belonged to Ashley's mother. Upon her death, she'd given the ten acres with the house and the outbuildings on it to Ashley, and she'd given the other ten acres to Karen. Which made sense because Ashley lived in town and Karen had no intention of returning. Ashley's goal had always been to purchase Karen's portion, but she worked for the Public Defender's Office. She wasn't exactly rolling in extra cash, but she had managed to purchase three of Karen's ten acres. Seven were still in her sister's name.

"The good thing about social media these days is that it's pretty easy to find people."

Ashley's heart started thudding in her chest, wild, animalistic beats, her fight or flight response.

"I won't leave you in suspense," Matthew said, a smile spreading across a cruel mouth. "You should be expecting a call from Karen." He glanced down at his Rolex. "Sometime in the next thirty minutes here." Then he turned and walked off, head held high, whistling an unfamiliar tune.

"That piece of shit," Katie said. "Do you really think he did that?"

Ashley's phone started ringing. She pulled it out of her laptop bag and looked at the screen. It read *Karen* and had a picture of Ashley's niece hugging Ashley's dog Princess when she was only a puppy. That was many, many years ago. When Ashley's mother had recently died, and Karen and her daughter returned for the funeral. Ashley hadn't seen them since, and she rarely heard from them.

"Yes, yes I do," Ashley said with a heavy sigh. She showed Katie her phone.

"Sometimes I wish murder was legal," Katie said, staring at Matthew's retreating form. Then she stiffened.

"What?" Ashley asked.

"Nothing," Katie said. "You talk to your sister. I just had an idea."

"I feel like this should go without saying, but whatever you do, don't get arrested."

"I won't," Katie said with a wide grin.

That wasn't very reassuring, but Ashley knew better than anyone that Katie was not one that could be controlled. If she had an idea, that thing was going to happen whether Ashley liked it or not. Katie strode off in the opposite direction of Matthew, which was at least a little heartening, but not much. She never could quite tell Katie's limits. She had always been a stickler for the law, but she was morally driven, which allowed her to justify when she stepped outside of what was strictly legal.

Ashley looked down at her phone. It had continued buzzing, gone to voicemail, then started buzzing again. Karen was not giving up. She'd call until Ashley answered or until her phone died. Ashley steeled her emotions, then pressed the answer button.

"Hello," Ashley said.

"How could you?" said Karen's familiar, yet unfamiliar voice. They'd never been particularly close, but years and distance had separated the sisters even farther. It now felt as though she was speaking to a stranger.

"How could I what?"

"Don't play dumb, Ashley. That realtor called me. He said he offered to lease my land. *My land, Ashley*. He wants to put windmills up, and those could generate between $5,000 and $10,000 per month. *Per month*. Do you have any idea what I could do with that money?"

"No. It's been what? Six years since we've spoken. I mean, I could guess. Perhaps you'd like to join the circus and be a performer. You might need cash to get a foothold in that industry."

"Sarcasm," Karen said, disapprovingly. "You always resort to sarcasm. That's something that will never change about you, I guess. I'll tell you what I would do with it. It could pay for my daughter's school tuition. That's what."

"Private school, Karen? Don't you feel like that's getting a little fancy? What's wrong with public schools?"

"Nothing where you are from, but everything in New York."

"Everything is an overbroad, overgeneralized response. It makes me feel as though nothing is wrong with the schooling. You just want your child to grow up with the richest, most pretentious brats the Northeast has to offer. That won't get her ahead in life. It'll simply teach her to always strive to keep up with the Jones's. Sorry, I mean the Kennedy's. The problem is that she never has been a Kennedy and never will be. All you are teaching her is that she's not good enough."

"Don't tell me how to parent, Ashley. You can barely take care of yourself, let alone a child."

Karen was right, of course, but Ashley wasn't going to admit it. "You know nothing about me, so quit acting like you do."

"Fine. You have a point. I don't know you, and I don't even think I like you anymore."

"You never quite did, big sis."

"I'm going to lease my land."

"That's fucked up on lots of levels."

"Don't use that language. And why? What's the problem with me leasing *my* land."

"Because you have no idea what's going on down here. That land is in my backyard. But not only my backyard, but that of other farmers in the area. One farmer just shot his neighbor over windmills. Walked straight up to his house, knocked on the door, and shot him point blank in the face. This shit is real down here. I know you don't like me, but perhaps you care enough that you don't wish that fate upon me."

Karen was silent for a long moment. "You made that up."

"I didn't. I'm representing the guy who did the shooting."

"Ugh, your job," Karen said with a groan. "Why do you still do that?"

"For the same reason you stay in New York. Because I like it."

"I don't know if I believe you."

"Look it up. All the local news stations are covering the trial."

"I will do that, but even if it is true, that doesn't mean I am changing my mind. It only means I'm thinking about it."

"Naturally," Ashley agreed. "Take your time. When the choice is between money and the life of a very annoying little sister, it's always a tough decision to make."

"I'm going to hang up before you infuriate me any further."

"Okay," Ashley said.

Then she lowered the phone from her ear and stared at the screen until it went dark. This was a disaster. Karen didn't have enough land for a lot of windmills, but she had enough for a few. The neighbors would never believe Ashley hadn't agreed with her sister. They would think she'd sold out like so many others in town. She'd essentially given up any chance at Judge Ahrenson's judgeship to keep the windmills off her property, but it seemed as though that snake Matthew Larson had found another way, and she was powerless to make it stop.

34

KATIE

Matthew Larson wasn't a local. He was a transplant like Katie. Someone who moved from a larger city to the small town of Brine for one reason or another. Katie had moved to escape the stigma of her father's conviction, for all the good that did when he followed her right to Brine after his release from prison. But Matthew, nobody knew why he'd moved to the small town. At least not at first.

Matthew had turned up in town four years earlier, hanging out a shingle like any small-town realtor. In a town the size of Brine, new professionals did not come often. Everyone noticed his arrival, and his sudden appearance had long been a topic of conversation down at Genie's Diner. Matthew had no family ties to the area, no friends either. Still, he'd thrown himself into the local community, spewing nonsense about putting down roots in the heart of the country. He'd joined rotary, and the local chapter of Habitat for Humanity. He'd played in the Thursday night dart league and bowled with a team on Saturday. He'd built relationships. Mostly with the higher ranking, land owning, richer members of society, but those were the people who made the decisions in an area like Brine.

After several years of schmoozing, Matthew had started putting out word about an anonymous client who wanted to purchase farmland. Some people sold only to later discover that the land purchase was meant for windmill farms. Nobody was pleased about the deception. Not those selling their properties who could have made a lot more money leasing it and receiving royalties. Not those living near the properties and not many of the townspeople. Some believed the windmills caused cancer. Others didn't want their view obstructed. Still others thought the blades would slaughter millions of birds and bats. Nobody was pleased with Matthew Larson.

Then came the money. Matthew's anonymous client cast off their shell of anonymity and started making offers to landowners. Most were not swayed. Katie had always wondered how Matthew and the oil company had convinced many hardheaded farmers to change their minds. Now, after seeing the tactics he had employed on Ashley, she understood. Or at least she thought she did. She needed to verify her suspicions with Nikki and Albert.

That was how she found herself sitting at Nikki Nelson's kitchen table, sipping coffee, and chatting at six o'clock on a Wednesday evening while in the middle of a murder trial.

"How is Lucas doing?" Nikki asked. "I couldn't see him from my screen. All I could see was that prosecutor and some of the jury."

"Yeah. He was behind the TV. Ashley didn't want him approaching the jury. They get skittish when people accused of murder get close to them."

"Understandably," Albert added. "Even though my son is not a murderer. He doesn't like it when anything dies before its time. Humans, plants, animals. You name it. I've even seen him cry once when he had to put down a rabid dog roaming our property. The damn thing nearly bit him, and he was still bawling his eyes out when he pulled the trigger."

"Well, that's sorta why I'm here."

"To prove Lucas's innocence?" Nikki asked. "How is that possible?"

Her expression was one of conflicted confusion, as if part of her wanted it to be so, but another part wanted the exact opposite. Which, Katie supposed, made sense. Nikki had grown close with Albert and she'd known Lucas all her life. Absolving Lucas of her father's murder would make her life much easier. Yet she still didn't want her father's death to go unpunished.

"Tell me about Matthew Larson," Katie said.

"That real estate guy?"

"Yes. Do you know how he convinced your father to lease the windmill property to his client?"

"Dad didn't know I knew, but I did. I always felt guilty about it." Nikki's gaze cut to Albert, then back to Katie.

"Why would you feel guilty?"

"It was because of me."

"What?" Both Albert and Katie said in unison.

"At first, Dad was completely against leasing the property for windmills. He'd made a promise to Lucas. A gentleman's agreement. They shook on it, and Dad always said a man is only as good as his handshake. That Matthew guy was insistent, though. He kept turning up all over the place, running into Dad at the grocery store or the lumber yard, acting as though it just happened to be a chance encounter."

"That's exactly what he's been doing to Ashley."

"Ashley Montgomery?" Albert asked.

Katie nodded.

"That son-of-a-bitch is even harassing my son's lawyer. When will this stop?" He shook a fist at the ceiling, like he was challenging someone up in the heavens to give him an answer.

"Well, he started noticing that I never left the property. That's when he started popping up all over the place around here. Not on the actual property, but on the road or in a hot-air-balloon—he did that at least fifteen times, by the way—pretending as though he just happened through our air space. It stressed me out. I have my problems, obviously," she gestured to the house around her, "And he was making it worse. I stopped being able to go out quite as far into the pasture. I stopped being able to feed the animals."

There was no doubt she was telling the truth, despite Charles's public accusations about her mental health. It had been the same with Ashley. Matthew stalked her, looking for his way in, and after plenty of time and effort, he found it. In her sister. A person nobody in Brine quite remembered, but somehow Matthew was able to find.

"The worse I got, the more concerned Dad became. He started to worry about my future, how I would survive once he was gone. He was old, like

Albert." She looked over at the heavily wrinkled man beside her. "No offense."

"None taken, sweetheart."

"So, he worried about me, and then Matthew started leaning on that, saying that I would never survive unless I had a fixed income."

"That's how he convinced your dad. He exacerbated your health condition, then used it to get what he wanted."

"Exactly. I tried to explain it to Dad. I tried to tell him that Matthew was the reason I'd grown more homebound, but he wouldn't listen. I guess my ability to see death coupled with my fear of leaving the house made him think I was incapable of understanding the situation. Even if I could understand, he definitely thought he had a better grasp on reality than I did. Maybe he was right in some regards, but not this one."

"It is shameful behavior, but I don't see how any of this will help my boy," Albert said.

"Who is your son's doctor?"

"Doctor? Why?"

"Just trust me."

"Doctor Mason. Over there on first street. Why?"

"I need to go see him."

"What for?"

"I don't know yet, I just feel like I need to follow up with him on Lucas's mental health."

"Isn't it too late for a mental health defense? I mean, the trial is halfway through," Nikki said.

"I don't know. I'll have to ask Ashley. But it doesn't matter anyway unless I find something, and I don't know that I will."

Doctor Mason was the only general practitioner in town. Everyone who lived in Brine any significant amount of time had seen him for one thing or another. Like many small-town doctors, he was part of the fabric of the community, and he cared about it. That's why he was on call virtually twenty-four hours a day. She could call his cell at any time, and he'd pick up, but she also didn't want to bother him late if it could be avoided.

"I probably better go," Katie said, glancing at her watch. "It's nearly seven o'clock and it will take me thirty minutes to get back to town."

"Okay," Nikki said. "I have one more question."

"What's that?"

"What do we do about the auction tomorrow?"

Katie had completely forgotten about the land sale. It was set to start the next day at ten o'clock. Still, she didn't understand Nikki's question. There was nothing she or Ashley could do to stop the sale. "What do you mean?"

"Can I bid on it?"

"What?" Katie was taken aback.

"Yeah. That land is right next to mine. I'd like to have it."

"But you can't farm it."

"Lucas can when you and Ashley get him out of this mess."

That was extra positive thinking, but Katie didn't voice the opinion. It was likely a fantasy—on both accounts—because that oil company would outbid Nikki. There was little doubt of that, at least in Katie's mind, and Lucas was probably never getting out of jail. Still, the pleasure in Albert's face was worth keeping her mouth shut.

"I actually don't know about that. You'll have to ask Ashley. She's the wizard here. I'm just the information gatherer."

"I'll give her a call once you leave," Nikki said, picking up her cell phone and holding it in the air.

"I'm leaving now."

They said their goodbyes and Katie left Nikki's home with less positivity than Nikki, but more than she'd had when she arrived. A plan was starting to form in her head, but she needed to speak with one more individual. Doctor Mason. That was a call she made on her drive home, and what she discovered shook her to her core.

35

ASHLEY

April 28
Day three of Lucas's trial

Ashley delivered her opening statement with as much excitement and fanfare as she could, considering she was still unable to provide much information. To do so even now might tip her hand, and surprise was the most effective tool remaining in her defense toolbox.

She couldn't say much, so she focused on Lucas's innocence, using the theme *you can't judge a book by its cover.* She hinted that this trial went far deeper than anyone realized, and they were soon to find out through defense witnesses. She'd been skeptical her opening would gain any traction, but by the time she finished and sat back down, she was sure nothing she had said carried much sway with the jury. But it wasn't her words they would find important, it was the words of her witnesses, or so she hoped.

"Call your first witness," Judge Ahrenson said. He had a quizzical expression on his face, as though he was trying to work out why Ashley had reserved her opening. Part of her was wondering the same thing.

"Defense calls Nikki Nelson to the stand."

Katie was back up at the defense table. Ashley needed her to usher witnesses in and handle technology. She popped up from her seat next to

Lucas and wheeled the large TV screen back in front of the jury. Ashley came around to the front of the screen so Nikki would be able to see her. Then Katie pressed the *on* button and the screen filled with Nikki's now familiar face.

"Good morning, Ms. Nelson," Ashley said. She was silently relieved to see Nikki present, dressed, and ready to testify. Katie had obtained some bombshell information from Nikki the night before. Information that could turn the tide of this case. It would be Ashley's luck for Nikki to disappear, fall apart, or refuse to testify.

"Good morning."

"Who is your father?"

"My father was Gerald Mock."

"Where do you live?"

"On a farmstead west of town about thirty minutes."

"Who is your neighbor?"

"My neighbors were Lucas Campbell and Albert Campbell."

"How long had Lucas and Albert lived in the house next to yours?"

"All their lives. I was born and raised out there, so was Lucas. Same goes for our dads."

"So, you've known one another for quite some time. Is that right?"

"All my life."

"Has there ever been bad blood between either of the families?"

"No. Not until recently."

"What happened?"

"The windmill company and Matthew Larson, that's what happened."

"Objection," Charles said, jumping out of his seat.

"What's the objection?" Judge Ahrenson said, looking down at Charles over his sharp, hawk-like nose.

"Relevance."

The judge's gaze cut to Ashley.

"The family feud between Lucas and Gerald's family is relevant to Lucas's state of mind."

"It goes to intent and you know it," Charles shot back.

"I'm not sure why that's of concern to you, Mr. Hanson. Seems like you'd want that testimony, right?" Judge Ahrenson said.

"Not the way she's doing it." Charles hooked a thumb toward Ashley.

"You had your chance to present evidence, Mr. Hanson. It's Ms. Montgomery's turn. She has a right to do her job."

"But—"

"I am allowing the testimony." He looked back at Ashley. "Go ahead."

Ashley nodded and snuck a glance at the jury. A few members were shifting uncomfortably in their seats. Whether that was because they were uncomfortable with conflict or if they were starting to tire of Charles, she didn't know.

"So, tell me, Nikki, what happened with windmills that had these life-long friends and neighbors feuding."

Nikki explained how the Campbells sold a chunk of their land to her father, and how there were no legal stipulations, but they had an informal handshake.

"What happened to that informal, handshake agreement?"

"My dad honored it for a while, then he leased the land to the oil company."

Ashley glanced at the jury, catching them in the corner of her eye without moving her head. Several people had crossed their arms while a few more shifted their weight.

"How did that happen?"

"Objection," Charles shot back up to his feet. "Hearsay. Calls for speculation."

Judge Ahrenson turned to the TV screen. "Ms. Nelson, do you have first-hand knowledge, meaning did you witness anything, or did someone tell you what happened?"

"I have knowledge."

"Overruled."

Someone coughed from within the jury pool. Charles was falling right into Ashley's trap. The more he objected to the windmill testimony, the more the jury would think that he didn't want them to know, that he was hiding something. This testimony was important, but building distrust for the prosecutor was even more important.

"Why did your father lease the property to the oil company?"

Nikki sighed heavily, and a tear slid down her cheek. She was the picture of a grieving child. Ashley couldn't have asked for a better witness. "It was because of me."

"What do you mean?"

Nikki explained her agoraphobia to the jury and how it came out of grief after losing her mother. She told them how she was getting along just fine so long as she stayed on the property. Then Matthew Larson started showing up. Everywhere.

At this point, several jurors had open expressions of sympathy for Nikki, who had lost both of her parents in such a short span of time, and some were turning to look toward the audience like they were looking for Matthew.

"Explain to the jury how your condition and Matthew's behaviors have to do with your father backing out of his gentleman's agreement with Lucas?"

"He aggravated my condition, then used it as a way to convince Dad to agree to the windmills. He claimed I'd need income for the rest of my life, and that's why dad did it."

"Did Lucas know about Matthew's involvement?"

"I assume he does now."

Ashley issued a self-deprecating chuckle. "I didn't word that very well. Did Lucas know about Matthew's involvement at the time?"

"No. He blamed Dad."

"Why didn't you explain it to him?"

"I couldn't leave the house because of my agoraphobia, and he wasn't answering my calls. He's also a farm boy through and through, so he didn't have an online presence and rarely checked his email."

"How did you know he blamed your father?"

"Anyone would blame my father."

"Objection, speculation," Charles said.

"I think the cat's already out of the bag," Judge Ahrenson said, "But sustained. Jury, you should disregard the witness's last statement."

Ashley didn't mind this turn of events either. Once again, it highlighted testimony that Charles did not want the jury to know and would likely be a point of interest because of it. If you ever want someone to listen, tell them they can't.

"I don't have any further questions," Ashley said.

"Cross?" Judge Ahrenson's gaze swung to Charles and the remainder of the courtroom did the same.

"Thank you, your honor," Charles said.

"Now, Nikki, would you say you were close with your father?"

"I lived with him. I don't know how much closer you can get to someone who isn't your spouse."

"I don't mean physically close. I mean emotionally close."

"Not particularly, but I think that's common with women. We tend to be closer to our mothers."

"You were present on January 30, correct?"

"Yes."

"You heard a gunshot, right?"

"Yes."

"Did you see your father as he was shot?"

"No. I knew it was going to happen, so I stayed in the kitchen."

"You *knew*."

"We've already been over this. He had an aura. I didn't know he was going to get shot. I just knew he'd die, and I didn't want to see it happen."

"What if he died of a heart attack? It would have been possible to help, right?"

"No. I'm not a doctor. And like I said, my interventions never work. I've tried in the past, back before Mom died and I was able to leave the house."

"Okay," Charles said in a *you're crazy, but moving on* sort of way. "The Defendant shot your father, didn't he?"

"That's what you say."

"Well, what did you see?"

"I already told you. I didn't see anything. I stayed in the kitchen."

Charles shook his head like a parent might when disappointed with a child. "No further questions."

"Re-direct?" Judge Ahrenson said.

"Just one question. How many shots did you hear?"

"One."

"Nothing further," Ashley said.

"Thank you, ma'am," Judge Ahrenson said, "Your testimony is completed, and someone here will shut off this screen."

Katie hopped up, switched off the TV, and then wheeled it off to the side.

Judge Ahrenson glanced at the clock on the wall. "It's about time for the morning break. Let's recess. We will reconvene in ten minutes."

Everyone in the courtroom rose and watched as the jury filtered out. One or two members looked at Ashley from the corner of their eye. This was the first time any of them had even attempted looking at the defense. Maybe she was starting to break through.

36

KATIE

Ashley didn't leave the table during the break, so Katie didn't either. Ashley spent the time going over notes and looking up, scanning the crowd every few minutes. She was looking for someone, but Katie knew better than to interrupt her when she was so deep in thought. If there was anything Katie could do to help, Ashley would ask.

Nine minutes later, everyone was back in the courtroom, standing as the jurors filed back in. All but two kept their heads down and their eyes averted.

"Call your next witness."

"Defense calls Theresa Walker."

Theresa was already in the courtroom. She'd come at the very start of the break and sat directly behind Ashley, Katie, and Lucas. Ashley had seen her come in, so she wasn't the person she had been scanning the crowd trying to find. Theresa rose from her seat and walked up to the bench.

"Please raise your right hand," Judge Ahrenson said.

She did so.

"Do you swear or affirm to tell the truth, the whole truth, so help you?"

"I do." Her voice was shaky.

"Have a seat." The judge nodded to the witness box next to him.

Theresa did as instructed, and Ashley waited for her to get situated before she started questioning.

"Ms. Walker, where are you employed?"

"I'm a jailer, here at the Brine County Jail."

"Do you know Lucas Campbell?"

"Yes. He's an inmate at the jail."

Ashley had been agonizing over this line of questioning for days. Part of her didn't want the jury to know that Lucas was in custody, but she also needed Theresa's testimony. Ultimately, Katie convinced Ashley that the jury would already subconsciously know Lucas was in jail. It was a murder charge, the most serious of all offenses. If murder wasn't worthy of pre-trial incarceration, then nothing was.

"How long has he been there?"

"Since January 31."

"How has he behaved?"

"Objection, irrelevant," Charles said.

"What's the relevance of this line of questioning, Ms. Montgomery?" Judge Ahrenson asked.

"If you allow me a little leeway here, your honor, I promise you will see where this is going."

"I'll allow it. But you should keep whatever you are doing here on a tight leash, Ms. Montgomery."

"Yes, your honor."

All eyes swung back to the witness. The room was still, silent.

"I'm sorry, can you repeat the question?"

Theresa was nervous. Anyone could see that. Her voice quavered and she kept fidgeting with the hem of her shirt.

"Yes. How has Lucas behaved in jail?"

"For the most part, good. I had no issues with him until he started taking that medication."

"Please explain."

"He was having trouble sleeping, and I think it was someone from your office who brought in his prescription sleeping pills."

"What kind of pills?"

"Zolozien."

Katie glanced over at Charles. He was leaning forward with his hands pressed down on the table, eyes bouncing from Ashley to Theresa as they asked and answered questions. He had no idea where this was going, and it was putting him wrong-footed when it came to objections.

"Did Lucas take the Zolozien?"

"Yes. We gave it to him in the dosage listed on the side of the bottle, one pill at nighttime."

"May I approach your honor?"

"You may."

Ashley glanced over at Katie, and she produced a plastic baggie containing a prescription pill bottle. Ashley took it and stood, striding up to Theresa.

"I'm showing you what's labeled as Defense Exhibit A. Do you know what this is?"

"Yes. It is the Zolozien pill bottle."

"Is this the same pill bottle that contained the Zolozien pills you gave Lucas in the jail?"

Ashley handed Theresa the baggie, and she flipped it over, studying the pill bottle from all angles. "It looks like it."

"Your honor, I'd like to offer Defense's Exhibit A into evidence."

Judge Ahrenson's eyes drifted to Charles. "Any objection?"

"Yes. Relevance. I fail to see what the point is in all this testimony or this exhibit."

Katie shook her head. Charles had no idea what was coming. Ashley's strategy was working, at least when it came to the prosecutor. The jury might be another story, though.

"I'll allow it. Exhibit A is accepted, but Ms. Montgomery..."

Ashley looked up at the judge.

"Tight leash."

"Got it."

"Defense Exhibit A is accepted into evidence."

"Did you notice any changes in Lucas after giving him the Zolozien?"

"Yes. Every night he sleepwalked."

"Objection!" This time Charles shot out of his seat.

Judge Ahrenson's eyes swung to the prosecutor. He didn't even bother asking the basis of the objection. He just sat there, coldly considering Charles.

"The State requests that the Court take a matter up outside the presence of the jury."

Half the jury shifted in their seats, and one person actually groaned. They were growing tired of Charles.

"Very well," Judge Ahrenson said. He turned to the jury. "Ladies and gentlemen of the jury, please follow the court attendant to the jury room. I don't know how long this will take. We will call you back when it is time to return."

The jury stood and followed the court attendant out of the courtroom. Not one of them seemed pleased with the development. When they were gone, everyone returned to their seats.

"What's the problem, Mr. Hanson?" Judge Ahrenson said once the loud creaking of the benches in the gallery had subsided.

"She's using an insanity defense and she hasn't noticed insanity or diminished capacity," Charles said, pointing at Ashley like a petulant child.

The rules of criminal procedure required defense attorneys to file formal notifications well before trial if they intended to use certain defenses. Insanity and its cousin, diminished capacity, required such notice.

"No, I'm not," Ashley responded, coolly, calmly.

"Yes, you are. Why else would you bring up medication if not to prove that he was under the influence of that medication, so he's not guilty."

"Yes, Ms. Montgomery. What is the relevance of the line of questioning if not to go to the Defendant's state of mind at the time of the offense?" Judge Ahrenson asked.

Ashley sucked in a deep breath, then released it slowly. This, too, had been a gamble. Ashley and Katie had discussed it multiple times, going back and forth on potential strategies. They could have noticed an insanity defense, that would have been the safe route, but that would have tipped Charles off and delayed the trial as he had his own expert from the state's side evaluate Lucas. Again, they'd decided on the element of surprise, but they also risked losing the evidence entirely.

"Mr. Hanson is right, the defense did not notice insanity or diminished capacity, but it is our position that this step was not necessary. That's because we are not claiming Lucas was insane at the time of the offense. We aren't claiming that he was so severely mentally ill that he didn't understand the nature and the quality of his actions. We are also not claiming diminished capacity. That would require a showing that Lucas was under the influence of some medication or drug, and that made him unable to form the proper intent. That's not our claim either."

"Then where are you going with this?" Judge Ahrenson asked. "If the medicine didn't affect his state of mind, then how is it relevant?"

"Because he was asleep."

"That's insanity," Charles shouted.

"No. It's more of an alibi defense," Ashley responded, her tone still calm. "He wasn't there because he was sleeping."

A small smile quirked into the corner of Judge Ahrenson's mouth. It seemed pretty clear by his expression that he was impressed with Ashley's ingenuity and would likely rule in her favor.

"Alibi has to be noticed, too," Charles whined. He, too, saw where this was going.

"Alibi does have to be noticed," Ashley responded, "But it also requires us to list where the Defendant was, and who can vouch for their presence. Here, we would have had to list a dead person and the scene of the crime. It isn't exactly an Alibi defense either."

Judge Ahrenson was silent for a long moment, considering the arguments of the parties. Then he spoke. "I agree it isn't insanity and it isn't diminished capacity. It also isn't alibi. It's a little of all three. However, the Rules of Criminal Procedure don't call for notice of a defense that is a little of each. Only the defenses specifically listed in the rules must be noticed. Since this defense does not fit snugly in any of the three categories, I'm going to allow the testimony."

He paused for a moment, waiting for any additional remarks from the attorneys, then he motioned to the court attendant. She came closer to the bench.

"Bring the jury back. We're ready for testimony again."

The jury returned, and Katie couldn't help thinking of the Catholic

Church and all the movement. Standing, kneeling, standing, kneeling, sitting. That's what the jury seemed to be doing during this trial.

"Your witness," Judge Ahrenson said to signal that Ashley could start questioning again.

"Thank you, your honor. Now, where was I?" Ashley paused, tapping her index finger against her chin. "Oh, yes, sleepwalking."

Theresa nodded. She'd seemed frightened before, but after seeing the heated exchange between prosecution and defense, she looked positively terrified. As much as Katie hated to admit it, it seemed entirely likely that the Sheriff's Department would find a way to fire Theresa after all this. They would claim it had nothing to do with the trial, of course. It would start with the jail administrator getting nitpicky about her work, writing her up for things that had never been an issue in the past. Eventually, she'd be terminated.

"Tell me, did Lucas sleepwalk that very first night you gave him Zolozien?"

"Yes, he did."

"What did he do?"

"He's in a cell by himself. He doesn't quite fit in with the other inmates, so I've got him alone. Anyway, he started banging his fists against the bars. He'd hit them over and over again, making this loud thumping noise. I was busy booking in a drunk driver when it started, so I couldn't get over there right away. When I finally did, I found Luas standing there, his fists bloody."

"What did you do?"

"Naturally, I was shocked. This wasn't normal behavior for him. I told him to knock it off."

"Did he stop?"

"No. Then I noticed that he wasn't even looking at me. His eyes were open, but he was staring straight through me."

"So, then, what did you do?"

"I didn't know what to do. I've been told never to wake someone who is sleepwalking, and I felt sure that was what was happening with him. I called the doctor that attends to our inmates. She happened to be on her way over to deal with an unrelated issue with another inmate. We woke him up together. When he came out of it, I'm telling you, he was completely shocked. His demeanor changed back to the Lucas I knew, and he started crying. I mean, really broke down sobbing."

"Do you know why he was crying?"

"He didn't say, and I didn't ask questions—it's not my place—but I thought—"

"Objection. Speculation."

"Sustained."

Theresa looked from the prosecutor to the judge, her eyes wide in a frozen, deer in headlights sort of expression. Katie studied the jury. They were considering Theresa with open sympathy.

"Did Lucas have any other sleepwalking episodes?"

"It happened every time he took that medicine."

"The Zolozien?"

"Yes."

"After seven bouts of it, he decided he didn't want to take it anymore. He said he didn't care that he wasn't getting any sleep. He couldn't keep waking up like this, having no idea what he was doing, especially after what happened to Gerald."

"He said that?" Ashley asked, "'Especially after what happened to Gerald?'"

"Yes. He did."

"What did that mean?"

"Objection, speculation."

The judge sustained the objection, but Ashley didn't seem bothered by it, and there was little doubt as to why that was. She'd made her insinuation, and the jury had understood. Any time a jury member looked at Charles, they scowled. If they'd liked him in the beginning, that had changed through Theresa's testimony. Ashley was making headway, or so Katie hoped, but trials could change on a dime. Any wrong step could backfire and result in Lucas spending the rest of his life incarcerated.

37

ASHLEY

The court didn't take a break after Theresa's testimony, which was fine with Ashley. The next few witnesses would be quicker.

"Defense calls Doctor Benjamin Mason to the stand," Ashley said.

Katie ushered the doctor into the courtroom and guided him up to the witness stand. Several of the jurors smiled at him, and one even waved. Charles fumed over at the prosecution bench, his nostrils flaring, but he didn't object. He'd probably noticed that he was mostly losing the objections, and they only made him look like he was trying to hide evidence.

"Please step up to the bench," Judge Ahrenson said.

Doctor Mason complied, and the judge swore him in. He was a small man, standing only approximately five feet five inches. He was thin and wore his characteristic gold colored wire-rimmed glasses. Most of his hair was gone, but there was a bit stretched along the back of his head and a tuft right on top, all of the purest white. He stepped up into the witness box and had a seat, turning his kind green eyes to Ashley.

"Good morning, doctor."

"Hello there, Ms. Montgomery," Doctor Mason said, adjusting his glasses.

"I have some questions for you about a patient, my client here, Lucas Campbell." Ashley patted Lucas lightly on the back.

"Yes, good to see you again, young man." The Doctor nodded at Lucas.

"Have you treated Lucas in the past?"

"Normally, I couldn't answer that question—HIPAA and all that—but since Lucas has signed a release of information for me to talk to really anyone that will listen, I'm free to answer your questions."

"Okay."

"Oh," Doctor Mason chuckled. "I failed to answer the question. Yes. I've seen Lucas in the past."

"How long have you been his doctor?"

"All his life. I started working with him when he was just a little tyke." Doctor Mason held his hand out and lowered it to the floor, demonstrating a toddler-sized height.

This was invaluable testimony. Not only for what would come later, but because Doctor Mason was humanizing Lucas. The jury was technically prohibited from drawing conclusions based on a defendant's arrest and incarceration, but that wasn't realistic. The presumption of innocence was a nice theory, like Karl Marx's idea that everyone works and shares, but that idea did not carry through to practice.

"Are you still his doctor?"

"Yes."

"May I approach, your honor?" Ashley asked.

"Yes."

Ashley stood, first heading for the court reporter. She was the keeper of exhibits. She picked up an exhibit and brought it over to Doctor Mason.

"What I am showing you is Defendant's Exhibit A. Do you recognize this pill bottle?"

"It's a prescription pill bottle. The ones they hand out down here at the local pharmacy."

"Is that the pharmacy that Lucas Campbell uses?"

"That's where I've always called my prescriptions for him."

"What is the prescription for?"

"Oh, my, you're going to make me put on my reading glasses. Hold on." He reached into the small pocket at the front of his shirt, and switched his round, wire-rimmed glasses for a pair of two small ovals. Then he stared down at the bottle, a frown forming on his face. "Why, this is Zolozien. A mighty high dosage, indeed."

"Who is the prescribing doctor listed on that pill bottle?"

"It says my name, but I didn't approve this script. I would never approve something like this for Lucas."

"Why not?"

"Because he has a history of sleep problems, among those was sleepwalking, and this kind of medication can cause sleepwalking."

"How do you know that?"

"It's a well-known side-effect. I believe that there's even litigation out there about it. I'm sure you'd know more about that as a lawyer, though."

"Why is sleepwalking a concern to you regarding Lucas?" Ashley asked.

"It matters because Lucas has nearly killed himself sleepwalking. It was mostly in his younger years, but he once walked outside and laid down in the middle of the road. Luckily, the car that drove through saw him and stopped before hitting him. Then there was another time that he left the house and walked halfway to town in bare feet. By the time his father tracked him down, the bottoms of his feet were bloody messes. There are more stories. I won't bore you with them all. I'm just saying that I have known of his condition for a very long time, and I also have known that he seemed to grow out of it. Still, I would never prescribe a medication like this."

"So, it's a forgery?"

"Yes. It has to be."

"Other than you, who else would have access to your records?"

"My nurse and my office manager."

"Would either your nurse or office manager have access to your prescription pads?"

"They aren't supposed to. I keep them locked in my office, but I suppose someone could have taken the key and stolen one or two without my notice."

"Are either of those employees in romantic relationships?"

"Well, my nurse is my wife, so yes she better be." He chuckled and some of the jurors chuckled along with him.

"What about your office manager?"

Charles opened his mouth to object, but then seemed to think better of it.

"She's dating that fella nobody seems to like. That realtor, Matthew Larson."

Several members of the gallery gasped at the revelation, and Judge Ahrenson gave them a hard look.

Ashley turned and looked at Katie, who was sitting next to Lucas, trying to keep her expression neutral. This information came from Katie's hunch and some deep digging. Ashley would have never followed up on this information as potential leads. She simply didn't have the time, and what time she had wouldn't have been wasted on something she would consider a pipe dream. But it wasn't a pipe dream. It was a bombshell.

38

KATIE

It was nearing eleven thirty. Katie expected the Judge to call for a break, but he didn't. He excused Dr. Mason and told Ashley to call her next witness. Ashley turned and scanned the gallery. Her eyes bounced from one person to the next. It was the first time throughout the entire trial that Katie had seen even a hint of anxiety in her friend.

"Where is he? Where is he?" Ashley mumbled. "I shouldn't have taken this risk."

"Who?" Katie whispered back.

Ashley merely shook her head. "I don't see him."

"Do you need me to stall?"

"Ms. Montgomery," Judge Ahrenson said. "You can call your next witness."

"Yes, your honor," Ashley said, but she didn't turn back around to address him. Instead, she continued scanning the crowd, a furrow etched deeply in her brow. It lasted several, tense moments, then her gaze locked on someone, and all the tension left her body. She spun back around, facing the judge, and said, "Defense calls Matthew Larson."

Everyone seemed to react to that. Several jurors leaned so far forward that they were nearly falling out of their seats. Members of the audience shifted their bodies, the benches groaning beneath their weight as they turned to look around. Even Judge Ahrenson's eyes widened with surprise.

Katie had to fight the urge to smile. She and Ashley had not discussed calling Matthew as a witness, so she had no idea what tricks Ashley had up her sleeve. Whatever they were, it would surely lead to an unexpected defense. Of that, she was certain. Whether it turned out to be successful or not was certainly not a foregone conclusion, though. Ashley was taking a serious risk.

"Mr. Larson," Ashley said, standing up and turning all the way around, so she faced the back of the courtroom. "Come on up here and join us."

"Do I have to?" Matthew sounded scared. Katie could hear his voice, but since they were both still seated, she could not see him.

"Yes. You've been called as a witness for the Defense," Judge Ahrenson said, sitting back and rising to his full height.

"I don't want to."

What a baby, Katie thought, but it was working wonders on the jury. Some of them were even scribbling notes on their notepads.

"You will come up here and testify or I will hold you in contempt of this court and place you in jail until you change your mind. Do you understand me?"

Part of Katie hoped he would refuse to testify. Matthew jailed felt almost as good as Ashley questioning him under oath, but not quite.

"Fine." Matthew stood, and Katie caught the first glimpse of his face. It was as white as a sheet of clean printer paper.

He moved up to the front of the courtroom, trudging so slowly it seemed like he would never reach the front, but he eventually did.

"Raise your right hand," Judge Ahrenson said. With the other witnesses he had asked them politely, using *please* and a softer tone of voice. All that geniality was gone now, and he bellowed the words like he was Zeus passing judgment from atop Mount Olympus.

Matthew reluctantly raised his hand. It was limp at the wrist, like that would somehow absolve him of his obligation to tell the truth.

"Do you swear or affirm to tell the truth, the whole truth, so help you?"

"I do," he grumbled.

"Sit." Judge Ahrenson nodded toward the witness box. When Matthew had reluctantly claimed his seat, the judge turned to Ashley, his blue eyes sparkling with excitement. He was enjoying this, and he wasn't even attempting to hide it. "He's all yours, Ms. Montgomery."

"Matthew Larson," Ashley said, "Look at you. Finally in the hotseat."

"Objection. That wasn't a question," Charles said.

"Jeopardy rules apply, Ms. Montgomery," Judge Ahrenson said, but he was smiling and even chuckling a bit as he said it.

"Yes, your honor. How does it feel to finally be in the hot seat?"

"I don't like it. Why am I here?"

"I'm asking the questions today, Mr. Larson. Your job is to answer them."

"Okay."

"There was an auction earlier today, wasn't there?"

"Objection. Relevance."

"Overruled."

Charles was right. Ashley hadn't laid the background for a causal connection between any auction and this case, but Katie sensed the judge was going to let her run wild with this witness. Rules of evidence weren't going to apply. Not that it really mattered. If the jury acquitted and Ashley won, the state couldn't appeal. If the State won and Lucas was convicted, Ashley wouldn't complain about the judge allowing defense evidence that should have been excluded. Besides, he was about to retire. What did it matter to him anymore?

"Answer the question," Judge Ahrenson said.

"I don't remember the question."

Judge Ahrenson issued an exaggerated sigh, then said, "Read it back to him."

The court reporter pressed several buttons on her steno machine, then looked down at the tape. "The question pending is, 'There was an auction earlier today, wasn't there?'"

A silence followed.

"Well, answer the question," Judge Ahrenson said.

"Yes, there was."

"Whose property was up for sale?" Ashley asked.

"The land belonging to Lucas and Albert Campbell."

"Are you now the proud owner of that property?"

"Objection," Charles said, but he seemed defeated. "Relevance."

"Overruled."

"Yes. I purchased that property."

"For how much?"

"Fifteen thousand dollars."

"You purchased twenty acres, a farmhouse, and all the outbuildings for fifteen thousand dollars. Excuse my language, but that is one hell of a deal," Ashley said.

One of the jurors chuckled and brought a hand over her mouth, trying to hide it. Not that it would have mattered to the judge.

"Yes. I got a good deal."

"Anyone else out there bidding on it?"

"No. I thought the neighbor might, but she didn't show."

"She didn't show because she's an agoraphobic, isn't she? She can't leave the house."

"If you say so."

"That's not news to you, is it? Her agoraphobia."

"It isn't."

"You used Nikki's condition to get the victim in this case, Gerald Mock, to lease his property to one of your clients, didn't you?"

"Objection. Relevance."

Several members of the jury visibly winced when Charles spoke up. Why was he continuing to object? The Judge was clearly giving Ashley free reign to do whatever she wanted. The objections were only further convincing the jury that Charles and the State were the villains, Lucas and Ashley the victims.

"Overruled."

Again there was a silence.

"I'll repeat the question," Ashley said, leaning forward and pressing her palms into the table. "You used Nikki Nelson's mental health to convince Gerald Mock to lease the windmill property to your client, didn't you?"

"Yes."

"But you weren't satisfied with Gerald's property, were you?"

"If you are asking if my client wanted more land, the answer is yes."

"You have been trying to get me to sell some of my property, haven't you?"

"Yes."

"And what did I tell you?"

"No."

"Then what did you do?"

"I discovered your sister owned seven of the acres, and she's likely going to lease it to my client."

"You found another way, didn't you?"

"Yes."

"Because that's what you do, isn't it?"

"I'm a salesman, Ashley. That's what salesmen do. We work on commission. If we all took the first 'no' we got, we'd all be in the poorhouse."

"Well, that certainly isn't a problem plaguing you these days—the poorhouse—is it?"

"No."

"You wanted Lucas Campbell's property, right?"

"I own it now, so yes."

"But back before Lucas's arrest. You were trying to get him to sell or lease his property to you or your client, weren't you?"

"Yes."

"But he wouldn't, would he?"

"No, He's the most stubborn person I've ever met."

"But you found another way, didn't you?"

"I don't like what you are implying."

"You have a girlfriend, don't you?"

"Objection," Charles said.

"Overruled."

"Yes. I am dating someone."

"You've been dating that person for close to a year and a half, right?"

"Something like that."

"That person works as an office manager for Doctor Benjamin Mason, doesn't she?"

"Yes."

"She had access to Lucas's files. She knew of Lucas's childhood sleep-walking condition, didn't she?"

"Objection."

"Overruled." The judge wasn't even interested in hearing the basis for Charles's objections anymore. Like everyone else, he just wanted to hear what Matthew would say.

"She works for the doctor, so yeah, she has access to all his files."

"Did she tell you about Lucas's history with sleep disorders?"

"Yes."

"Working in a doctor's office, she would also know the side effects to Zolozien, wouldn't she?"

"Yeah."

"Did you have her steal an empty prescription pad from Doctor Mason and forge a Zolozien prescription for Lucas?"

"I didn't *force* her to do anything. She saw how distraught I was. My client needed more land, and they were threatening to hire a new realtor. She wanted to help."

"And then you had her call Lucas and tell him that the doctor had changed his mind, didn't you?"

"I did."

Katie glanced over at Charles. His face had gone completely white, and he was sitting back in his chair, looking at Matthew with a dumbfounded expression.

"I didn't commit any crimes, though," Matthew insisted. "I mean, she might have, but I didn't do anything wrong."

The sad thing was that he was right. Unless his devoted girlfriend squealed on him, he'd probably leave her holding the bag. Although, she was going to lose her reputation, her job, and possibly her freedom. Some women are completely loyal to their boyfriends, which had always baffled Katie, but consequences like those she'd be facing might chip away at that devotion.

"You knew Lucas would take the medicine because he had come to the doctor with complaints of insomnia, right?"

"I knew about his inability to sleep, yeah."

"And the weather at that time, January in Iowa, is mighty cold, isn't it?"

"Yeah."

"You hoped Lucas would wander out of the house and freeze to death, didn't you?"

"I hoped something would happen that would get him to change his mind about selling the property. You don't understand about that area of the county. We learned that wind corridor is the best in the area."

"Like dying or imprisonment for life after shooting his neighbor," Ashley continued, ignoring the second half of his answer.

"I didn't know what would change his mind."

"You also knew that Lucas needed money and the farm was about to be foreclosed on, didn't you?"

"I did. That was a matter of public record."

"So, you decided you wanted a cut of the money. You wanted to buy the property and lease the land to the windmill company yourself, didn't you?"

"I've done all the work. I deserve more than the chump change I've been getting on these commissions."

"Thank you, Matthew," Ashley said with a Cheshire grin. "I don't have any further questions for you. It's possible that Mr. Hanson over here will have a few, though."

Everyone turned to Charles. He hadn't moved from the last time Katie had looked over at him. He still looked as though the world was crumbling around him.

"No questions."

"Get out of my witness box," Judge Ahrenson said.

Matthew stood and started making his way toward the back of the courtroom where he had been seated. As he passed people in the gallery, they leaned away from him, often whispering something in their neighbor's ear while watching him pass. When he took his seat beside Tucker Caine, Tucker scooted over, creating space for two people to sit between the two. Even he now realized that there was no political gain in buddying up with Matthew Larson.

"Do you have any other witnesses?" Judge Ahrenson asked Ashley.

Ashley's gaze shifted to Lucas. "Possibly one."

The judge nodded, knowing. "Ladies and gentlemen of the jury, now has come the time for us to break for lunch."

They stood, some stretching, and followed the court attendant out of the courtroom. When they were gone, the judge turned back to Ashley.

"Do you have some record you want to make?"

Without outright asking it, the judge was asking if Lucas was planning to testify. Defendants had a right to testify. If a Defendant chose not to exercise that right, the judge would make a record of it outside the presence of the jury. This was so that on appeal, when the court of appeals only had the written record to rely upon, they would know that the Defendant had been given an opportunity and declined.

Ashley glanced back at Lucas. "I don't know yet, your honor. Can we take the lunch break to think it over, then return with an answer before we bring the jury back in?"

Judge Ahrenson nodded. "That's acceptable."

The judge stood and left the courtroom. Then the gallery slowly emptied of people. When Katie looked again, both Tucker Caine and Matthew Larson were gone. She wondered if they'd return. She hoped not, but that Matthew Larson was insistent. She wouldn't put it past him to show up thinking that the prosecutor would save his reputation. Seeing Charles' reaction, Katie seriously doubted that.

39

ASHLEY

Ashley made it a habit to counsel clients against testifying in trial, especially if things were looking good. It wasn't an easy task because it went against human nature. People wanted to explain themselves. Nobody was a villain in their own story. They always had an excuse for their behavior. Many thought that if they could explain themselves in their own words, the jury would understand.

The problem was that quite often the jury did not understand. They couldn't. They didn't come from the same background. They weren't born into families with severe, debilitating mental illness or homes full of violence. They weren't sexually assaulted when they were children or raised by parents high on drugs. They weren't offered methamphetamine at the tender age of ten and addicted by eleven. These were the lives of so many of Ashley's clients, and there was no way that a jury could fully understand what it was like to be them. Ashley couldn't even grasp it.

But Lucas, he was different. This whole case had been different. The jury not only understood Lucas's frustration toward the windmills, they'd been living it themselves. It was the sleepwalking part that gave her pause. The defense was unusual, that's why it was unexpected, and that was what gave it power.

"What are you thinking?" Katie said.

Ashley had been alone in the courtroom, but Katie had just returned. She'd popped out to use the restroom. Lucas's guards had taken him to do the same. He'd be back soon, though.

"About Lucas testifying."

"Let's talk it out," Katie said, dropping into her chair at counsel table. "Are you leaning toward 'yes' or 'no?'"

This was one of the things Ashley loved about working with Katie. So much of Ashley's job happened in her head, and sometimes she got bogged down. It helped to say the words, puzzle them out aloud. She'd never really had that opportunity with other people.

"A little of both."

Katie cocked her head to the side, puzzled, because, honestly, how could it be both? "Explain."

Ashley sighed. "Things have been going remarkably well. I think we've at least got half the jury members on our side or leaning our way. That's enough to hang them, which would be a win in the sense that Lucas wouldn't be a felon—at least not yet—but a loss in the sense that he remains in custody, and we have to do this whole dog and pony show again and next time Charles will know what we are up to. We'll also have a different judge who won't allow even half this evidence. This defense won't be effective twice."

"And then what?"

"Lucas ends up convicted."

"It sounds like you have no choice. You have to put Lucas on the stand," Katie said.

"How did you get there?"

"If you end evidence here, the best case scenario is a hung jury. You just said yourself that a hung jury is just the long road to a conviction. That doesn't do Lucas any good. So, why not throw the dice and try for the acquittal? If Lucas bombs on the stand, then so what? It ends up shortening the process, but the result remains the same. The way I see it, your only option is to take the chance."

Katie was oversimplifying it because Ashley had no real data from which to draw her conclusions. The idea that she had only half the jury convinced could be dead wrong. She could have all or none, she didn't know for sure. Yet Katie did have a point. The risk was probably worth taking.

"It'll ultimately be Lucas's decision, but I think you're right," Ashley said.

"Well, then, it's a good thing they are bringing Lucas back now."

Lucas sat down and all three waited for his guards to step back far enough to allow them a private conversation.

"How do you think we are doing?" Lucas said, looking from Ashley to Katie, and then back to Ashley. He was seated in the middle with his chair slightly back to allow them all into the conversation.

"Good," Ashley said, "But not quite good enough. Or at least that's my assessment."

"Ditto," Katie said.

"So, what do we need to do?"

"I think you should testify," Ashley said.

"Are you sure about that? I'm not very good at public speaking. What if I clam up?"

"That's a possibility, I'm not going to lie," Ashley said.

One of the other risks in a defendant testifying is the pressure. Sometimes the anxiety of having so many eyes upon them could make them stammer and sweat, fidget and freeze. All of which could be misinterpreted as signs of untruths, when, in reality, they only showed anxiety.

"But it's your best shot at winning," Katie said.

"We know it is a risk," Ashley said, "And that's why only you can make this decision. We're just here to guide you."

"So," Katie said, "what do you want to do?"

40

KATIE

"Is there any record you need to make, Ms. Montgomery?" Judge Ahrenson asked.

Ashley turned toward Lucas, getting one last affirmation, before she said, "No, your honor. My client has decided to testify."

"Very well." He seemed to approve of the decision. Judges weren't supposed to convey their thoughts one way or another, but the jury wasn't there yet, so it had no practical effect on the trial. "Bring the jury back."

Within minutes, all thirteen jurors were in their chairs looking at Ashley with curious expressions. They didn't have seating arrangements, but Katie found that people often went back to the same chair they'd originally occupied. It was something most people did without thinking. Perhaps a comfort thing.

"Call your next witness," Judge Ahrenson said.

"Defense calls Lucas Campbell."

Lucas stood. He wore a light blue button-up shirt and a pair of beige slacks, both borrowed from Katie's father. His hands visibly shook. He balled them into fists, then released them, and as he did, Katie could see that he still wore a wedding band around his ring finger. His expression was solemn as he approached the witness stand, all eyes on him.

The room was deathly quiet. Nobody spoke. Nobody moved. There was no coughing out in the gallery. No creaks of benches or sniffles of noses. It was like someone pressed the pause button on everyone other than Lucas, who slowly trudged toward the stand like a man on his way to the gallows.

"Do you swear or affirm to tell the truth?" Judge Ahrenson said once Lucas had lifted his right hand.

"I promise."

The word *promise* caught Katie's attention. It was different than the way every other witness had responded. They had all said "I do" or "I will." There was something powerful about adding a promise to a swear.

"Please take a seat." Judge Ahrenson nodded to the witness box then turned his gaze to Ashley.

"Hello, Lucas," Ashley said.

Her tone was so calm that it baffled Katie. She knew that Ashley's insides were as tight and twisted as her own, yet she betrayed no sign of that anxiety. She supposed that was just one of the many things Ashley had learned throughout her fifteen years as a defense attorney.

"Umm, hello." His voice shook.

"You're a little nervous, aren't you?"

"Yes."

"Why are you nervous?"

"I'm a farmer. I don't do a lot of public speaking."

"Just focus on me, answer my questions truthfully and honestly, and you'll be alright. Can you do that?"

Lucas swallowed hard and nodded.

This strategy of Ashley's was genius. Many of the witnesses had addressed the jury directly, especially the professional witnesses like the forensic guys and law enforcement officers. Lucas did not have the confidence to do that, so Ashley was explaining the difference before the jury had a chance to give it much thought.

"You'll have to answer out loud," Ashley nodded to the court reporter.

"Sorry, yes. I can do that."

"You know why you are here today, right?"

"Yes."

"So, I won't belabor that point, okay?"

"Okay."

"I want to talk about what you remember about January 29 into the early morning hours of January 30.

"Okay."

"What did you do that day?"

"I got out of bed around eight o'clock in the morning. It was winter, so I didn't have anything to do out in the fields. I tinkered around with some of the farming equipment, repairing anything that needed work."

"I noticed that you said 'got out of bed' instead of 'woke up.' Why is that?"

"I wasn't sleeping well. I had a lot on my mind. There were some ongoing issues that were weighing on me. It had been a long time since I was able to make it all the way through the night. My divorce was finalized that week, and I received final notice that the farm was in foreclosure. If I didn't come up with twenty thousand dollars by," he paused, thinking, "I guess it was earlier today, the entire property was going to auction."

"What else did you do?"

"I had a doctor's appointment at ten o'clock."

"What was the appointment for?"

"Just my yearly physical."

"Who is your doctor?"

"Doctor Mason."

"Did you go to your appointment?"

"Yes."

"What was the result of that appointment?"

"What do you mean?"

"Did he prescribe you any medications?"

"No. My blood pressure was pretty high. I explained to him that I was going through a lot and I hadn't slept through the night for as long as I could remember."

"What was his recommendation?"

"Yoga. Setting a nightly routine. Drinking a cup of warm milk before bedtime. Those kinds of things."

"No medicines then?"

"No. And I really didn't expect anything different. I would have liked for him to order something—anything—because I was getting delirious from lack of sleep, but he didn't."

"What did you do after you left Doctor Mason's office?"

"I went home and made some lunch. I made ramen noodles. Dad and I ate together."

"And then what?"

"Then I puttered around the farm some more until I got the call from Doctor Mason's office."

"What call?"

"It was his office assistant. She was calling to tell me the doctor had changed his mind and ordered some Zolozien. She said the script was sent in to my usual pharmacy, the Hy-Vee there on highway twenty, and I could pick it up in an hour or so."

"Did you ask her why the doctor changed his mind?"

"No. I didn't want to push my luck."

"What do you mean by that?"

"Like I said, I was getting desperate. I was so exhausted, yet I couldn't sleep. I don't know if you've ever had problems sleeping, but it is torture lying awake at night watching the clock tick closer and closer to the next day without any relief."

"What did you do?"

"I went back inside and told Dad that I was going back to town. He wasn't super happy about it since I'd just driven back, and the price of gasoline is sky high. I didn't like it either for that very same reason, but I was that tired. I valued nothing above a good night's sleep, that's how desperate I'd become."

"Did you get the medicine?"

"Yes."

"Did you return home after that?"

"Yes."

"Then what did you do?"

"It was nearing suppertime, so I made another batch of Ramen noodles for me and Dad."

"Sounds like you were eating a lot of noodles."

Lucas shrugged. "That's all we could afford."

"What did you do after dinner?"

"Dad and I played a couple games of checkers, and then I went upstairs to go to bed."

"Did your father know about your Zolozien prescription?"

Lucas shook his head. "I didn't tell him. I knew he wouldn't like it. He'd try to talk me out of taking it because of my background with sleepwalking. But, like I said, I was so desperate, I didn't want to hear reason or logic. I just wanted to solve the problem, and taking a pill was a whole lot faster than taking up yoga or getting my body acclimated to a routine."

"What happened after you took the pill and laid down?"

"I went to sleep."

"What do you remember next?"

"I remember waking up to a deputy screaming at me to get down on the floor and put my hands behind my back."

"Did you do that?"

"Yes. And I noticed I was covered in something sticky with a strong metallic smell. It turns out that it was blood, but I didn't realize that at the time."

"Deputy Pitch mentioned that you were eating a bag of Doritos. Where did that come from?"

"I don't have any idea."

"Did you have anything like that in the house?"

"No. Not in a long time. If we did have chips—and that's a big *if*—it would have been an off brand. I didn't have two extra pennies to rub together, let alone five dollars for a bag of expensive chips."

"Was there a convenience store nearby?"

"Not for twenty miles or so."

"Could you have gotten them inside Gerald's house?"

"I doubt it. Honestly, I haven't really given the chips much thought. I missed so much that night. I was covered in my neighbor's blood. The chips were the least of my worries."

"Thank you, Lucas," Ashley said. "I don't have any further questions."

"Cross examination?" Judge Ahrenson said to Charles.

"Yes, your honor." He was smiling, but it was a cruel sort of smile. One that Katie did not expect to go over well with the jury.

"Well, well, well, we've finally got you in the hot seat," Charles said. It was a play off Ashley's words to Matthew Larson earlier that day, but several of the jury members sat back and crossed their arms rather than leaning forward with interest.

"You're saying you don't remember anything about shooting Gerald Mock in the face?"

"I don't."

"You don't remember doing this to him?" Charles pulled up the worst, most gruesome close-up photo of Gerald's face.

Lucas winced, his eyes darting away. "No."

"You *say* you don't remember it, but you aren't denying that you did do it, are you?"

Lucas's gaze darted toward the defense table.

"Don't look at your attorney. She can't answer this question for you. Only you can."

"No. I'm not denying it."

That was bad, but not unexpected. They knew cross-examination was going to be a bitch. The question was how damaging it would be in the end. Katie looked over at the jury. Several of them were writing something in their notepads. That was not a good sign.

"This is a gunshot wound," Charles said, pointing at the inflated picture of Gerald Mock. "Have you ever shot a firearm before?"

"Yes. Many times. I live in the country."

"Then you know that guns aren't exactly quiet."

"No. They aren't."

"A firearm like this." He picked up the shotgun that had previously been introduced into evidence. "Has a kick to it, too, doesn't it?"

"Yes."

"Yet, you didn't wake up at the sound of a shotgun, did you?"

"No."

"You didn't wake up when the gun kicked you, did you?"

"No."

"Help me out here, because that doesn't make a lot of sense."

"I don't know how to explain it, Mr. Hanson. All I can say is that sleep-walking is not like normal sleeping. I didn't wake up when I walked a half mile barefoot over gravel while wearing only boxer shorts and a t-shirt in negative temperatures either. That doesn't make sense, but it still happened."

"But you did wake up when Deputy Pitch shouted at you to get on the ground."

"Yes."

"What was different about that?"

"I don't know. Maybe he had been repeating it long enough to break through the medication."

"Or maybe you are lying."

"Objection," Ashley said. "It is wholly improper to use that word with a witness, and Mr. Hanson knows it."

"Sustained. I'd like counsel to approach the bench."

Ashley stood, and she motioned for Katie to follow. Charles Hanson arrived next to the judge about the same time.

"Mr. Hanson, you are walking a thin line here," Judge Ahrenson said in a tone far too low for the jury to hear. "It is improper to call any witness a liar, but this isn't just any witness. This is the Defendant. You cannot call him a liar. I have half a mind to grant a mistrial right here and right now, but I won't. I won't because I suspect that is your goal here. I will not reward bad behavior."

Katie was taken aback. She hadn't considered that Charles might try to make the case end in a mistrial. It meant that he was worried about the verdict, but it also meant that he'd be stepping over the line of proper court behavior every chance he could get from this point forward. Katie didn't like it, but she had to admit that it wasn't a bad strategy. It gave him a redo, and next time he'd be prepared.

"I know what you are thinking," Judge Ahrenson said, glaring at the prosecutor. "You're thinking you might lose anyway, so why not push the boundaries. I would caution you against that sort of behavior, Mr. Hanson. You may end up getting your mistrial, but you're also going to be defending yourself in front of the ethics board."

Ashley's eyes widened and Charles apologized profusely, looking cowed. The Judge's threat had teeth. Improper court behavior was a viola-tion of the rules of ethics, and those reported by judges were taken seriously. Charles may want to win, but he likely wouldn't stake his law license on it.

"Do we have an understanding?"

"Yes," Charles said.

"Good. Now, get back over there and finish up with this witness."

They all returned to their seats, and Charles said, "No further questions, your honor."

"Re-direct?" Judge Ahrenson said, turning back to Ashley.

This was Ashley's chance to respond to Charles's questions. Ashley had always said re-cross was a double-edged sword. She could try to soften the worst answers, but in doing so, she would also highlight them.

"No further questions."

"Very well, you may step down, sir." Judge Ahrenson said to Lucas.

Lucas stood and walked back to defense table. He collapsed into his chair like his legs could no longer hold his weight for a second longer.

"Any further evidence, Ms. Montgomery?" Judge Ahrenson asked.

"No, your honor. The Defense rests."

41

ASHLEY

"Smoke and mirrors, folks," Charles said at the start of his closing argument. "That's all the defense's case is, an illusion. A clever trick of the hand, telling you to look over here." He waved his right hand in the air. "While the truth lies here." He lifted his left hand. "How do we know that? We look at the facts."

"We know for a fact that the Defendant, Lucas Campbell, shot Gerald Mock. We know he used a shotgun." He walked over to the evidence table and lifted the tagged firearm. "We know one shot was fired at point blank range, doing this to poor, unsuspecting, Mr. Mock." The television monitor sprang to life displaying Gerald's mangled face, brought to life by one of Charles's staff members who was now at counsel table, helping him.

Ashley would do the opposite. She would deliver her closing without anyone else at counsel table. Katie had been a great help with witnesses, but she wanted the jury's last look at Lucas to be him all alone, looking like an average Joe suffering under the wrath and the might of the state government.

"Gerald was unarmed," Charles said. "All he did was answer his door. Then *bang*, his life was over. We know all these things are true. They are fact. How do we know that? The evidence."

Charles took in a heavy breath, then released it. "Lucas was there when the firearm went off. We know that because he was covered in blood. Criminalists from the DCI laboratory told you that without a doubt, the blood belonged to the victim, Gerald Mock. The criminalists also told you that the Defendant had brain matter on him, also a DNA match to Gerald Mock. The Defendant was there when the firearm went off."

"The Defendant fired the firearm. We also know this because ballistics experts compared the shotgun shell and casing to the firearm propped inside the doorway of the Defendant's residence. This gun." He picked up the gun and held it up in the air. "Was absolutely positively one-hundred-percent the gun used to quite literally blow Gerald Mock's brains out. This gun." He shook it in the air. "That is registered and owned by the Defendant. This gun." He shook it in the air again. "That has the Defendant's fingerprints. And if that's not enough evidence to prove that the Defendant was the one to pull the trigger, another criminalist told you that a swab of the Defendant's hands was positive for gunshot residue. The Defendant had this gun, he brought it over to the victim's residence, and then he pulled the trigger at point blank range."

"These are all the things we know. There has been testimony from the defense, excuses, for why the Defendant shot his neighbor. He was mad about the windmills. He'd been duped. He was losing his farm. He was sleepwalking. Excuses, excuses, excuses. They might drum up some sympathy for the Defendant, but they don't excuse him doing this." He pointed to the picture of Gerald's body. "To his neighbor. Nobody has any right to do that. Not to anyone. Not to their worst enemy. And that's what I want you to think about when you go back to deliberations. Think about poor Gerald. He didn't deserve this. When you return, I am asking you to return with a guilty verdict for murder in the first degree. Thank you."

Ashley's heart started fluttering. It always did right before she started her openings and her closings. This was the closest trials got to public speaking. If that wasn't enough pressure, there was the added component that this was the only moment she'd have to sum up her entire defense. It was her only chance to tell the jury what facts were important.

"Ms. Montgomery," Judge Ahrenson said. "Your closing statement."

Ashley took a deep, steadying breath, and then she stood and walked toward the jury. These few moments before she began speaking were always the worst. When all eyes were on her, and she had to focus on every step to ensure she didn't trip and make a complete fool of herself. Yet once she started talking, many of those concerns faded away.

"The State would have you believe that we, Lucas and I, are two magicians trying to trick you into believing something that isn't true. Smoke and mirrors, he said. Yet, not *all* magicians are liars and crooks. What about Houdini? He was not all smoke and mirrors, and neither is our defense."

"You know that because the evidence tells you so," Ashley said, moving along the rail that separated her from the jury. "Sleepwalking has been a lifelong condition for Lucas. Doctor Mason verified that. He also verified that Lucas was known to do life threatening things while he was sleepwalking. You learned that Lucas was desperate to get some sleep. That he had a whole lot of life stressors that were preventing him from getting sleep. You also learned that he was tricked into taking the Zolozien pill that led to this fateful night. Tricked by a man who wanted, and later obtained, his farm at auction. That's the real criminal here. Matthew Larson."

"You all know Mr. Larson. You know what he's been up to in this town. He's pitted neighbor against neighbor, using sneaky tactics to snatch their property out from under them. And that is what happened between Lucas and Gerald. A blood sucking, money grubbing outsider moved into this town and destroyed the tranquility. Lucas may have pulled the trigger, but he didn't know he did. Matthew Larson, though, he should have anticipated it. He did, in fact, anticipate *something* bad would happen. And that's what makes him culpable. So, at the end of the day, when you go back to your deliberations, think about that. Who is the guilty party here? It isn't Gerald. It isn't Lucas. It's Matthew. And we, the defense, are asking that you return with a not guilty verdict."

Ashley turned and returned to her seat, her heart beating like it wanted to burst out of her chest and run across the room. She sat down and Lucas leaned over.

"Thank you," was all he said, and a single tear streaked down his cheek.

Ashley patted him on the hand as Charles rose from his seat to address the jury again. The prosecutor always got a chance to respond to Defense's closing. Ashley thought that was bullshit, but the theory behind it was that they made the accusation and they had the burden, so they got to speak twice.

"I don't have a lot to say here other than this was all a choice for the Defendant. Even if you believe the smoke and mirrors argument, the Defendant had a choice. He chose to take that pill knowing he had a dangerous sleepwalking condition. He chose to keep it a secret when his father was home and could have stayed awake or tried to stop him from going over to Gerald's house with that gun. He chose to keep a firearm in the house. These were all his choices. If he had chosen differently in even one of these instances, we wouldn't be here today. Gerald would be alive and well, feeding his cows, and living his life. But we aren't. And why is that? Because of the Defendant's choices. He may have been tricked in some regards, but these were all facts that he had within his complete control. Find him guilty because that's what he is. Guilty as charged."

There it was. The hole in Ashley's defense. She'd been so hoping that Charles wasn't smart enough to catch on, but she'd been wrong. He'd found the way the jury could have sympathy for Lucas but still convict him of murder in the first degree. And he'd taken a page out of Ashley's book, surprising her with it. He hadn't shown any signs of catching on until the very end, when Ashley would have no chance to respond. It sucked, but there was nothing she could do at this point other than watch the jury as they filed out and hope that she'd done enough to convince them.

42

KATIE

The jury had the case, and Katie watched helplessly as they left the courtroom, each person dropping their cell phones into a basket held by the court attendant as they left. They would no longer be allowed to use the internet or contact outside sources. Deliberation was set to begin.

Once the jury was gone, the courtroom emptied. After having spent several long days watching the presentation of evidence, nobody wanted to spend any more time cooped up in that stuffy room.

"Let's go," Lucas's guards said as they sidled up to the defense table.

"He should stay here," Ashley said. "The jury could come back quickly."

"That would be a bad thing, wouldn't it?" Katie asked.

"It would mean that the jury was all in agreement from the jump. That they didn't have anything to debate, which could either be incredibly good, or incredibly bad."

"So, we want them to stay out for a long time?" Katie asked.

"A long time or a very short time."

"Okay."

They waited in the courtroom, twiddling their thumbs. Ashley had her laptop out and looked like she was catching up on work, but Katie knew better. She could see Ashley's screen and saw that she really wasn't doing anything other than shifting from one search bar to another. It was difficult to think, to focus on anything other than when the jury might come back.

The jailers took Lucas back after the first hour. Ashley was out of excuses to prevent it.

Katie leaned back in her chair and stared up at the ceiling. It was an old courthouse, built during the inception of the town. A great deal of money had been spent on its creation. It had towering ceilings, ornate crown moulding, and hand-painted murals. The cost of creating even the ceiling in today's world would be astronomical.

By the second hour, Katie was up and pacing. She moved back and forth along the length of the courtroom, up and down the aisle, trying to burn off some excess energy. Finally, she stopped beside Ashley and said, "What is taking them so long?"

"I don't know, but it's frustrating. This is one of the worst parts of trials. The waiting. It's like purgatory. The trial is not yet over, so it feels impossible to move on and start focusing on something different. Yet, this jury may not even have a verdict today. The judge could send them home overnight and ask them to reconvene in the morning."

"That long? I don't think I can handle it. What are they talking about anyway?"

"That's the million-dollar question," Ashley said. "I'd love to be a fly on the wall."

"There isn't much they *can* talk about, is there? I mean, they either believe him and they find him not guilty, or they don't, and they convict, right?"

"Not exactly. You saw the jury instructions. There are a lot of lesser included offenses."

"What are the lesser offenses?" Katie asked.

"Well, murder can't occur without an assault, so assault."

"That would be ideal."

"Ideal, but a bit of a longshot. It's a simple misdemeanor, the lowest level of crimes aside from traffic offenses. While the jury isn't told punishment, they would know assault is much less serious than murder and they might not go for it for that reason."

"Okay."

"They could convict him of murder in the second degree."

"We don't want that, though, do we?"

"No. The jury often thinks they are giving someone a break when they render a second degree murder conviction, but they aren't, at least not in Iowa. The sentence is so hefty that it amounts to a life sentence anyway."

"Is that what you think they are doing? Going through lesser included offenses?"

Ashley shrugged. "I have no idea what they are doing. They could have a decision but are holding out for a free dinner. These things are impossible to predict."

After the third hour, even Ashley had lost her cool and was up pacing along with Katie. By the end of this ordeal Katie felt sure she would have walked five miles.

"I wish I could have a glass of wine," Ashley said.

Katie perked up. "There's an idea. Let's go have a drink. Mikey's Tavern is just down the street. We could pop in and be back before the jury's done."

"You can, but I can't. I'm still technically in trial. I can't come back intoxicated."

"I didn't mean get sloshed. I just meant one drink."

"Still a problem for me. But you go ahead," Ashley made a shooing motion. "One of us deserves to relax a little."

"No. I'll stay here," Katie said, and she was glad that she did.

Within a few minutes, the court attendant returned and said four words that had Katie momentarily relieved. "They have a verdict."

Then her stomach started twisting into knots.

43

ASHLEY

The jury filed into the courtroom, all silent, solemn. Ashley did not try to interpret their expressions. She didn't even look at them. There was nothing to be gained from trying to determine the result before the judge made the official announcement. There were so many potential options. Guilty as charged. Murder in the second degree. Going armed with intent. Willful injury causing death. Willful injury causing serious injury. Willful injury. Reckless use of a firearm. Assault with a weapon. Assault causing bodily injury. Assault. Not guilty.

"Is that everyone?" Judge Ahrenson said, his eyes sweeping across the jury box and settling on the court attendant.

"Yes, your honor." The court attendant said.

"Very well," Judge Ahrenson turned to speak to the entire courtroom. "You may be seated."

Feet shuffled behind Ashley and the bench seats in the courtroom gallery creaked as the onlookers in the packed courtroom reclaimed their seats. Ashley, Katie, and Lucas remained standing until after the entire jury sat down.

Once everyone was settled, the Judge turned back to the court attendant. "Has the Jury reached a unanimous verdict?"

"Yes, your honor," she said.

He motioned for the court attendant to approach, and she came forward, handing him a stack of documents, careful to keep them face down. The jury verdict forms. A stack of thin pieces of paper, one of which would decide whether Lucas would spend the rest of his life in a cage.

Judge Ahrenson put on his reading glasses, looking down at the stack of documents. Then he began flipping through. Nobody in the courtroom moved, all frozen with anticipation. Ashley was finding it hard to even breathe in that moment.

Once he'd reached the last page, the judge looked up. His gaze traveled from Ashley, to Lucas, and then settled on Charles. The judge started flipping back through the documents again. He passed the earlier ones quickly and started slowing down near the end. Ashley tried to remember, were the more serious offenses at the front of the verdict forms or the end? She couldn't remember. Judge Ahrenson stopped on a page, then cleared his throat.

This was it. This was the verdict. Ashley's stomach twisted and her heart pounded.

"The jury has signed jury verdict number eight," the Judge said, his expression grave.

Was that good or bad? Ashley couldn't remember. She wished he would just say it already. She was on the cusp of a heart attack, and Lucas had to feel worse.

"Assault with a weapon."

All the air whooshed out of Ashley's body, like something had hit her in the chest.

Lucas turned to her, his brow furrowed. He didn't know what it meant.

"Who is the foreperson?" the Judge asked.

A middle-aged man seated near the front stood up. "I am."

"Is this the unanimous decision of the jury?" Judge Ahrenson asked.

"It is."

"Very well. Would either party like to poll the jury?"

After the announcement of the verdict, the defense or the prosecution could choose to "poll" the jury. What that meant was that the judge would go through each juror's name and make them pronounce out loud on the record that this was their verdict. Ashley declined. Charles did the opposite.

Lucas leaned over to Ashley as the judge started reading through the names, and jurors raised their hands and stated their agreement.

"What does this mean?"

"It's a win, Lucas. Assault with a weapon is an aggravated misdemeanor. A maximum of two years in prison. There is no mandatory minimum."

"So, I could serve two years in prison?"

"No. Six months would be the max. Prisons are full, so they are kicking people out as quickly as they can. Plus, you've already got a good deal of time served here in jail awaiting trial. If the judge sends you to prison—and that's a big *if*—you'll only do a couple months."

"I don't understand, though. How can they have this verdict? It doesn't make any sense."

"It makes perfect sense," Ashley said. "They hated Matthew Larson and blame him for the things that happened here. Yet they also bought the prosecutor's argument that you had a choice whether or not to take the pill. They wanted to punish you for that choice, and so they came up with something that would allow for that."

"I'm grateful, but that doesn't seem legal."

"It's the way the system works."

"All members of the jury have announced their agreement with the verdict," Judge Ahrenson pronounced, cutting through Ashley and Lucas's conversation. "That will be the order and judgment of this court. The jury is excused. There are a few housekeeping matters the Court needs to take up with the parties."

Everyone stood as the jury filed out. Ashley shot to her feet, her body seeming a thousand times lighter than it had been only moments before. Once the last juror had left, they all sat back down.

"I'm going to set sentencing for May 25th. Will that work for everyone's schedules?"

"Yes, your honor," Charles said sulkily.

"Yes, your honor," Ashley said.

"Now there is the business of release. Since the jury's conviction was for something other than a forcible felony, it means that I do not have to hold him between conviction and sentencing."

"That's true, your honor, but considering the facts, you should," Charles said. "This was a murder case, and the verdict indicates that the Defendant is guilty of a weapons charge."

"Oh, sit down, Charles," Judge Ahrenson said. "I sat through the trial. Remember? I have a decision. I'm going to release Lucas pending sentencing. That will be the final order and judgment of this court."

Judge Ahrenson stood, and everyone stood with him. He descended from his bench and headed for his chambers. Before disappearing behind the heavy wooden door that separated the two rooms, he turned and winked at Ashley.

In that moment, she knew he was going to grant Lucas time served. He wouldn't have his farm back, but he would have his freedom. It wasn't everything, but it was fair. At least fair enough.

EPILOGUE

May 1

It took a few days for the trial excitement to blow over. Lucas Campbell's trial had been the talk of the town, and his release from jail only served as another source of gossip. The townspeople seemed to find him interesting, but they certainly didn't want him as a neighbor. Lucas left Brine almost immediately after his release. Ashley hadn't heard from him since, which was probably a good sign.

"What are you up to today?" Katie's voice cut through Ashley's thoughts.

Ashley looked up to see her long-time friend standing in her office doorway, leaning against the doorframe.

"The usual," Ashley said with a sigh. The time between a large trial and everything else was a transition. Ashley's brain had been so focused on one case and its every intricate detail that it was hard to turn back to the bigger picture.

"Have you heard back from the committee?" Katie asked as she came into Ashley's office and flopped down on one of the ratty chairs across from her desk.

"Not yet." The Judicial Nominating Committee had met and likely had the names of the two individuals they would send to the governor to choose which of the two would replace Judge Ahrenson, but they hadn't released their results. "I don't think that's a good sign."

"Oh," Katie said.

Just then Ashley's phone started to ring. It was nearing the end of the day, so Elena had already left the office. Ashley picked up. "This is Ashley Montgomery."

"Ashley, it's Judge Ahrenson."

Ashley's heart flitted, then began pounding. Much like it had as she stood there with Lucas, waiting for the jury to read their verdict. Yet she forced her voice to sound calm. "Oh, hello, Judge."

"You know why I'm calling, don't you?"

"Yes. And you don't have to say it. I didn't get through."

"Actually, it's quite the opposite."

"The opposite?" She repeated the words as though they were foreign.

"Yes. You've made it through. You and Magistrate Mirnka. You remember her, don't you?"

"Umm, yes." Ashley said. She'd tried one case in front of Magistrate Mirnka as a preliminary hearing not too long ago. Ashley had found the magistrate to be well prepared, understanding of issues, and willing to do what's right. She would make an excellent district court judge. "But wait, I thought for sure Charles Hanson would get through."

"Nope. Lucas's trial buried him."

Ashley didn't agree with the reasons the Committee used to block Charles's ascension, but she was unconcerned. Charles would have made a terrible judge. He was too affected by politics. It was ironic that it was those very same politics that were holding him back.

"What about Tucker Caine? He was hellbent on keeping me from getting through."

Judge Ahrenson chuckled. "He put his eggs in the wrong basket, the Matthew Larson basket, and lost all credibility. That's another thing about politics. They are fickle. Your allies turn on you on a dime. He had great sway with this whole town, including that committee, but now he'll probably be fighting to save his spot on city council in the next election."

That was the true meaning of Karma, but Ashley didn't voice her thoughts.

"Well, I suppose you have some calls to make, and some celebrating to do," Judge Ahrenson said.

"I do," Ashley said with a smile.

"Stop by my office sometime tomorrow. We've got to start preparing for step two. You've got one more candidate to beat."

"Thank you. I really mean that. Thank you for supporting me."

"I didn't do anything that you didn't already earn on your own."

Ashley cradled the phone, then looked up. Katie wore a smile, but there was a sadness in her eyes. "You got through, your honor?" Katie said.

Ashley nodded. "I'm not 'your honor' yet."

"You will be."

"We'll see. I have a fifty percent chance. Those aren't great odds."

"Don't downplay your achievement because of me," Katie said, shaking her head and popping out of her chair. "I'll be sad to lose you right when we are back working together, but I'm still proud of you."

"Thank you."

Katie moved toward the door and motioned for Ashley to follow. "I have something to show you."

Katie led Ashley to the front of the office where a large bunch of flowers and a cake that read *Congratulations* sat on top of the counter. Elena and Katie's father stood near the cake. Next to them stood Ashley's once client turned houseguest turned college student, Rachel Smithson. She was the closest thing Ashley had to a daughter.

"Rachel!" Ashley said. "I didn't know you were coming back."

"Katie arranged it," Rachel said with a sheepish smile.

"I have one more thing." Katie handed Ashley a card. "It came in the mail earlier today. It's from Lucas's ex-wife."

Ashley ripped the envelope open and opened the card. A picture fell out, fluttering to the floor. Ashley bent down and picked it up. It was a photo of Lucas, Kristy, and their daughter all standing together, giant smiles on their faces. It was a recent photograph; Ashley could see that from the lines in Lucas's face and the age of the child. Lucas was more at ease in this picture than Ashley had ever seen him. She handed the photograph to Katie, then turned to the card.

Inside, there were only a few words written. *Thank you for bringing him back to us.* It was signed by Kristy Campbell.

"I guess there is such a thing as a happy ending," Ashley said, wiping away a tear that broke free from her eye. "At least for Lucas."

"I guess so," Katie said rocking from her heels to her toes. "But not only for Lucas. We've got some cake to eat, some celebrating to do, then we focus on the next stage of achieving yours."

Ashley waved a dismissive hand. "The governor has sixty days to choose. There's plenty of time between now and then to worry about all that. Definitely enough time for another big case."

"Speaking of big cases..." Katie said, her voice trailing off. "Have you seen the news?"

"No."

"I think one is already on its way."

UNCONDITIONAL REVENGE
ASHLEY MONTGOMERY LEGAL THRILLER #6

A deadbeat with a criminal past. A husband with a dark secret. When two seemingly unconnected cases collide, Ashley Montgomery will risk everything to right her wrongs and chase down the truth in this riveting legal thriller.

When Oliver Banks is charged with attempted murder after hitting a pedestrian with a car, defense attorney Ashley Montgomery is hesitant to take his case. Something is off about Oliver, and when troubling new information emerges she begins to suspect he might be entangled in something far worse than this one crime.

Struggling to keep her PI agency afloat, Katie agrees to investigate a new client's husband. Bruce Ross has been spending all his time in the garage but refusing to let anyone inside, and his pregnant wife Vivian is concerned about his behavior. But as Katie learns more about the family, she begins to suspect that Vivian isn't telling the whole story either...especially when she discovers a connection between the Ross family and Ashley's client, Oliver.

As they work to uncover their clients' secrets, Ashley and Katie soon realize that the two cases are intertwined. Now they must work together to figure out the big picture...before a secret plan results in a terrible tragedy.

Get your copy today at
severnriverbooks.com/series/ashley-montgomery-legal-thrillers

ABOUT THE AUTHOR

Laura Snider is a practicing lawyer in Iowa. She graduated from Drake Law School in 2009 and spent most of her career as a Public Defender. Throughout her legal career she has been involved in all levels of crimes from petty thefts to murders. These days she is working part-time as a prosecutor and spends the remainder of her time writing stories and creating characters.

Laura lives in Iowa with her husband, three children, two dogs, and two very mischievous cats.

Sign up for Laura Snider's newsletter at
severnriverbooks.com/authors/laura-snider

Printed in the United States
by Baker & Taylor Publisher Services